WHITE FEATHERS

A Dystopian Urban Fantasy Novel

Angels of the Apocalypse
Book 3

CINDY CARROLL

Hanlon Creek Press

White Feathers
Angels of the Apocalypse Book 3

by Cindy Carroll

ePub ISBN: 978-1-06-884517-8

Print ISBN: 978-1-0688451-8-5

Edited by Lawrence Editing

All characters in this book are fiction and figments of the author's imagination. www.cindycarroll.com

For my husband, always

A week after a misunderstanding almost destroyed the planet, Sarah Malak stood at the bar, waiting for the bartender at Baron's Jazz and Blues bar to pour her drinks. Technically, it was more than a misunderstanding. Bombs were lobbed at Russia. They just didn't come from the US like everyone thought. After sending the horseman War back to limbo, she and her fallen angel sisters deserved a break. Increased violence in the city meant Rachel could be called into a homicide at any time. Becky might need to cover a breaking story for the TV station. Leah, the youngest of the group, was rarely required to put in extra teaching hours at the high school. And Sarah was always ready to help at the hospital when they needed her. Lately, they'd needed her a lot.

Sarah glanced around at the customers sitting at the tables in front of the stage. Busy for a Wednesday evening in the last week of January, the band was taking a break, so the owner's playlist pumped out of the speakers set at strategic spots around the club. Did any of the clientele tonight have souls? She probably should have let Becky get the drinks so the reporter could do a soul check. She and Rachel hadn't earned enough power back to be soul detectors. Becky and Leah knew how to get their angel power back. She and Rachel were still trying to figure it out.

Back at the table, their usual at the back of the place so they always had a good vantage point, she plunked the drinks down.

"I should have let you get them," she said to Becky.

"I'll get them next time."

Sarah took her seat, snaked out a hand to grab one of Rachel's fries, then popped it into her mouth. "These are so good."

Rachel pulled her plate closer, wrapping her hands around it protectively. "If you wanted fries, why did you get onion rings?"

A commotion at the front of the club drew their attention. About to answer, Sarah stopped and stood again. Everyone in the booths by the door was kneeling on their seats, facing the windows, peering outside. The band, who had just taken the stage again, put their instruments down and rushed to the door.

Fear rippled across the floor. Someone gasped. A gunshot split the air. Everyone jumped.

Rachel bolted out of her chair and turned to Sarah, Becky, and Leah. "Stay here. Make sure everyone in the bar is okay."

"You know I'm not staying here. Someone out there might need medical attention."

Rachel glared at Sarah, then sighed. "Fine."

Sarah and Rachel raced to the side door, burst outside, and sprinted around the building instead of trying to push through the crowd inside the club.

Chaos reigned outside. A crowd gathered around a man who lay in the street, a gaping hole in his coat evidence of the bullet's target. Sarah slowed when she reached him. Rachel raced past, following the direction of the pointed fingers from the crowd. Helpful bystanders urged Rachel on.

"I need room, please." Sarah bent to assess the man's wound. He was in his mid-thirties, fairly fit. "Sir, can you tell me what happened?"

She pulled his coat aside to reveal the wound. She had to keep him talking until the paramedics arrived. Stop the bleeding. If the bullet hadn't gone clean through, he would need surgery, but she needed to make sure he was stable enough for that.

He grimaced in pain. "I wanted a bottle of water."

His head turned, and she followed his gaze. A bottle of water had rolled to the curb, the label on it covered in red splotches of blood.

"I need to check if the bullet went clean through."

The man nodded. Sarah put her hand under him, checking his back for exit wounds. Her hand came away clean. Retrieving the bullet would be the hospital's job. Without the proper equipment and a surgical bay, she couldn't risk removing the bullet here.

Becky bent down beside her, shoving a first aid kit into her hand. "Is there anything I can do to help?"

Sarah nodded. She liked this more helpful side of Becky now that she figured out how to get her angelic gifts back.

"Keep pressure on the wound while I find some gauze."

Becky pressed her hands on the hole in the man's lower abdomen. He groaned, scrunching up his face with the pain. "Sorry."

Sarah yanked open the kit and rummaged inside for pads of gauze. She found five pads, a few bandages, ointment for burns, and not much else. She ripped open the packaging on the gauze, then nudged Becky's hands aside long enough to put them over the wound.

"I'm calling nine-one-one." Leah's voice remained calm.

Sarah's stomach knotted. The increasing lack of respect for life since they'd arrived on Earth was like a needle to her heart. With an apocalypse in full swing, it would get worse before it got better.

"Do you have anything else?" Becky asked. "The gauze is soaked through."

Sarah pulled out the cloth bandages. At least there were still a few of those in the kit. She took one triangular bandage out of its packaging and gave it to Becky.

Sarah checked the man's pulse and breathing. His heart rate was elevated, his breathing rapid.

"I can take over," she said to Becky.

Becky stood while Sarah placed her hands on the bandage to staunch the bleeding. Where was that ambulance?

The crowd moved in closer, camera phones out. No doubt the whole incident in various clips would be on the internet before the man even made it to the hospital.

"Give them some room." Rachel's authoritative voice broke through the murmurs of the bystanders.

The few people closest to Sarah and the man moved back. Rachel took up a position, arms extended at her sides, and she moved forward, forcing the crowd to retreat.

Rachel looked over her shoulder. "The shooter got away. I called in a description of the suspect to the 50th Division. Constables patrolling the area will hopefully pick him up."

The scream of a siren pierced the night air, the plaintive sound growing louder the closer the ambulance got.

Finally, red and white lights strobed in the street behind Rachel.

The crowd parted for the EMTs, and Sarah looked up at Jason Hickey as he approached her. He was the EMT who had looked after Rachel when a gang member had shot her. His lips were pressed into a thin line, a bag slung over his shoulder. He kneeled beside her.

"Hey, Dr. Malak. What have we got?"

She rattled off the victim's vitals and her observations. "There appears to be no exit wound."

"Thanks. We'll take over."

She stood, moving out of the way so Jason and his partner could do their job. Once they had the victim stabilized as much as possible, they lifted him onto a stretcher. Sarah followed them through the crowd to the ambulance, helping to load him into the vehicle.

"I'm going with him." She climbed into the back and sat beside him.

"Sarah?" Rachel asked.

"I'm not sure how long I'll be. Get my food to-go. I'll eat when I get home."

Jason shut the back doors of the ambulance. The sound of the driver and passenger doors closing prompted her to grip the side of the gurney. The ambulance lurched forward, the siren screaming again as they raced through traffic.

An hour on her feet in the OR at the hospital left Sarah with a surge of adrenaline, excess energy she didn't want to waste. Her patient from outside the bar, Ed James, was still in recovery, so she roamed the emergency room, checking on other patients, helping the doctors and nurses who were already ragged but still had hours left in their shifts. If she could help a few of them get a short break, a breather to grab a coffee, she was more than willing to put in some time.

When they'd brought him in, she'd asked to be the doctor of record. Mr. James was a father of two and a husband. His wife had been called, and Sarah wanted to be able to return to the ER waiting room with news of his successful surgery. Until he was awake and talking again, she didn't want to give his wife any news.

On her way down the hall, she spotted a woman with a bottle of water from a patient's tray duck out of the recovery area and hustle away. Sarah stopped at the curtain and pulled it aside to look at the patient. The woman's eyes were closed, but the cookies on the plate were gone. Had the patient eaten them? Or had the water thief eaten a little snack?

Since she was at the hospital, she took the elevator up to the fifth floor to check in on some patients she'd admitted last week. It wouldn't stop her from checking on them again in the morning when she was back for her shift, but it would give her peace of mind before leaving, making sure they were still on the road to recovery.

She stopped at Laura's room. Becky's intern from the television station had been beaten to within an inch of her life and still had a lot of healing to do. At this time of night, the intern was fast asleep when Sarah checked on her. Still without a roommate, the curtain dividing the two beds was pulled all the way back to the wall. Sarah observed Laura from halfway across the room, not wanting to get close enough that she might disturb her. The woman's vitals, all displayed on the various machines hooked up to her, looked good.

Sarah ducked out of the room in time to see the

woman who took the bottle of water shove a pair of gloves into her purse. Boxes of gloves were attached to walls all around the hospital, but this was the first time she'd seen someone who wasn't a medical professional grab them. She didn't know every person who worked at the hospital, so it was possible the woman was staff. Monitoring the woman to see where she went, Sarah pulled out her phone and called security, informing them to keep an eye out for the glove snatcher.

Satisfied with her patients' progress, Sarah pocketed her phone, then hit the call button on the elevator to go back to the ER. Nurses, calm in the chaos, rushed back and forth. Doctors, the weight of the world's sick slumping their shoulders, ducked in and out of curtained off areas to examine patients.

Sarah stopped at the emergency desk. "Avril, need me to help with anything?"

Relief washed over the nurse's face. "We have another gunshot wound in curtain one. A stabbing victim in curtain three. And we had four patients come in, all presenting with flu-like symptoms. Take your pick."

Thinking about the tips Becky received about the flu vaccine a few weeks ago, Sarah picked one of the four patients presenting with similar symptoms. It could have nothing to do with the vaccine, but she needed to make sure it wasn't the flu. If it was, it would only confirm the tipster's hint that the vaccine wasn't as effective for this season. Doctors and hospital staff already knew that because of the memo the public health department for the city sent out.

She checked the file to see which curtain hid her newest patient. They were in bed four, halfway down the hall and to the right.

When she ducked past the curtain, the woman on the

other side looked up, sagging with relief. Her face was flushed with fever.

"Hello, Kelly. I'm Dr. Malak. It says here you've had a fever for a few days."

Kelly nodded. "Aches and pains too. I'm exhausted."

Sarah grabbed the stethoscope from around her neck, put the buds in her ears, and listened to the woman's chest. The lungs sounded clear, and she had a good heartbeat.

"It's flu season, so I'm going to do a swab to make sure it's not that."

"What if it is?"

"There are some antivirals you could try, but mostly it means rest and fluids until it goes away." Sarah glanced through the woman's chart. "Did you get a flu shot?"

"Yes. And the booster too, a week ago."

Sarah noted that in her chart. "I'll be right back with the flu testing kit."

Sarah pulled the curtain aside and jumped back to avoid colliding with another doctor, who was speed-walking to a curtain farther down the hallway. While seeing Kelly, the ER had gotten busier. If she believed in that sort of thing, she would have wondered if it was a full moon.

She hurried through the hall, past the nurses' station, to the supply cupboard where the hospital kept the kits for testing various viruses. Locked at all times, she punched in her code to open the door. A soft click sounded. She found the kit she wanted, made sure the door was secure again, then raced back down the hall to her patient.

She took the swab, then propped up the pillow on the bed to make Kelly more comfortable while she waited.

"I'll be back in about twenty minutes with the results."

Kelly nodded. "Thanks."

Unable to do anything else for her patient, Sarah left the curtained area and grabbed another chart. The other three people with similar symptoms still waited to be seen, so she attended to each of them, performing the swab test for all three.

After putting in a full shift and not having dinner, her eyes refused to stay open and her stomach grumbled with every step she took. Once she got the results back from the tests, she would clock out again. She grabbed a coffee from the vending machine in the waiting area. The jolt of caffeine should be enough to keep her on her feet for at least an hour. Long enough to give the patients their results and for her to get home.

She picked up a few more folders from the triage nurse. In the space of an hour, she deftly sutured a stab wound on a man's arm, inflicted during a bar fight over a woman, diagnosed pneumonia in a six-year-old girl, requested a psychiatric consult for a forty-year-old man, and checked on patients she'd had admitted even though they'd been assigned attending doctors.

When the test results finally came in, she sagged into a chair behind the check-in desk to go over them. All tested negative for the flu. It was probably a cold. She pushed herself up from the chair to deliver the news and discharge them from the ER. Either the flu vaccine worked, or the booster did its job. Later, when she was more awake, she would check out the results more in depth and compare them with any other rush of patients in ERs across the city with similar symptoms.

Outside again, she took a deep breath of the winter air. The cool night invigorated her, waking her up long enough for the short walk back to the loft. After she'd clocked out again, she texted Rachel to make sure they weren't still at Baron's. Though she missed the talk and drinks, she felt pride in helping a busy emergency room.

Sarah was so tired she could barely pull the loft door open. Since she left that morning, the door had gained a thousand pounds and refused to budge. She took a deep breath and put all the strength she had left into yanking on the door. On her second try, the door slid open, Leah on the other side with a smile on her face.

"About time you got home."

"Sorry. I couldn't leave them in a lurch. I can't believe how busy the ER has gotten over the past couple of weeks."

Sarah dropped her purse on the table by the door, trudged over to the sofa, then dropped onto the soft cushions with a heavy sigh. Every muscle in her body ached, screaming out for sleep, but her stomach argued for food with a loud grumble.

"It's the same with the homicides in the city. By this time in a usual year, we'd only be at ten to twelve. Now we're at twenty."

"I'll get your food. Do you want me to heat it? I put it in the fridge since we didn't know how long you'd be." Becky already had the fridge door open.

Sarah shook her head. "I'll be asleep by then. I can eat it cold."

Rachel sat at the other end of the sofa, her nose wrinkled. "How can you eat pasta cold?"

Becky offered Sarah a cardboard food container and a fork, then sat in the chair beside the sofa. Leah took up a spot on the floor facing the sofa on the other side of the coffee table. Thankful they'd stayed up until she got home, she smiled. It was nice to have company when she ate. A twinge of guilt twisted her stomach for bailing on them, even though she hadn't been needed at Baron's.

"Easy, like this." Sarah opened the container and dug into her Fettuccine Alfredo.

It would have been better hot, or at least warmed, but she didn't want to wait to eat. Waiting even a few minutes meant going to bed that much later. Her eyes fought to stay open as she chewed. Cold, the food's flavors didn't dance over her tongue like they normally did. Right now she didn't care; eating was strictly for nourishment tonight.

"I get why they can't have everyone in the ER. They need some doctors to be fresh and ready to come in if there's a mass casualty, but it really runs the rest of us ragged."

Sarah popped another forkful of pasta into her mouth, chewing slowly. Her body could barely manage that. Her bones had that overtired, dull ache about them. The kind she knew would disappear the minute she allowed her body some rest. But her stomach continued to growl.

"You work too hard. The world needs you to be a doctor, but they need angel you more," Leah said.

Eyes gritty, drooping closed, Sarah forced them open and nodded. "I can't cut back yet. I need to check with other hospitals tomorrow to ask about an influx of patients with flu-like symptoms."

Becky perked up in her chair. "You think it's because the tipster was right? The vaccine wasn't as effective?"

Too tired for a complete shrug, Sarah twitched her shoulder. "Maybe. All four of my patients also had the booster. And their tests came back negative for the flu. I'll know more tomorrow."

It felt like she'd worked thirty-six hours in the past twelve. She finished her last bite of food and put the container on the table. Leaning back into the cushions took effort, and once there, she didn't want to get up again. But she couldn't sleep on the sofa.

"Lately, the ER has been busier than usual, mostly because of the increased violence in the city. Two months ago, we might have had a few domestic violence cases in a week. Now there are a few every other day.

Rachel nodded sadly. "Though War is back in limbo, at least for now, Conquest is still running around the city. Father Ianetti has enough ingredients to keep calling them, so as angels, we need to work on a permanent solution. If the priest's pattern holds, he's already summoned Famine."

"Based on last time, he'll call War back. So we have to snuff out Famine as quickly as possible. I have a bad feeling about the flu-like symptoms," Sarah said.

Chapter Two

Thursday morning, Sarah woke up at 5:00 a.m. Though a little early for her, considering when she went to bed, she was energized. Lying in bed, she tossed and turned, sleep refusing to come back. She threw off the covers, put her feet over the side of the bed, and did a few sitting stretches. If she got up now, she could get a jump start on her day, make breakfast for her sisters, get to work early and maybe get through paperwork on time for a change.

Silence filled the loft. No one else was up. She pushed herself off the bed and padded to the kitchen, enjoying the quiet of the place. With four of them living there, it was rarely below fifty decibels.

She pulled out the ingredients for breakfast, but before cooking, she idled over to the enormous windows and pulled the curtains apart. They were closed in the evening before they went to bed, but she and her sisters liked them open during the day. Letting in the light, especially during the winter, was important to them. Too early for the dappled rays of the sun, at least Leah could bask in the warmth of her bed before she left for work and feel the sun on her cheeks during her commute. For Sarah, Becky, and Rachel, the winter meant leaving before the sun came up and returning after it set.

Though she didn't need coffee yet, she put on the machine to brew a pot because it would be the first thing her sisters reached for. Surprised she had so much energy, she wasn't about to look a gift horse in the mouth.

By the time she had the food on the breakfast island, stirrings of movement emanated from the bedrooms. She pulled out maple syrup, butter, and orange juice from the fridge. Final touches for a rare midweek breakfast. Usually, they were so busy all they had time for was toast and coffee, if that. Most of the time, they grabbed something when they got to work. Even though she worked at a hospital, the cafeteria food wasn't that appetizing.

Becky arrived in the kitchen first, shuffling through the living room, eyes half closed, inhaling deeply. Leah and Rachel followed, equally tired.

Becky sat on the stool closest to the bedrooms, facing the kitchen. "Sarah, this is amazing. When did you get up?"

Sarah poured coffee for each of them, plunked them onto the island, and went to the fridge to retrieve the cream.

"About an hour ago. Maybe I still have an adrenaline rush from helping at the hospital. I feel completely rested."

Rachel sat beside Becky, poured a large amount of cream into her coffee, and took a sip. "That hits the spot. I need this added energy to get through the day."

Leah sat on the other side of the island, Sarah settling in beside her.

After Leah prepared her coffee and took a sip, she turned to Becky. "Can you pick up more of the Mt.

Hermon limestone today from the occult shop? We used most of it to send War back."

Becky finished her coffee and shoved her mug toward Sarah, but before she could get up, Becky pulled it back and poured a second cup for herself. "It was on back order before, but I'll stop in to see if they got in any more since I bought all they had."

Another bloom of white spread across Becky's wings, in one of the few patches that were still black. Becky and Leah had figured out how to earn their power back and now, at every opportunity, they did things to make that happen. It was a good thing. But frustrating because she and Rachel still had no clue how to get theirs back. Though it appeared to be random, it wasn't. Every time she managed to get even the tiniest amount back, she reported to Becky, who added the data to her spreadsheet.

"Thanks. It's going to be hard enough to find the ancient grains we need. I've been looking for a week and still can't find them."

They'd discovered a few weeks ago everything they needed in order to summon the horsemen and how to send most of them back. With the priest also summoning, some of the ingredients were hard to get, especially since he'd purchased all the stock of some items. Sarah poured a large amount of syrup over her pancakes, cut off a forkful, and shoved it in her mouth. The sweetness sliding over her tongue made her want to do a little sitting dance on her stool.

Thankful Becky cleared away the dishes, Sarah relaxed on her stool. Once Becky loaded the breakfast dishes in the dishwasher, she popped a cleaning tab into the slot, closed the machine, and hit the button for a normal wash. Once a horseman was summoned, the summoner needed recovery time. The priest had most likely recovered enough from summoning War to have summoned Famine by now. More anxious than ever now that she suspected Famine was Earth side, Sarah took a deep breath. She would be no good at the hospital if she was distracted. Still, it was hard to ignore the bad feeling that gnawed inside her stomach.

Famine, known to the rest of the world as Zach Wheatley, sat in the waiting area of Queen City University Research Group, waiting for his perfunctory interview for the position of Lead Lab Tech. Fluorescent lights starkly emphasized the objects in the room. A reception area with a heavy metal door behind it stood between the general public and the actual lab. The walls, painfully white, shone under the harsh lighting. The waiting area provided three chairs and no reading material. With his influence, the interview was a formality, unless the person interviewing him had a soul. Not as easily swayed to do what the horsemen wanted, a souled person would make his job a lot harder.

It wasn't like the lab had a vast selection of potential employees to choose from, but they wanted what they wanted.

The person before him came out of the office to the right, a grin on her face. A grin of confidence. If things went according to plan, he would bury that confidence. When she walked past him, the scent of rosewater clung to her, turning his stomach. Retched were the souled, for he could not sway them. At least not as easily as he could the unsouled. His own confidence rose a few notches.

Five minutes after the woman left, the phone at reception rang. After a brief conversation, the receptionist stood and told him to go in.

He ran his hand over the briefcase in his lap, magically beefing up his résumé and his abilities with so many credentials Dr. Lina Hayes wouldn't be able to resist hiring him. He didn't bother to knock on the door; he had been told to go right in.

The sickly sweet smell of decay greeted him. It wafted through the air, surrounding him like a warm security blanket. A smile pulled at the corners of his lips. Sitting behind a large oak desk, Dr. Hayes was a middle-aged woman some might call handsome. White tendrils, escapees from the tight bun sitting atop her head, framed her square face. Blue eyes sparkled when she saw him. A bookcase behind her housed dozens of volumes dealing with science, epidemiology, viruses. His gaze stopped on the pulp fiction books hiding on the bottom shelf.

She stood and extended her hand. "Mr. Wheatley, thank you for coming in on such short notice. The lab has been swamped lately with new projects coming in, and we have a few positions to fill rather urgently."

"That's perfect. I can start tomorrow, provided this goes well, of course." He waved a hand between them and smiled.

She moved her mouse and clicked something. Her eyebrows drew together. "I don't seem to have a copy of your résumé."

He schooled his face into a sheepish grin. "I'm a little old-school with some things." He pulled out a paper copy of his résumé from his briefcase.

A smile curled her lips up, and she leaned back in her chair. "How refreshing."

He placed the crisp white paper on the desk and pushed it toward her. The moment she reached the salient part of his CV, her eyes widened. "Impressive research credentials for someone so young."

"I started young and did extra classes to graduate early from high school. I knew where my passion was." On the off chance she was still on the fence about hiring him, he moved his wrist infinitesimally, shooting her with a burst of magic strongly suggesting she hire him.

"Couldn't wait to get your hands on the research, huh?"

Famine smiled. If only she knew. "Something like that. Unless you research a problem, you can't come up with a solution. It's like a puzzle. And I love puzzles."

Pressing the tip of her finger to her lips, she nodded. "We handle the vaccines for most of Canada here. The lab works with Queen City University Group. In the down times, after flu vaccines have been given out and before we ramp up our efforts on the new one, we have a seed department. That's where you'll be for now."

Though annoyed he wouldn't be placed in the vaccine lab right away, it was inevitable that he end up there. When the pestilence hit, they would be dragging people off the streets to do lab work. Possibilities ran through his mind for the seed work. What better type of seed could there be than one that provided more nutrients than any other? If it only grew once, forcing farmers to buy more each year, at increased prices, that would serve to help the famine along. It wouldn't be apparent right away, and by the time they realized it, it would be too late to do anything. If the humans survived that long.

He plastered a look of surprise on his face. "I'm hired?"

A wide smile followed a slight nod. "Welcome to the team. Delia will get you set up with a security badge. IT will have an account set up for you within the hour. You'll use that user name to log into everything from your email to the lab computers."

When she stood, he followed suit, accepting the hand she extended in a firm handshake. "Glad to be part of the team."

As he walked through the door back to the reception area, he heard her speaking with the receptionist. He sidled over to the desk, waiting patiently while Delia spoke to Dr. Hayes. Thirty seconds later, the receptionist hung up the phone and greeted him with a warmer smile than the one she'd bestowed on him when he arrived.

"I'll take your picture for the security badge." She grabbed a small digital camera from the top drawer of her desk and nodded to the cream-colored wall behind him. "Stand against the wall with a neutral expression. I'll take a few to make sure we get a good one."

Famine suffered through two hours of getting set up for his position and in the end, he had a shiny badge, a state-of-the-art laptop, a research station, and access to everything he needed to help move the pestilence along. In the very near future, Queen City University Research Group would become the busiest lab in the country save for the Public Disease and Health Agency of Canada and it would take them time to figure out exactly what hit them.

Drained from the morning's activities, Sarah sat in the doctor's lounge at Queen City Hospital, chugging down her fourth cup of coffee. With the sugar and carb rush of her breakfast long gone, she contemplated more appropriate nourishment to get her through the afternoon. It had been nonstop since the second she stepped foot in the ER. It was like there was a full moon out there and the entire city was under its influence. But it was almost midday and the full moon had been last week.

She settled for the banana she'd brought from home, pulling it out of the fridge along with a small carton of milk. Eating the fruit faster than recommended, she washed it down with three gulps of the milk. The snack would have to do until she had more time. Even though she should return to the ER, follow up with her patients, see new arrivals, she settled back in the chair, waiting for her food to settle. A brief respite was better than none. Right now, the lounge was exactly how she liked it. Empty save for her.

A nurse burst through the door, scattering the calm the lounge had provided. Sarah sighed, remote hope that the nurse was looking for someone else fleeing when the woman focused on her.

"Sorry to pull you away from your break so soon. A pile of new patients has arrived." She looked down at the scrawl on her left hand. "A stab wound, car accident, upset stomach, a few patients complaining of head and body aches."

Sarah sat up straighter. "High fever?"

The nurse nodded.

Sarah bolted out of her chair, tossed the remnants of her snack in the garbage, and straightened her lab coat. "I'll take the fever and body aches. What curtains?"

"Seven and eight."

Sarah hustled out of the room, raced down the hall, swung right at the nurses' station, rushed down the corridor, and stopped at curtain seven. Preliminary chart in hand, she pulled the curtain aside and stepped through. A woman in her early fifties sat on the bed, hunched over, her face contorted in pain.

"Mrs. Jeffries, it says here you're suffering from some aches and pains."

The woman sat a little straighter and rose her head to look at Sarah. "I ache all over."

Face flushed from an apparent fever, the woman's overall appearance screamed flu, but Sarah listened for the whispers to tell her what was really wrong. Many illnesses presented with the same symptoms. It would take more than a swab to diagnose this woman. Sarah was sure a quick flu test would come back negative. The same as the other four patients she'd seen recently.

Acids swirled in her stomach, bringing a bout of nausea. Rachel had her feelings, and they were usually right when it came to the crime in the city. Sarah's instincts about the sick were equally on target. And the recent flu-like symptoms bothered her.

"Any vomiting? Cough? Sore throat?"

The woman shook her head, frowned, then nodded. "I threw up once. But no cough or sore throat."

"Sneezing?"

"No."

Sarah pulled a digital thermometer from her pocket and pointed it at the woman's forehead. The readout flashed the result—two degrees above normal. After performing a thorough exam, her conclusions were the same as they had been last night.

"I'll be right back with a flu rapid test kit."

"You think it's the flu? But I had the vaccine."

"And I see from your chart that you had the booster as well about a week ago. I want to rule it out."

The woman sighed and leaned back onto the bed, pulling her legs up as well to stretch them out. It was just as well. Her patient needed rest and liquids, whether it was the flu or a cold.

After making sure Mrs. Jeffries was comfortable and checking her blood pressure, Sarah hurried down the hall to the supply cupboard to grab a flu test. She signed for two of the kits for now. If she ended up examining all the patients with similar symptoms, she'd have to go back and get more. There were only so many things she could carry in the pockets of her lab coat.

Sarah disturbed her patient long enough to get a swab, then let her rest again. While she waited for the results in the lounge, she called two other downtown hospitals and learned they'd had an influx of patients with flu-like symptoms as well. A hunch like this that panned out in a way that was not optimal made her stomach churn. She called a few other hospitals in other parts of the province and received the same information.

All of this had something to do with Becky's tips. She was sure of it. The tipster mentioned the flu vaccine not being as effective. But why were so many people getting sick who had also had the booster? She needed to get Becky's expert to analyze the booster before she was forced to administer more of them. Every time someone came in for one, she deferred or tried to talk them out of it, telling them they should wait until a later date. Delay tactics would only work for so long before someone noticed what she was doing.

Twenty minutes later, test results in hand, she raced back to her patient.

"Negative for the flu."

Mrs. Jeffries sighed. "Then what is it? The aches are constant and the fever is exhausting."

"We can try a bunch of more tests, but it appears to be a viral infection of some kind. Your body has a fever because it's trying to fight it off. These sorts of bugs usually clear up in about a week."

The woman pushed herself up, grimacing as she swung

her legs over the side of the bed again. "There's nothing I can do?"

"Painkillers, fluids, and rest. If it gets worse or you develop more symptoms, call your doctor or come back and see us."

Sarah helped her patient off the bed and walked with her down the hall until she came to the next curtain containing another person with the same symptoms. She waited until Mrs. Jeffries turned left at the nurses' station and was out of view. Healing the woman with magic crossed her mind, but she had to conserve power. And there were so many patients coming in with the same symptoms she couldn't heal them all.

After performing the same tasks on her second patient, John, a man in his early forties, and getting a negative flu test, she discharged him as well. Before heading to another patient, she used the phone in the lounge to call Toronto's public health unit. A pleasant woman took all the information, placed her on hold for ten minutes, then came back to let her know her observations hadn't alarmed the public health doctors. It was flu season.

She hung up the phone and plopped down in the nearest chair. A low grumble in her stomach reminded her to eat something. The snack she'd had earlier hadn't been enough to see her through the day.

She hustled to the hospital's cafeteria for a quick lunch. Grabbing a salad and a sandwich, she observed the workers behind the counter, the cashier, other patrons sitting at tables. A table at the far end of the cafeteria stood empty. It had the best view of the small park across the street. She settled into a chair and ate her food but noted a few people who looked flushed. Others grimaced as if in pain. Still, others pushed plates away, their food half eaten.

A bad feeling settled in the pit of her stomach, almost

taking away her appetite. She hurried through eating, not even enjoying the tanginess of the dressing or the crunch of the celery in the tuna salad. Ten minutes later, she grabbed her tray, put it on the counter for washing, and dropped her garbage in the bin on her way out.

Back in the ER, the nurses and doctors raced around, treating a new batch of patients. A young nurse approached her, eyes widening with relief.

"Four-car accident. Driver from the sports car didn't make it, but we have six other patients from the scene who need attention."

Sarah took a deep breath and nodded. "Give me a chart and show me the way."

On the outside, the Grange gang headquarters was a dilapidated warehouse, its brickwork scorched by years of neglect and graffiti. Inside, the air was thick with the scent of stale beer and unwashed bodies. A testament to how the gang had thrived under Conquest's leadership. Caleb, as the new leader, seemed to be letting the gang members use the place as a flophouse. Rachel sat in the middle of it all, her gaze never wavering from Caleb.

The meeting room had all the equipment and accessories an office conference room might have. Caleb sat on one side of the large conference table. She and Williams sat on the other. It pained her how far down Caleb had fallen. For a split second, she wished Becky were there to see how Caleb's soul fared. When Rachel had first met Caleb, the young man had a soul that was bright. But the longer he controlled a gang and participated in gang activity, the more tainted his soul would become.

"Caleb," she said, her voice as cold and hard as the

concrete floor beneath their feet. "We need to talk about Vince."

"Vince?" Caleb's voice held a note of mockery. "You mean the lowlife who got himself killed?"

Vince might have been a lower-level gang member, but he was still a Grange member. Word on the street pinned the murder on a former Esskays member. An orphaned gang member looking to make a name for himself to start a new gang.

"He was one of yours," Rachel said. "Doesn't that mean something?"

Caleb snorted, his dark eyes glinting under the harsh overhead lights. "What could it mean? He's dead. End of story."

Rachel clenched her fists at her sides. "No," she said. "You and I both know it's not the end. The way I see it, you have two choices. Retaliation and peace. Retaliation will only lead to more violence."

Detective Williams, standing beside her, nodded in agreement. "She's right, Caleb. This cycle has to stop somewhere."

Caleb shrugged nonchalantly, leaning back in his leather chair. "And why should I listen to you two? You're cops. You don't understand our world. You think I'm scared of a little war?"

Rachel leaned forward, her gaze never leaving Caleb's face. "I understand more than you think," she said.

Surprise flickered in his eyes before he quickly masked it with indifference. She knew he didn't believe her—how could he? He was a gang leader; she was an angel in exile.

"It's not about fear. It's about unnecessary violence. Besides," Rachel said, "I'm still investigating your father's death."

At this, Caleb laughed uproariously, slapping his thigh

in amusement. "That's rich," he said when he finally managed to catch his breath. "Good luck with that."

Rachel frowned at him, taken aback by his reaction. "You don't care at all who killed him?"

"He did me a favor," Caleb said with a shrug. "And frankly, I wouldn't be surprised if you never found out who did it."

Rachel tensed and she crossed her arms over her chest. Her gaze pierced Caleb's. "I know who did it," she said, her voice steady and unyielding. "It's just a matter of finding the proof."

Caleb scoffed, and he leaned forward with a gleam in his eyes. "You should leave now," he said, his eyes darting to the door. "Before our hospitality runs out."

Rachel held his gaze for a moment longer before standing up and walking out of the room, Detective Williams following closely behind her. As they made their way to their car parked outside the gang headquarters, Williams turned to her.

"What was that all about?" Williams asked as they climbed into their car. His brows furrowed in concern. "You can't just accuse him of murder. We need evidence."

"I know," Rachel said, staring out the window at the passing cityscape. She didn't know what had come over her; she had acted on instinct, something deep within her telling her that Caleb was hiding something.

In the dim light of the car, Rachel could see Williams studying her. His eyes were filled with concern, his mouth set in a thin line. He was a good man—a family man— dedicated to his job and making the streets safer for his family.

But this was more than just a job for Rachel. It was her redemption, her chance to earn back her wings and stop the apocalypse from ravaging the world she had grown to care about.

She turned to Williams, meeting his gaze with a nod. "We'll find the evidence," she said. "And we'll bring Caleb Bishop to justice."

"It will be tough finding the evidence. I'm sure, if he is guilty, he did a good job of covering it up," Williams said. "But if it's out there, we'll find it."

As they left behind the gang headquarters and Caleb Bishop, Rachel couldn't shake off the feeling that they were descending deeper into a world of darkness and danger, one that threatened to consume them all if they weren't careful.

The radio crackled to life, a harsh voice cutting through the silence of the car. "We got a lead on the Denton case. Forensics just came back with evidence. Richard Black's prints were all over the murder weapon."

"Yes!"

Rachel loved when criminals did stupid things. And leaving your prints all over a gun you used to kill someone with was stupid. Even if the weapon had been wiped clean, she would have eventually been able to trace it back to Richard Black. One of the many suspects in one of the dozens of homicides she and Williams were investigating.

She glanced at Williams, his grip tightening on the steering wheel.

"We're on our way," he said into the radio, his voice steady and calm.

"We've been after Black for months," Williams said as they turned onto Shuter Street. "This could be our chance to finally put him away."

Rachel nodded, her gaze fixed on the road ahead. "Let's hope so."

But even as she spoke, another call came through on

the radio. "Shots fired at 111 Shuter Street. All units respond."

Rachel's blood ran cold. That was Black's address, where they were heading.

Williams jabbed the button to turn on the emergency lights, and slammed on the gas, sending them hurtling down the street toward danger and uncertainty. Rachel gripped her seat, her mind racing.

As they neared the address, flashes of blue and red lights reflected off the buildings. The sound of sirens filled the air, a chilling reminder of what was at stake.

She swallowed hard, steeling herself for what lay ahead. She had faced countless dangers before, but this felt different somehow.

As they pulled up to the scene, Rachel couldn't shake off a deep sense of foreboding. Something dark and dangerous was unfolding here—something that threatened to pull them all under.

Chapter Three

Hours into her shift, Sarah leaned against a wall near the end of the corridor for a breather. She didn't want to take up a chair a patient might need, and if she ventured into the lounge again, she'd be tempted to disappear into a sleep room to get some shut-eye. The lack of a full night's sleep caught up with her sometime around three in the afternoon. Since then, she'd guzzled coffee like it was the most delicious beverage she'd ever tasted.

A commotion at the end of the hallway pulled a groan from her lips. She pushed herself away from the wall and hurried down the corridor, quickening her step when she spotted Rachel's raven black hair. Her sister had a firm grasp of a man's arm, his hands shackled behind him. Interest piqued, Sarah flashed her sister a smile and nodded to the nurse at the desk. It amazed her how calm the nurses continued to be even during the most chaotic shifts.

"I'll help Detective Malak. Has the patient's information been taken already?"

The nurse checked her computer, then nodded. "Richard Black. Curtain three is available."

Sarah jerked her head to the right and marched down the corridor, stopping halfway. On the left side of the corridor, she pulled the curtain aside.

"What seems to be the problem, Detective?"

Rachel released her iron-like grip on her suspect so he could sit on the bed to be examined. "Gunshot wound to the shoulder."

Sarah pulled on a pair of blue surgical gloves in order to examine the man's wound. Before she could begin, a nurse hustled through the opening in the curtain to hand her a chart.

"Thanks."

After a perfunctory perusal of the man's information, she plunked the chart down on the table beside the bed.

"Vitals on the way in looked okay," she said.

But since arriving, the man's color had drained. She listened to his heart, checked his pulse. They were both of concern.

"You should lie back."

Though he glared daggers at Rachel, his eyes softened when they looked at Sarah. He nodded and leaned back.

"It is busier out there than I've ever seen it." Rachel nodded to Sarah's patient. "He was shot by a woman who said he killed her husband."

"Are you allowed to tell her that?" The man groaned when Sarah touched the area around the entry wound.

"It will be public record. You are being arrested for murder."

His nostrils flared. "She shot me!"

Rachel nodded sadly. "Yes, so we had to arrest her too. Sad really because we were already on our way to arrest you with the evidence we had. She didn't need to do anything except wait."

Sarah wrote something in the chart, then focused on Rachel. "It's been super busy here too. Not just violent crime, but accidents, that flu-like thing that seems to be going around."

Without taking her eyes off her prisoner, Rachel paced the small curtained area at the foot of the bed. "The gangs are taking over." She paused, leaning into Sarah so the patient couldn't hear. "More people are choosing to be nasty because it's fun. Lingering effects of having two horsemen topside, perhaps. But Conquest still has influence."

Sarah nodded. "It's going to get worse." She finished writing in the chart, then turned her attention to her patient. "I'm sending you up to the OR. The bullet is lodged in your shoulder. It will have to be removed. You're lucky she was a bad shot."

Before he could retort, Sarah left the curtained area, made the arrangements, then returned to check his vitals again.

A few minutes later, a porter came to escort him to an operating room. Sarah tucked the chart in the hanging folder at the end of the bed and moved aside so the porter could get the bed out. Once he was transferred to an operating table, the gurney would be sanitized and brought back for another patient. Until then, they were a bed down.

Outside the curtain now, Rachel stared at her, eyes wide. "You're not going to perform the surgery?"

"I'm needed here. And the OR doctors are great."

A tingle rippled over her wings and a sense of calm washed over her. She made a mental note to tell Becky of the power boost. The younger angel would be able to figure out how she could get more back intentionally if there was enough data in her spreadsheet.

From the look of anger on Rachel's face, the older angel deduced what had happened. Rachel leaned closer and whispered in her ear.

"That's not fair. I bust my ass with work, closed more cases this past week than I've ever closed in a week before, and you get your angelic gift back for handing off a patient to someone else."

Sarah shrugged. "You'll figure out what works for you eventually."

"Eventually isn't soon enough. You figured out what does it for you?"

"No. I'll tell Becky and she'll figure it out. Better call to have a constable here to watch Mr. Black when he gets out of surgery."

Rachel pulled out her phone and called it in. If the guy died, she and her partner, Detective Williams, would likely get the case. Michael Williams had been Rachel's partner since she and her sisters had taken on their human personas months ago. A great detective, Williams was also intelligent, witty, and a family man. While Richard Black was still alive, the woman who shot him was Division 50's case. If he survived, Rachel would spend every moment she could building a case against him for killing the woman's husband.

"I'll probably be late tonight," Sarah said. "The sick and injured keep coming. Don't you have to escort your suspect to the OR?"

Rachel nodded and raced down the hallway to catch up to her suspect.

———

The door to Baron's weighed more than a concert piano. Sarah yanked with every ounce of energy she had left and barely budged it. Rallying her muscles, she took a deep breath, pulled again, and the door swung open, releasing a soothing beat that made her foot tap. If she had the strength to tap her foot in time to the music, she had the strength to eat.

Despite the dim lighting in the place, she spotted her sisters at the back of the club at their usual table. Plates of food already covered the surface, including a burger and fries in her usual spot. She pushed through the crowd of music lovers, feeling like a salmon swimming upstream. Exhausted, she plopped down in the free seat closest to the back door and facing the bar.

"Thanks for waiting for me until I got home." Sarah picked up a french fry, noting the other meals looked like they hadn't been sampled yet. The second she popped the fry into her mouth, her sisters dug into their meals.

Becky's stomach grumbled. "You called just in time. I was about to attempt cooking. And these were brought out a few minutes ago. Any longer and I would have devoured my food and started on yours."

A twinge of guilt prickled her neck at being so late. They tried to eat together as often as they could—it helped cement the sister bond they'd built into their histories—as often as their work schedules allowed at least. Which was most of the time unless Rachel was on a tough case, or Sarah was stuck at the hospital past her shift. Becky's job rarely required her to stay at the office after she'd finished the six o'clock news. For anything else that needed to be done for the TV station, Becky worked on those items at home. And Leah was home before all of them most days even though the high school was more of a commute.

In between bites, Rachel put her fork on her plate and focused on Becky. "How's Laura doing?"

Becky finished chewing a bite of her pasta. "Fully recovered thanks to Sarah. I'm still tempted to suggest she and her fiancé move the wedding up by a few months."

"Probably a good idea to move it up. But how would you explain why?" Sarah asked.

The hollow pit in her stomach was a little less hollow now that she'd eaten a few bites of food. Sarah racked her brain for the name of someone she might warn. Professionally friendly with most of the staff at the hospital, she couldn't call anyone a friend. Most of her spare time was spent with her sisters, researching how to send horsemen back to limbo and performing spells to do just that. Once, a few weeks ago, she'd gone out with a group of doctors to let off some steam after a particularly tough night in the ER. Rachel had her partner. Leah had the teachers at school and her students.

She shoved the thoughts aside for now and looked at Rachel. "What's going on with the gangs? They've been keeping our ER hopping. And I'm sure the rest of the ERs in the city are the same."

"With the Esskays gone, the Grange is running the city. Caleb is turning out to be more ruthless than Victor."

Becky nodded. "Conquest taught Caleb everything he knows."

"It's even affecting the schools now. The board is talking about postponing the history trip for the teachers until the summer. They want us here over March Break just in case. Might need a bit of angel magic to convince the board to let us go." Leah took a sip of her pop.

"Yes," Rachel said. "We'll need stuff you can get on that trip to help stop this apocalypse."

From her vantage point, Sarah had a perfect view of

the bar and the TV above it. The scroll across the bottom of the screen mentioned a sickness in Russia, thought to be connected to the bomb that hit the area over a week ago. She pointed to the screen.

"What do you think that's all about?" she asked.

Becky and Rachel swiveled to see the screen.

When they turned back around, Becky shrugged. "The devastation wasn't as bad as they thought it would have been for a bomb. But the sickness isn't radiation related. At least that's not mentioned in the scroll."

"Almost flu-like symptoms. Sort of like what I've been dealing with lately at the hospital." Sarah frowned. The illness in Russia couldn't be a coincidence. "It is flu and cold season, but it's unusual that so many people around the bomb site are getting sick."

"I'll look into it tonight when I go back into work. They've got me covering the delicate 'peace' talks between the US and Russia this week."

Rachel narrowed her eyes at Becky. "Since we got here, I don't remember you doing the news at eleven."

Becky shrugged. "Now you will."

Sarah leaned back in her chair, took a sip of her decaf coffee wishing it were a stiff drink, and turned her attention away from the TV when the scroll across the bottom switched to celebrity news.

Alarm bells clanged in her head, but the source of the alarm remained elusive for now. When she got to the hospital in the morning, she would look into the patients who had come in with the fevers and body aches. Check with the other hospitals in the area again to see if they had any more. A knot forming in the pit of her stomach told her this was just the beginning. Things were going to get a lot worse.

Back at the loft an hour later, Becky bustled around the place, getting ready to go back into work. Rachel and Leah sat at the island, facing the kitchen. Sarah faced the living room, watching with amusement as her sister rushed into the bedroom and the bathroom, looking for her laptop. Working the late shift caused her sister to become befuddled, which was a drastic change from the picture-perfect anchor she portrayed to the public and at home.

"Beck, it's right where you left it before we went to Baron's." Sarah pointed to the laptop bag sitting on the floor against the end of the sofa.

Becky let out a deep breath. "Thanks."

Sarah nodded. "It was nice of you to take Kevin's shift tonight."

Becky marched to the door, grabbed her coat from the closet, and shrugged into it. Slinging the strap of her bag over her shoulder, she smiled. "He's been wanting to spend more time with his wife. Given the circumstances, I thought it would be the right thing to do. Don't wait up."

Becky yanked the loft door open, an unmistakable shiver tracing down her back as she stepped over the threshold. Annoyance bubbled in Sarah's stomach. When Sarah took over someone's shift or stayed late, the only reward she got was a sense of accomplishment at having helped someone.

Rachel's eyebrows drew together and she pointed at Becky's wings. "It's not fair."

Sarah slid off the stool and marched to the fridge. "Have some dessert to take your mind off it."

Rachel's eyes lit up and she wiggled on her stool. "We have dessert? What is it?"

Since they'd been eating in more, the fridge was stocked with everything they needed to make balanced meals and decadent desserts. Two upper shelves held various baked treats along with puddings, custards, and whipped cream. She reached in and pulled out a glass pie dish.

"Apple pie. With ice cream or custard."

Rachel opted for pie with custard, warmed in the microwave for thirty seconds, while Leah asked for pie with vanilla ice cream. Sarah prepared both, plus her own, chocolate fudge pudding with whipped cream. She placed the desserts on the island and before she sat down, Rachel and Leah dug into their sweet treats.

"No seconds," Sarah said. "We need to make sure there's enough for Becky when she gets home."

A shiver zinged through her wings. She covered it with an exaggerated yawn. It was another instance for Becky's spreadsheet and one Rachel didn't need to know about at the moment. The eldest angel was already miffed about having the least amount of angel mojo.

Once they finished their desserts, they moved to the living room where the seats were more comfortable and it was easier to watch Becky's newscast. Rachel sat on the sofa, in the corner closest to the kitchen. Leah sat cross-legged on the floor on the other side of the coffee table, facing the sofa, her laptop centered on the table already open, waiting for input. Sarah plopped into the easy chair. It was by far the best seat in the house, with easy access to the kitchen and a direct line of sight for the television. She was the only one who didn't have to turn their head to see the newscast.

A bit early for the late-night news, the end of a movie rolled on the screen. Rachel pointed the remote at the TV and turned the volume down.

"Leah, how are our supplies? Do we have enough to send War and Famine back?" Sarah asked.

The youngest angel's fingers flew over the keyboard as she finished typing. Her fingers moved to the touchpad, and she clicked to open a spreadsheet. "You think War is back?"

Rachel leaned forward on the sofa. "If the priest hasn't summoned him yet, he will soon. He brought back Conquest after we sent his ass back to limbo."

Leah scrolled through their list, frowning. "The everyday ingredients are fine. But we're low on holy basil. And we need more holy oil, holy water. The limestone from Mt. Hermon is still on back order. I took all they could spare to vanquish War. Then there's the new stuff we need for Famine and Death."

Sarah nodded. "Make a note of what we need for all of them and we'll stock up with what we can."

Leah typed something into the computer, presumably making notes as Sarah had suggested. "The stuff to vanquish Death will be harder to get. Luckily, a little angelic mojo put me in charge of the history teachers' trip for March Break."

Rachel got up from the sofa and wandered into the kitchen. Cupboard doors banged open and shut. The crunch of a bag filled the loft. She returned with a family-sized bag of chips.

"Where did those come from?" Sarah asked.

Rachel shrugged. "You must have missed them behind the cereal." She turned to Leah. "The Israel Museum and The Vatican I can see. But how are you explaining Mt. Hermon?"

"There's an ancient historical site at the base. Besides, they're just glad they're getting away for a week with everything planned for them."

Sarah waved at Rachel. "Turn it up. She's on."

Rachel raised the volume until it sounded like Becky was in the room with them. From the television, she smiled at her audience, reading the news prompter with such ease it looked like she was talking to an old friend about the day's events.

"Tensions are mounting between Russia and the United States of America, but mediator Penny Cooper is confident she can get both countries to back down from their desire for mutual destruction. Canada has already sent peace keepers to Russia's borders with numerous other countries to ensure hostilities don't erupt."

Sarah shook her head. No matter how skilled the mediator was, with War at the heart of the conflict between the two nations, a war might still happen.

Thursday after the evening mass, Father Ianetti sat in the middle pew on the left-hand side of the nave and listened to the silence. It had been at least an hour since the last parishioner pushed through the heavy wooden doors at the front of the church. They clanged shut, echoing in the high ceilings. But the clanging died down until it stopped completely. Even the rest of the church staff—junior priest, receptionist, office manager—had left. It was in the quiet times that his creative mind roared to life, figuring out plans, going over details.

The fitness band on his wrist buzzed with a reminder that it was time. He smiled at the band, a gift from a worried member of his flock last week who thought he wasn't getting enough steps in a day to keep him in peak health. Not part of the Omega sect yet, the parishioner was playing a vital part now with the reminders he was able to set, the monitoring of his heart health he was able to keep track of.

He pushed himself up with a groan. He wasn't getting any younger, and the summoning spells drained him more every time he did one. Still not at one hundred percent after calling Famine from limbo, he silently cursed whoever had sent War back. It had to be the sisters who had come to talk to him about his predictions about the apocalypse. The detective and the reporter. He didn't know what the other two did and didn't care. He cared that they kept interfering in his plan to give the Earth a do-over. Angels was the only explanation. It was sad really, that warriors of God were trying to stop something that would benefit humans in the long run.

The thought crossed his mind more than once to let Conquest take care of them, but the horseman had made it clear he had better things to do. Nuisances must be left to meddle, unless he could figure out a way to prevent them from interfering himself.

He padded down the center aisle of the nave, took a right at the first pew, and ambled down to his office, all the while listening for stragglers. Sometimes, the receptionist worked late instead of returning to an empty home. Her husband left her months ago and she couldn't bear the empty apartment.

Stillness filled the air. No lingering sounds filtered through the old walls. Tonight, she had listened to him and left. Maybe she even stopped at a restaurant for a late dinner with the office manager. They tried every day to get him to join them. Family. That's what they were here. And when children were naughty, they had to be taught a lesson. All of God's children needed to be taught a lesson.

His room was dark save for a patch of moonlight filtering in from the small window beside his bed. He flicked the switch beside the door, flooding the room with soft yellow light. Undressing, he folded each garment, smoothed the material, and placed them on the foot of his bed. A bath, drawn over an hour ago, waited for him in the en suite.

Taking a deep breath, he lowered himself into the cool water, shifting to get comfortable, but the grit of the salt dug into his legs. For the other summonings, he stayed in the ritual bath for an hour. He didn't have that kind of time or the fortitude to endure the cold water for more than ten minutes. Not when he had to perform the ritual outside with no coverings. He took a deep breath and slid under the water until it covered his head. A few seconds later, he pushed against the end of the tub to propel himself above water again, sputtering for air.

When he couldn't take the chill any longer, he gingerly got out of the bath, being careful with his footing on the floor. Slip and falls could be dangerous, especially when there was no one here to hear him.

A towel hung from the rack beside the tub and this was one time he wished his modest quarters included a towel warmer. He grabbed the thin material and wrapped it around his shivering body. He dried off as he walked back into his bedroom, making sure every last drop of water was absorbed, then pulled on his robe.

The trunk at the foot of his bed held everything he needed for that evening. Hours ago, when there had been a lull in parishioners, he'd gathered what he needed and placed them on top of his sweaters. A groan of hinges filled the room when he lifted the lid. He picked up the paper bag with his ritual items, closed the trunk, and hurried to the courtyard in the back of the church.

After double-checking to make sure the gate to the small courtyard was locked, he used a flat stone to act as an altar, placing a pewter bowl the size of cupped hands in the center of the rock. Next, he created a pentagram with powered chalk. He placed the black pillar candles in a circle on the outside of the pentagram. Once he was happy with the setup, he put his athame in front of the bowl, dug into the bag to retrieve his lighter, and took a deep breath.

Not wanting to spend more time in the winter weather than he had to, he rushed through lighting the candles, mixing the herbs in the bowl, burning the sigil for War, and slicing the tip of his finger to provide the five drops of blood. At the last possible moment, he dropped his robe, then started chanting the incantation to seal his circle and summon the horseman from limbo.

If the sisters kept interfering, he could do this a thousand times if necessary, if it didn't kill him first. He had enough of everything to keep bringing the horseman back until the job was done. It wasn't enough to set the apocalypse in motion. The Omega sect had done that decades ago, with a timetable set for now, when the estimated world population would grow into the unsustainable. With the Omegas and horsemen, his prediction of the end of the world would finally be proven true.

A slight breeze whispered over his skin, raising the hair on his arms with goose bumps. He kept up a steady stream of the incantation until he'd uttered the words seven times. Though he'd been whispering, the sudden silence weighed heavily in the air when he stopped.

Prepared for what was to come, he braced himself for the horseman's arrival. Seconds ticked by. The night stilled. The breeze stopped. Suffocating, hot air filled the circle of his pentagram, ripping the breath from his lungs. Gasping, he fell to the ground on one knee, his head throbbing, lungs bursting.

A wisp of red smoke formed in the space between the

circle and an old maple tree by the back wall of the courtyard. The smoke formed into a horse. Hoofbeats pounded in Father Ianetti's ears. War popped back into existence, filling the circle with Father Ianetti. Air flooded into the priest's lungs again and he sagged with relief.

War glanced around the courtyard. "How long have I been gone?"

"A little over a week."

Jeans formed over the horseman's muscular legs. A T-shirt, then a lightweight coat covered War's chest. Rugged boots formed over his feet.

"You don't look so good, old man."

Father Ianetti waved his hand in the air, shaking his head. "I'm fine. I'll be able to call Death's reapers."

"See that you do. How far behind are we?"

"Not too far. Famine is working from the inside. Conquest is doing what Conquest does."

"Rest up, Father."

Before Father Ianetti could respond, War marched out of the courtyard, into the night, in search of his brothers. Father Ianetti waited in the circle, on the ground, and pulled his robe under him to shield his naked body from the cold grass. A half hour later, when he'd mustered enough energy, he gathered his things, pulled the robe on again, and shuffled back inside.

Chapter Four

Friday morning, after a sound but short sleep, Sarah roamed the hospital halls an hour before her scheduled shift. A second cup of coffee called to her as she walked past the doctor's lounge. Once she checked on her patients, the ones who had been admitted instead of being sent home from the ER, she would reward herself with a double shot of caffeine.

All her flu-like patients had been released, but there was a burn victim on the fifth floor who would remain at the hospital for a few days to make sure his dressings were changed regularly and that infection hadn't set in. Once she determined sending him home would help his recovery, she would release him. She was sure his girlfriend could handle the job of home nurse.

She finished her non-official rounds with ten minutes to spare before her shift started. Enough time to pop into the lounge for a quick coffee and the muffin she'd picked up from the hospital cafeteria when she arrived.

She plopped down in the first vacant chair, beside Dr. Goretti. Also a workaholic, Dr. Patrizia Goretti usually beat her into the hospital even though she lived forty-five minutes away, when rush-hour traffic was good and the weather didn't interfere. Sarah admired that kind of dedication in anyone but especially a healer.

The doctor's long brown hair was pulled into a ponytail that fell halfway down her back. Sparkling hazel eyes twinkled when she smiled and raised a mug.

"Morning, Dr. Malak. How are your patients from yesterday doing?"

"Improving. How about yours?"

"Doing well. Must be our magical healing hands."

Sarah chuckled. Magic would be a more thorough way for her to help the sick, but the good old-fashioned way would have to suffice. Slightly rested from her brief respite, she pushed herself up from the table, poured herself a cup of coffee, and grabbed her muffin from the fridge. She returned to her seat at the table. As breakfasts go, it wasn't what she would recommend, but it would do for now.

After wolfing down her food and guzzling the coffee, Sarah stood. She stretched from side to side, bent over and touched her toes, stood tall, and took three calming breaths. One of the things she loved about the ER was every day was different. She never knew what kind of patients she would have, what challenges she would face, and that excited her. But a nagging feeling in the pit of her stomach told her what at least a few of her cases would be.

"Ready to help the sick?" she asked Dr. Goretti.

Her colleague nodded and stood. "Let's do it."

The morning was a blur of patients. A nonstop stream of the sick and injured lingered in the ER waiting area for a doctor on duty to see them. Sarah took as many as possible, churning through them as fast as she could effectively treat and diagnose them. Almost half were people with headaches, pains, and fever.

Her latest flu-like patient sat behind curtain eight, waiting for Sarah to take a look at her. With so many of them coming in, it would be easy to chalk this up to another of the same and send them on their way. But if flu was suspected, she needed to run the kit. Since the first one arrived, she'd kept a supply of kits in her lab coat pockets and hidden under trays in the curtained off ER areas so there was always a kit on hand.

She pulled the curtain aside, stepped into the enclosed space, and smiled at her patient. "I'm Dr. Malak. What seems to be the problem today?"

"Blinding headache. I have a bit of a fever. And aches and pains."

Sarah put the stethoscope buds in her ears and listened to the woman's chest. Then she shone a light in her patient's eyes, nose, and throat. The digital infrared thermometer gun confirmed a fever.

"Did you happen to get a flu vaccine this year?"

Her patient shook her head. "No. I forgot."

Interest piqued and theories crumbling, Sarah pulled out a flu testing kit. "We'll do a swab to make sure it's not the flu."

The woman nodded. "I did get the booster, though, a little over a week ago. I figured it was just another flu shot, but better."

Sarah nodded, frowning. She couldn't really fault the woman's logic. If the original flu vaccine didn't work and the government was recommending people get the booster, why wouldn't they think it was just another flu shot? Only improved from the failed one. Her theory rose like a phoenix from the ashes.

"It might be a cold or another virus. Once we get the results of the flu test, I'll come back in to see you."

The woman nodded and opened her mouth so Sarah

could take the swab. When Sarah tucked the sample into a bag to take to the hospital's lab, her patient leaned back in the bed, exhausted.

"Rest here for now. I'll be back soon."

Before she could leave, her phone buzzed with a message from Becky.

Tipster says to check the booster

B

I'll see what I can do.

S

Sarah left the area and hurried to the lab to drop off the sample. On her way back to the ER area, retching sounds filtered down the hallway from the waiting area.

A page went over the hospital's public address system, calling for a porter to clean up the mess.

A desire to test her theory overwhelmed Sarah and she stopped at the nurses' station. "Vanda, can you give me as many of the fever, achy, headache patients as possible?"

The petite nurse looked up from the computer and smiled. Big brown eyes shone with empathy. "Sure. We've got a lot of them."

"Can we start with the patient who threw up? Without seeing their intake chart, I'm pretty sure they are one of the fever, achy patients."

"Good guess. I'll send them to curtain three."

Sarah thanked the nurse, then hurried down the corridor to check in on her other patients. The girl in curtain two was still waiting for an X-ray after falling from her bike. And in curtain four, her patient waited for an ultrasound. Two other patients waited for their flu kit results. And now she would be adding another to the list.

She ducked into curtain three. The man who had vomited in the waiting area lay against the pillows of the gurney. The bed was raised slightly so he was in a semi-sitting position. A green pallor tinged his face.

"Hello. I'm Dr. Malak. How long have you been feeling ill?"

The man struggled to sit up straighter. "Two or three days."

"Have you traveled anywhere?"

"No. I've been at work."

She asked him a variety of health-related questions, ending with the flu shot question. He'd had a flu shot and a booster. Like most of the patients coming in with similar symptoms, the booster had been administered about a week and a half ago.

He agreed to a flu test and managed to keep from gagging while she took the swab.

"How is your stomach feeling now? Should I get you a bowl in case you vomit again?"

He shook his head, stopped, and put his hand to his stomach. "I think I'm okay."

"Lie back. I'll get some water sent in and a bowl just in case."

After promising to return once the results of the test came in, she ducked out of the curtained area. She found a nurse and asked about sending in water and a bowl, then hurried to the lab to drop off the kit. While there, she picked up the results of the ones she'd left over half an hour ago.

So far, she'd examined six people with the same symptoms, seven if she included the vomiting patient. And all the tests came back negative for the flu. Despite the vomiting, she was sure his test would have the same result.

Before going back to the ER, she popped into the

lounge, pulled out her phone, and called Public Health. The woman who took her call was as helpful as an umbrella in a hurricane, explaining she would make note of the situation and get back to her.

Sarah contemplated taking a five-minute rest, refueling with more caffeine, but she couldn't spare the time right now. She stopped at the nurse's station for another patient file.

Vanda handed one over. "Curtain five. Scarborough City Hospital wants to send patients here. They're swamped."

"Mass casualty? I hadn't heard anything about an accident."

Vanda shook her head, sending brown curls dancing on her shoulders. "No. With flu-like symptoms. They can't keep up."

Sarah's chest tightened. A tingling sensation swept over her hands. "I'll send the director over to give authorization."

"Thanks."

Sarah tucked the file under her arm and marched down the corridor to her next patient. Her stomach churned, the bad feeling growing. If all hospitals in the city were dealing with the same thing, outbreaks would headline the six o'clock news. Somehow, she needed to get a sample of the booster to Becky for testing by her contacts.

Though it was early evening, Sarah's bones screamed at her to sleep as if it were closer to midnight. Her shift had ended less than an hour ago, and she sat at the back of Baron's with Rachel and Leah, waiting for Becky to arrive, facing the bar. Since Becky had to be on air at 6:00 p.m., she was always the last to arrive.

Sarah took a sip of her decaf coffee. Decaf because she wanted to fall asleep as soon as her head hit the pillow. She smothered a yawn.

A little after 7:00 p.m., Becky waltzed into the place like she owned it, stopping and chatting to customers as she made her way to the back of the bar. Her *celebrity* status still occasionally caused a stir with some of the new patrons of the place. The regulars were accustomed to the news anchor frequenting the bar.

It took Becky five minutes to make it to the table. She pulled out the empty chair and plopped down, blowing red tendrils of hair out of her face. She picked up the drink that sat there waiting for her. They usually drank the same thing, so whoever arrived first ordered drinks. It cut back on the waiting.

Rachel picked up her beverage. "So what's the big deal? It's flu season."

"What did I miss?" Becky asked.

Leah nodded at Sarah. "Overabundance of flu-like symptom patients in the ER today."

Becky's brow wrinkled. "And that worries you because my tipster was right and the vaccine wasn't as effective?"

Sarah shook her head. "It's true that it's cold and flu season. But it's never been this bad, at least not in recent years. And we have at least two horsemen running around. Maybe three. I'm concerned about the booster. There's another sample in the fridge at home for you to take to Dr. Karimi."

Becky nodded. "I'll take it tomorrow and remind him it's urgent."

Leah's eyes widened. "You think Famine is behind it?"

"Not necessarily. Everyone so far seems well nourished, but I do think it's part of the overall apocalypse plan."

Becky wiggled in her chair, put her drink back on the table, and frowned. "Speaking of the plan, I've been looking into the doomsday Omega sect. Members have been hard to find because they tend to hide the Omega tattoo most of the time. But I have discovered a few in the city, in interesting positions. There's a member of the board at the hospital, a member of parliament from Toronto, the head of research and development at Ralston from the 1980s."

Leah perked up. "When the agreement to destroy weapons of mass destruction and biological agents was signed."

Becky nodded. "I've found more reapers, too who go back a long way. But I don't think they're doing anything to actively help the apocalypse along. They're just not hindering it either."

Sarah frowned. "A board member from the hospital? That's not good. I wonder how many others there are at the hospital."

The TV above the bar scrolled news of the day, capturing Sarah's attention. No mention of a health crisis yet. Public Health was still looking into her concerns.

Something about the bar bothered her. It was different somehow. Then she realized Mario, the usual bartender during the week, wasn't there. Steve, the owner, emerged from the door beside the bar, a smile on his face, and he walked around, greeting tables.

When he finally made it to their table, she nodded to the bar. "Where's Mario tonight? I don't think I've ever not seen him back there during the week."

Steve nodded. "He's out sick tonight."

"That's too bad. Do you know what his symptoms

are?" A business didn't have a right to ask what an employee's symptoms were, but sometimes employees offered. She took a chance that Mario would be the sharing type.

"He said he had a fever, aches and pains, a massive headache. He mentioned he was going to take some over-the-counter meds and try to get some sleep."

Not wanting to alarm Steve, she smiled reassuringly. "Give him our best wishes for a speedy recovery."

Her stomach churned. Now that she took a moment to look around the place, there were fewer people than usual on a Friday night. Even when there weren't a lot of new people in the place, it usually took Becky at least ten minutes to make it to the table. Though the music from the playlist was loud—the band was taking a break—the crowd wasn't as thick as usual. Tables stood empty. She could see between people on the dance floor. They weren't squished against each other.

"I will tell him that." He squeezed her shoulder, smiled, and hurried off to see to another table.

Sarah pulled out her phone and tapped on Google, then frowned. She didn't know Mario's last name. Another tactic popped into her head. She searched for the bartender via people he knew. Steve, the wait staff, the kitchen staff. She checked the bar's social media accounts to see if Mario was tagged in any posts. Other members of staff from the bar were tagged in a post about their Tuesday night specials. She clicked there and fell down a rabbit hole of links until she finally found a mention of Mario that included his last name.

"How weird would it be to show up at his door to see how he was doing?"

They'd only been on Earth for a few months, but the staff at the bar felt like a second family. Outside of work, they spent most of their time at the bar and knew most of the people who worked there well.

Rachel leaned forward, an earnest expression on her face. "Weird. But if you want, I can find his address for you. I'd have to do it in a way that Williams won't find out, though."

Sarah sighed and leaned back in her chair. "No, that's okay. It's probably nothing. I'll check the hospitals to see if he came in. If he didn't, I'm sure it's probably just a cold."

A new scroll across the bottom of the TV above the bar caught her attention. It was a reminder for people to get the flu shot booster.

After dinner, Rachel insisted they return to their building but not to the loft to let the food settle or relax in front of the television with some books. Still investigating the apocalypse and how to stop it, but in a way that exerted little energy. No, she marched them down to the basement for training. Tonight, she'd settled on hand to hand.

Sarah and Becky sat on the benches nestled against the right wall of the training room, watching Rachel put Leah through her paces. The youngest angel was doing well against the eldest angel. Leah dodged a few blows, then landed a couple, knocking Rachel off balance.

With training came hydration. Sarah picked up a bottle of water and took a long gulp. Watching Rachel and Leah dance around each other on the mat tired her out. As it was, she could barely keep her eyes open. The shifts at the hospital were getting more and more hectic, the consequence of having horsemen in the city.

Sarah put the lid back on the water and turned her attention back to the training mat.

"Sarah, you're up." Rachel helped Leah stand up from a prone position on the mat.

She'd missed the move that landed the youngest angel on the floor. Leah was usually better than that, always keeping Rachel on her toes. It was late, and they were all tired. Which was why this was cruel and unusual.

"I'm too tired to train. I think we should all go to bed so we can be fresh in the morning."

Rachel marched over to the bench. "The others trained. It wouldn't be fair for you to get a pass."

"I took mental notes when you were training Becky and Leah. Every move, it's right here." Sarah touched a finger to her temple.

Rachel narrowed her eyes at Sarah. "I'd buy the note thing from Leah. But there's nothing like practice. Even I need practice. You're helping me too, not just yourself."

A shiver rippled through Rachel. Sarah hopped off the bench to examine the angel's wings. A white patch appeared close to her spine, where there hadn't been before.

Becky would take note of the power boost and go into analysis mode when they got back upstairs.

Now that she was standing, a wave of exhaustion threatened to take over. All she wanted to do was sink into a comfy bed and sleep for a week.

"I've been on my feet all day." Maybe now that Rachel had done something to get power back, she'd be in a better, more negotiable mood.

"You're always on your feet all day. It's part of your job. You still need to keep fit, stay prepared. Becky almost died fighting War. And Leah was thrown off the roof. We all need to keep sharp."

The logic behind Rachel's words filtered through the stubborn part of Sarah's brain, past her exhausted limbs, and settled in the part of her mind where her desire to stop the apocalypse lived. When Leah had flown off the roof, every instinct in her had screamed out a denial that the angel was dead. Thankfully, the fall hadn't caused damage so major that it couldn't be quickly healed with some angel magic.

But would they always be able to do that? Rachel still couldn't. Becky had most of her power back now, and Leah was closing in on her, but they needed all they could get to fight the horsemen. No matter how many times they sent the horsemen back, Father Ianetti could summon them again. Until the apocalypse was curtailed for good, Rachel was right. She needed to do her part.

Sarah sighed, rocking her head from side to side to work out the kinks in her neck. With a deep breath, she stretched her arms above her head, then lowered her arms, bending sideways at her waist, left then right.

"I'm not going to be any good," she warned.

"You'll be better than you think. Instinct will kick in."

Before Sarah could prepare herself, Rachel lunged froward, knocking Sarah back onto the mat. The wind knocked out of her from the contact.

Rachel helped her up and circled her. "Maybe it won't kick in."

Sarah observed Rachel, but her mind was on the patients at the hospital. How many more with the same symptoms had come in after she left? Would there be more in the morning?

Rachel charged her again and swept her leg along the floor, knocking Sarah's legs out from under her. She landed hard on her ass.

"Sarah, focus. You can't be distracted when you're fighting for your life."

Pushing herself off the ground, Sarah took a deep

breath. She shoved the hospital out of her mind, focused on Rachel instead. A twinge in her right hip mocked her. She was better than this. During their usual training sessions, Rachel wasn't able to beat the crap out of her.

Rachel charged again, but this time Sarah dodged out of the way and spun around so they faced each other again. Rachel smiled.

"Better."

From out of nowhere, Rachel threw a punch, but Sarah blocked it. Then blocked another. And another. Rachel threw them fast. Alternating sides, but not in a pattern that Sarah could discern. Sarah focused, never took her eyes off Rachel, and blocked every single punch. Then, to her delight, got in a few jabs, knocking Rachel back a step.

Sweat stung her eyes, and she wiped it away with the back of her hand.

The clock above the benches ticked over to 10:30 p.m.

"I think we should call it a night," Rachel said, holding on to her side where Sarah had landed more than one punch.

Sarah sighed and collapsed onto the floor. She could stay there for hours, but it would be uncomfortable when she finally got up. She raised her head. "I was just getting started."

Rachel laughed.

Thankful the training was finished, she picked herself up off the floor, marched to the bench, and took a swig of water. Now she was too pumped to sleep.

Sitting at the kitchen island in the loft, Sarah listened to the quiet, still too wired after her training session to go to bed.

Even after two mugfuls of hot chocolate. The empty mug sat in the middle of the island, the last dregs of chocolate powder sludge clinging to the bottom. No matter how many times she stirred, there was always some chocolate-enriched sediment at the bottom.

Her sisters had gone to bed half an hour ago, the calming effects of the hot beverage doing the trick for them. She hopped off her stool, grabbed the mugs, and put them in the dishwasher. A twinge of guilt niggled in her stomach when she popped in a cleaning tablet and pressed the on button. She liked to wait until the machine was full before turning it on.

Still too agitated to sleep, she padded to the living room area, plopped down on the chair facing the TV, grabbed her laptop from the coffee table, and opened it. The TV was on, tuned into the usual twenty-four-hour news channel from Becky's station, with the volume on low so it wouldn't wake the other angels. She liked to have something on in the background, especially when she was alone. She wasn't used to being alone in the loft, or anywhere really. At the hospital, staff and patients surrounded her. At home, there was always another angel in the loft, and they usually went to bed around the same time. Work schedules meant they all needed to get a decent night's sleep.

Right now, it was more worry than adrenaline that kept her awake. Her mind raced with questions about the patients. If it wasn't the flu, and it wasn't a cold, what could it be?

On the off chance it was something more serious than a cold, she pulled up an internet browser and keyed in the symptoms of fever and headache. In this case, Dr. Google would help her eliminate some possible causes before she hit the medical journals. A list of articles appeared with headache and fever bolded in the preview text. She eliminated a vaccine cause right away. None of the patients had recent vaccinations. And side effects from the booster would have abated after more than a week.

She frowned at the next option. Meningitis. They hadn't done any more testing other than the flu kit, and meningitis wasn't something they could diagnose without a test. Did they have an outbreak? No one mentioned sensitivity to light or seizures. She tried to recall other symptoms listed for each patient she'd seen. No one with a stiff neck. Her one patient had been vomiting, but that could have been anything.

Had she made a mistake sending them all home? Panic coursed through her that she'd missed an important symptom, but her gut instinct had told her they had a cold.

She scrolled to the next article and ruled out a bacterial infection without even clicking on the link to read the full text. No one was coughing or short of breath. Everyone had the same symptoms. Fever, headache, aches, and pains.

Though it took the test to rule out the flu, the longer she thought about it, going over the complaints in her mind from all her patients, she also ruled out cold. No one had mentioned a sore throat, a runny nose, sneezing. Based on the lack of those symptoms, she ruled out allergies as well. Stranger things had happened than mass allergies, even in winter, but it didn't present as an allergic reaction to anything either.

No. It was something else.

Digging deeper into the research, she abandoned Dr. Google and called up the medical research website she used at the hospital.

She typed in the few symptoms there, leaving out the vomiting because only one of her patients had had that.

Mononucleosis? After scanning the symptoms, she frowned and dismissed that as the cause. No one had swollen glands, no sore throats. The older patients hadn't been jaundiced.

Discouraged, she clicked on the next possible cause. Yellow fever. She ran through the patient histories in her mind, everything she could remember. Some of it fit, except the timing. Usually, symptoms presented three to six days after infection. How would she track down what they were all doing in that time frame? Maybe she could get a nurse to follow up with them. But the nurses were so overworked as it was and kept everything running smoothly. She didn't want to take a nurse away from their regular duties to follow up with patients. And she didn't want to give them extra work and take away some of their muchneeded lunch time.

She huffed out a breath, determined to look into the patients more when she got back to the hospital on Monday. What was one more thing on her plate? She could juggle it all.

She closed the lid of her laptop and put it back on the coffee table. A low hum, almost indiscernible, filled the room. When they were all milling about in the loft, she never heard it. But now, with the quiet of the night and her sisters soundly sleeping, the noise was there. Comforting somehow. But when she turned the TV off, the sound would wink out too.

She contemplated another hot chocolate. Maybe she should make it warm milk instead. The sugar in the hot chocolate might add to her inability to sleep. Though it hadn't hurt her sisters' trip to dreamland.

It was after midnight and she had to be at the walk-in clinic by ten. She could sleep in if she wanted, if she was even able to get to sleep in the first place.

Dreading going to her bedroom and staring at the ceiling for an hour, she took a deep breath. She couldn't stay in the living room all night. That would guarantee she got no rest.

Sighing, she picked up the remote to turn the television off. A scroll across the bottom caught her attention. It informed the viewer that Public Health had had numerous calls concerned about the recent symptoms, followed by a reminder that it was cold and flu season. The end of the scroll reminded people to get the flu vaccine booster.

Chapter Five

Saturday morning, almost full from a breakfast he'd brought with him to War's place, Famine sat at the dining room table with Conquest on his left and War sitting opposite him. The horseman still had only snacks in his cupboards, no proper food or drink in the place. Their "homes" were decoration really and a place to sleep, nothing more. The important work was out there, in the city.

War pushed his plate away and patted his stomach. "That was delicious. Thanks for bringing it."

Famine shrugged. "I had no choice if I wanted to eat properly."

War scowled. "I'll make sure there's something in the place next time."

Conquest chuckled. "You know he won't."

Famine smiled. He knew. It was like this every time they were on Earth. War and Conquest focused on what they wanted, how their talents could be used. No one thought about him. And if you asked Famine, he was the most important of all the horsemen. He killed more people worldwide than wars and conquests. And Death, he just ushered them home, but only if there was a mass casualty. His reapers did the day-to-day grunt work.

"For the purge to happen, there needs to be more deaths." War gathered the plates, then went to the kitchen to put them in the sink.

Conquest nodded. "I'm rallying the gangs. Creating new ones. Causing general havoc in the city. But that's only the beginning."

Famine shook his head, watching the two jockey for position on the apocalypse front. Sure, war was how some of the casualties would happen. And giving the police more work to do, striking fear into a city until no one wanted to be out at night, was all fun and games.

The behind-the-scenes work at the lab had been surprisingly interesting and tiring. He made sure he was there before anyone else every day so he could sabotage what needed to be sabotaged. Undo what needed to be undone. It was probably why he'd been so tired and so hungry lately.

War returned from the kitchen empty-handed. Famine hoped he'd at least have brought drinks. Or something to clean the palate after the greasy plate of food they'd just had.

"Patience. It takes time. Your war and your conquering will happen. But for things to really get going, there needs to be food scarcity. Disease running rampant. The entire world needs to live in fear. Having the city scared is peanuts."

Hmmm. Peanuts. He could go for a handful of those, but War didn't look like he was in a particularly amiable mood. Perhaps later.

"And how are you working on that?" War asked.

"The food stores in the US are already running low. It's

not in the news yet, but that's only a matter of time. They don't want people panicking, so they've downplayed how little food there is since the retaliation from Russia." He tipped his head at War. "Nice play, by the way."

War straightened in his seat. "Thanks. I could have used the hacker more if he hadn't been caught. I might look for another one to keep in our toolbox."

Famine nodded. "Good idea. We might need someone to make the farmers or stores think they are running out of seed."

"What the hell will that do?" Conquest asked.

Brute force and strength. That's all they cared about. While he focused on science, the mind, strategy that had nothing to do with guns or battles.

Famine sighed. "If we can get Ontario reliant on itself for most foods, we can introduce a curve ball. At the lab, I'm developing seeds that create foods with less nutrition. Some of them are out to farms already. People will need to eat more for the same nutrients, causing a shortage. The US can't ship as much food across the border because of shortages of its own. These seeds are hardy. Can grow in the most harsh conditions, so farmers all over the world will eat them up." He chuckled. "Pardon the pun."

Conquest shook his head and pounded a hand on the table, causing the salt and pepper shakers to rise off the surface a micron. "We don't have that kind of time. Omega has specific dates in mind for the collapse of humanity. And it's not years."

Famine leaned back in his chair. "Collapse will happen with war and disease. Disease has been in the works for decades. It won't take long for it to wreak havoc."

War grumbled. "And the priest needs time before summoning Death's reapers to join with Death again."

"How much time?" Conquest asked.

War shrugged. "More than it took for him to summon me after the angels sent me back to limbo. He really didn't look good when I left him. He'll need all his strength for the ritual, and even that might not be enough."

"He wouldn't have been chosen by Omega for the task if he wasn't up to it," Conquest argued.

War nodded. "True. But I don't think they realized how much energy it would take. And he's not a young man in his thirties."

Famine leaned into the table. "Which means we have some time to plant seeds, spread disease, create more fear."

The prospect of an apocalypse always left him with a tingling feeling in his stomach. It was the only thing that ever brought him close to feeling full. Satisfied. This time, it had to work. The end had to arrive as predicted.

War looked at Conquest. "Rile up more people. Famine will help spread disease and food shortages. The bombs did some of the work, hitting soil that was used for crops in the US. Taking out a lot of its food stores. I will find another hacker and see if I can get some of the countries surrounding Russia to renew their skirmishes." He turned to Famine. "We need some good old Canadian peace keepers going over there, don't we?"

"Yes, I believe we do. But only ones who have received the flu vaccine booster." A smile spread across his face. "We wouldn't want anyone getting sick and spreading it around, would we?"

Saturday afternoon, the brightly lit basement gym pulsed with an air of intense focus as Rachel stood in the middle of the room. Around her, the space teemed with various training equipment: punching bags hanging from steel chains, barbells stacked against the concrete walls, kettle-bells lined up neatly on rubber mats. Each tool bore testament to the grueling sessions they'd been through, their tarnish and wear marking the seriousness of their endeavor.

Sitting on the benches, eager to start, Darla, Ivy, and a few more of the sex workers watched as Rachel demonstrated the drills she would put them through, her movements precise, a dance of power and control.

Respect hung heavy in the air, tangible and solid as the iron bars of the weight racks. It emanated not just from her physical prowess but also from the knowledge and skill she imparted to those under her tutelage.

Darla stepped forward, determination etched into every line of her face. She moved through the drills with palpable eagerness, throwing punches, dodging blows, extricating herself from Rachel's hold on her.

"You're improving, Darla," Rachel said, her words cutting through the hum of exertion in the room. They were simple but carried the weight of approval and encouragement—fuel for confidence.

At Rachel's praise, pride bloomed across Darla's face. It was as if someone had flipped a switch, illuminating her features with a beam of happiness that outshone even the harshest fluorescent lights above them.

Rachel watched Darla return to her spot, chest heaving with exertion but eyes sparkling. The sight of their sweat-drenched bodies and the unyielding determination in their faces brought a wave of satisfaction washing over her. She looked around at the sex workers, each one stronger, more confident than when they'd first stumbled into this basement gym several weeks ago.

An ember of hope flickered within Rachel's heart. This training was about more than just learning how to throw a punch or dodge an attack; it was about empowering these women, giving them tools to protect themselves. Perhaps if they could fend off some of the dangerous clients, they wouldn't have to work as much, maybe even get out of the trade altogether.

"Who's next?" Rachel asked, her voice echoing off the bare concrete walls. From the group of sex workers, Ivy stepped forward. She moved with a grace that belied the harsh reality of their lives above ground, her eyes meeting Rachel's with unflinching determination.

A current of camaraderie rippled through the room as they watched Ivy move to the center. Darla, still catching her breath from her own training, clapped her hands together in encouragement. The sound bounced off the walls, reverberating around them like an echo of solidarity.

Under Rachel's watchful gaze, Ivy worked through the drills. Each punch she threw was sharper than the last; every dodge smooth and calculated. Sweat glistened on her skin, reflecting the harsh lights overhead, but she didn't falter. Her focus remained unwavering, her grit palpable even amidst the grueling exercises.

"Good job, Ivy," Rachel said, her words carrying the weight of approval. The sense of accomplishment that bloomed across Ivy's face echoed Darla's earlier triumph, a testament to the progress they'd made under Rachel's training.

As Ivy fell back into line, panting yet satisfied, the gym fell quiet once more. The sounds of exertion, the scent of sweat mingled with the sharp tang of metal equipment, became symbols not just of their struggle but also their resilience. For these women, each day was a battle. But here, in this basement gym, they were becoming warriors. The silence stretched out between them, heavy with anticipation for what would come next.

"Now, get into pairs and go through the drills. Take turns being the attacker and the victim."

The ladies jumped off the benches and paired off. They'd all come so far, but there was always more she could teach them. She would feel better if they didn't put themselves in danger, but at least she could empower them with skills to mitigate that danger.

She stood at the edge of the training area, her gaze sweeping over Darla and the other sex workers. Their muscles strained with effort, their faces etched with determination as they continued to push past their limits. A sense of pride swelled within Rachel's chest like a warm wave, washing away some of the chill that haunted her heart.

How much more could they learn if she used her angel magic? She visualized herself glamoring into one of their dangerous clients, forcing the girls to face the harsh reality of their situation head-on. It would be a cruel lesson, but it might make them understand why self-defense was so crucial.

However, even as she entertained this thought, the weight of her limitations pressed down on her. She had no idea how to regain the power she'd lost, and she needed to conserve whatever magic remained for emergencies. Plus, revealing her angelic abilities to mere mortals wasn't a good idea.

She wanted to do more, give more, help more, but the chains of her circumstances held her back. The frustration simmered beneath her skin, making her fingers twitch, her jaw clench.

"All right, ladies," she said, breaking the silence that hung heavily in the room. "It's time for round two."

Her gaze swept over Darla, Ivy, and the other sex workers, satisfaction warming her eyes like an ember's glow. The sweat-streaked faces before her were painted with exhaustion but also determination—a testament to their progress.

"Excellent work today," she said, folding her arms across her chest. The echo of her words hung in the air, amplifying the sense of accomplishment that filled the room.

"But physical training is just one part of our journey," Rachel said, "Next, we tackle financial education."

A murmur rippled through the group, curiosity piquing as brows furrowed and glances exchanged. An undercurrent of uncertainty, raw and potent, threaded through the room. She knew this was unfamiliar territory for them, but it was essential ground to cover.

She gestured toward the door to the gym. "Becky and Leah are waiting for you in the classroom-style room down the hall," she said, pointing out the path.

Their steps were hesitant as they moved, the lingering tension from their physical exertions still visible in their gait. But they followed Rachel's instructions nonetheless, leaving behind the familiarity of the gym for the unknown awaiting them.

"As important as your physical safety is, so is your financial independence and stability," Rachel said.

The echoes of their footsteps gradually faded as they left the gym, one by one. They moved with a boldness that hadn't been there before, their bodies straighter, shoulders squared. Their faces were flushed from exertion but also glowed with an unspoken triumph—a newfound confidence that was only beginning to emerge.

However, one figure lingered behind, her silhouette cast in stark relief against the harsh fluorescent lighting of the basement gym. Darla, usually so quick with a sassy retort or sarcastic quip, silently approached Rachel. Her face was somber and serious when she finally spoke.

"Thanks for this," she said, gesturing vaguely around the room. "For everything you and your sisters have done."

Rachel turned toward Darla, surprise flickering across her features before humility quickly replaced it. An invisible weight seemed to settle on her shoulders, making her stand taller, more resolute. "It's my pleasure," she said, her voice barely above a whisper.

With a nod, Darla fell into step beside Rachel, and together, they strolled out of the gym and down the long hallway toward the classroom-style room where the next part of their training awaited. The echo of their footfalls gave rhythm to the silence between them, matching the steady beat of expectation thrumming in their veins. As the last sliver of light from the gym disappeared behind them, the uncertainty of what lay ahead loomed even larger, casting a long shadow over the path they had chosen to tread.

The echo of their footfalls faded as they entered the classroom. A motley array of mismatched chairs and tables greeted them, hastily arranged into makeshift rows facing a whiteboard at the front. The air hung heavy with anticipation and uncertainty, mirroring Rachel's own emotions.

Darla broke away from her side, disappearing among the group of women already seated in the room. Darla, joined by other sex workers, took her seat, her eyes glinting with curiosity and anticipation. She adjusted herself on the hard chair, leaning forward as if ready to dive headfirst into the abyss of knowledge promised before her. Her colleagues' faces mirrored this sentiment, an eagerness to learn about financial independence dancing in every eye.

Rachel lingered at the back of the room, her gaze sweeping over the scene before her. Beside her, Sarah stood silent and stoic, watching the proceedings unfold with sharp eyes. An electric tension hummed between them, like a current waiting to be unleashed.

At the front of the room, Becky and Leah were poised before the whiteboard, markers in hand. They radiated confidence and authority, but beneath it all, there was a trace of vulnerability, a reminder of how much was at stake here. Fluorescent bulbs cast long shadows across the room, creating pockets of darkness in corners that seemed to hold their breath along with the women seated there.

As she watched, Rachel wondered what would become of this classroom once they no longer needed it. A memory flashed through her mind of Becky waving her hand and with a flicker of angel magic, the room had transformed before their eyes, turning from nothing into the makeshift learning space it now was.

With a nod from each other, Becky and Leah began their lesson.

Becky glanced at every person in the room before she spoke. "Before we get into the financial stuff, we want to cover steps for escaping abusive relationships."

Rachel stood a little straighter. At no point during the planning of the lessons had she asked what Becky and Leah would cover. Because she figured the physical training would be enough to get the women out of a difficult situation. But as she listened to Becky and Leah talk about determining if a friend is going to be on their side, slowly stocking necessary items in a home that is not theirs, and then how to save money without their pimp knowing, Rachel's respect for Becky and Leah sky rocketed.

They segued into finance. Their voices echoed off the concrete walls, bouncing around the room with words of Canadian investment options, tax savings accounts, retirement plans. They broke complex terms down into digestible pieces, jargon replaced with simple analogies that made understanding easier.

Pens scratched furiously over paper as Darla and the others absorbed the information being shared, scribbling notes and underlining key points. Every sentence spoken was another step toward empowerment, toward freedom from the chains of exploitation they'd been bound by for so long.

As the session progressed, hands shot up tentatively, questions tumbling out one after another. Becky and Leah answered each query patiently, confidently, their deep understanding evident in the way they explained complicated concepts effortlessly.

The importance of this makeshift class couldn't be understated. For these women, it wasn't just about learning how to manage money; it was about gaining tools essential to break free from the cycles of abuse and dependency. It was more than just a class—it was a lifeline thrown to those drowning in despair, offering them a chance to pull themselves onto the shores of self-sufficiency and independence.

As the financial training session drew to a close, Rachel and Sarah walked to the front of the room. One by one, the women left the makeshift classroom, their footsteps creating a rhythmic cadence on the cold floor. Silence settled like a thick blanket as the door shut behind them, leaving only Rachel, Sarah, Becky, and Leah behind. The air clung with anticipation, each woman lost in her thoughts, processing the weight of what had just transpired.

Rachel turned toward Sarah, Becky, and Leah. "Are you ready for your training?" she asked, her voice steady yet tinged with excitement. She smiled at their groans. As much as they hated it, they knew it was necessary in order to beat the horsemen.

Sunday morning, coffee in hand, Sarah breezed into the Nicolas Grove Clinic a block away from Queen City Hospital with ten minutes to spare. She started at ten. She had enough time to finish her coffee and make sure the exam rooms were prepped before patients were let in to see her and the other volunteer doctors. The clinic, associated with the hospital, provided much-needed care after hours for people who couldn't wait until Monday to see their family doctors. In some cases, the clinic was their family "doctor."

The hours worked well for her, enabling her to sleep in a little on Saturday and Sunday, have breakfast, and still feel like she had a full weekend. This was merely an errand in her day.

She smiled at the harried receptionist, who gave a brief nod and went back to checking in the lineup of patients who had probably been waiting since eight o'clock. The clinic didn't open until ten.

A steady stream of patients kept her busy for the morning. Eye infections, bronchitis, a case of suspected pneumonia. Most issues required a prescription. For a few others, she wrote requisitions for blood tests or X-rays.

After a quick lunch break, she finished the paperwork from her last patient, then walked out to the front of the clinic to let the receptionist know she was available to patients again.

"I have a patient waiting for you in room six." She handed a folder to Sarah.

Sarah nodded. "Thanks. If you need a break, let me know and I'll cover for you for a few minutes."

The woman's shoulders slumped and relief flooded her

face. "Thanks. It helps knowing you'll do that. I should be okay. Only a few hours left."

Sarah stopped in front of room six, opened the folder, and scanned the document for the patient's reason for being in the clinic. Her stomach sank. The flu follow-up shot. Still waiting for Becky to bring it to Dr. Karimi for analysis, she couldn't in good conscience administer the shot.

She took a deep breath and opened the door. "Hello, Howard. It says here you came in for a shot."

Becky's tipster wasn't wrong about any of the other things they'd brought to Becky's attention. The trail to Ralston and the weapons turned out to be worse than Becky had thought. Sarah's stomach clenched at the thought of injecting the person in front of her with something she wasn't one hundred percent sure about. If not for the tips, she would have been giving the shot out to everyone who asked.

"Yes, I'm going on vacation and it's been recommended to get the shot at least seven days before leaving."

Sarah's mind raced at the mention of the lead time. She didn't recall seeing it on any of the scrolls on the news channel. And they didn't give out many vaccines in the ER, so the number hadn't been mentioned there. She did remember it was mentioned once in a news bite.

Seven days. She would have to dive back into research to see what incubated for seven days.

Sarah sat in the chair in front of the exam table. "You did get the regular flu shot?"

Howard nodded. "But with the news that it's not as effective this year, I want to make sure I'm protected. I don't want to get sick on vacation. Or before I go."

"The media played that up a little more than necessary. The regular shot is still pretty good protection."

"And now I want more protection, like they're advising."

Sarah's mind raced for an excuse to turn them away. "I would love to give you one, but we ran out. This morning. There's been a high demand for it. You should come back next week."

Howard's face flushed red. "I'm going away next week. That's not enough time."

He huffed, hopped off the exam table, yanked open the door so hard she thought he might remove it from its hinges, then stomped down the corridor. She bolted off her chair to watch him at the reception area. A twinge of guilt niggled in her stomach.

He spoke to the receptionist, who remained calm, nodding every few words. Flailing gestures with his hands indicated the corridor, and most likely her.

This was not going to go over well with the hospital brass. If the complaint got back to them. How many of the patients actually knew the hospital ran the clinic? The clinic name didn't mention it at all. The only place one might put the two together was in the fine print on the website.

Sarah went through the rest of the day on autopilot, continuing to diagnose and treat everything that came her way. Dreading a patient looking for the same shot as Howard. Thankfully, by the end of the day, he was the only one.

She finished the paperwork, inputting all her patient information into the computer before leaving for the day.

Back at the loft, she dropped her keys in the bowl on the table in the entryway. Becky, Rachel, and Leah turned to look at her from the kitchen island. They sat around it, cups of coffee in front of them.

Becky frowned. "Hard day?"

Sarah filled them in on Howard.

"You did the right thing," Becky said.

Nodding, Sarah shuffled to the living room and turned the TV on, changing the channel to a cooking show. She hit record on the PVR so she could rewind as she cooked. Learning to make something new for dinner would help relax her, put the day behind her.

She padded back to the kitchen and pulled out ingredients for the new dish, improvising when she discovered they didn't have everything the recipe called for.

She might have to forego some volunteer work for a while. She couldn't keep denying the shot without an explanation. And explaining the reason she refused was out of the question. Eventually, the hospital board would demand to know why. Especially if they started receiving a lot of complaints. At least in the ER she didn't have to give it out usually. Decision made, she turned back to the onion she was chopping for dinner. A brief tingle through her wings brought a smile to her lips.

Chapter Six

A cloud of dread followed Sarah to the ER on Monday morning. Every time a new person came onto the floor, she expected to see her boss, their mouth in a tight line, requesting to see her. Maybe the patient from the clinic hadn't complained to anyone but the receptionist.

With her hands full, the moment she stepped on the floor, she didn't have much time to dwell. The ER was handling a two-car collision, a variety of cuts, some unknown illnesses. Unknown, at least until a doctor saw them. Some slip and falls. It was a typical morning in the ER, which meant anything could happen.

Vanda handed her a chart after Sarah turned in the information from her previous patient. "Patient is in curtain three."

Behind curtain three, a woman sat on the bed, cradling her left arm in her lap, a grimace on her face. At first glance, it could be a sprain, a break, muscle strain.

"Hi, Grace, I'm Dr. Malak. It says you were in a car accident. Did you lose consciousness?"

The woman shook her head. "I wish I would. This hurts like crazy." Grace barely lifted her left arm.

"Any numbness or tingling?" On closer inspection, the bone did look broken.

Grace nodded.

"I'm going to send you up to the imaging department to get some X-rays of that arm. It looks broken, but we need to see how badly and in how many places."

Sarah paged an porter to bring the patient up to X-ray, writing a few notes in her chart before reassuring the woman she'd be well taken care of, and Sarah would follow up with her before the woman left.

Back at the nurses' station, she perused the list of patients waiting to be seen and spotted a familiar name. Mrs. Jeffries. Sarah pointed to the name.

"She was in here last week."

Vanda nodded. "She's complaining of a rash now."

"I'll take her if you don't mind. I saw her on Thursday."

"Curtain four."

Sarah hurried down the hall and pulled the curtain aside to slip through. Mrs. Jeffries sat on the bed, mittens on her hands and an angry rash creeping up her neck and onto her face.

"I'm sorry you're still not feeling well, Mrs. Jeffries. Is it just the rash now? How are your other symptoms?"

The woman sighed, tears shining in her eyes. "They're still there. But now I have this." She waved the mittens up and down in front of her neck.

Sarah pulled on a pair of latex gloves, popped the earbuds for her stethoscope in her ears, and listened to the woman's heart. After grabbing a tongue depressor from the clear glass jar on the table at the back of the curtained area, she looked into the woman's mouth.

She took a step back and inspected the rash. "Have you had chickenpox before?"

The sores didn't look exactly like chickenpox, but that was the closest she could imagine. Shingles most often affected the torso. Of course, it might just be an allergic reaction to something.

"Yes. Do you think that's what it is? Or is it shingles?"

"Is the rash painful or just itchy?"

"Itchy."

"I don't think it's shingles. Have you had any medications lately that you normally don't have? Did you take anything for your other symptoms besides pain reliever?"

"Nothing. Some over-the-counter medications that I've always taken for headaches."

"Have you had measles?"

The woman pursed her lips and looked up at the ceiling. "I don't think so, but I was vaccinated for them."

Relieved to hear the woman had been vaccinated, Sarah went through other possibilities but kept landing on chickenpox. The rash closely resembled the textbook pictures of the disease. Maybe it had resurfaced and instead of erupting as shingles, it remained chickenpox.

"Have you been around anyone with chickenpox lately?"

"Not that I know of, but my sister does have kindergarten age children. I've been hanging out with them on the weekends to help her out."

Children were petri dishes of colds and disease. Illnesses spread through schools like wildfire, and in the end, with things like chickenpox, no one had to worry about getting it again.

"Have the fever and headache abated at all?"

"I went down to a degree above normal for a day. But the headache has persisted. I only came in today because the rash was driving me crazy. I want to scratch my skin off."

Sarah leaned in again and took a closer look at the bumps on her patient's skin. They reminded her of text-book chickenpox. Though it was rare for a woman in her fifties to contract it again, it wasn't unheard of.

"How much of your body is covered with the rash?"

"It's everywhere." She frowned. "Except for the soles of my feet and my palms."

Sarah nodded. "I can't imagine how itchy and uncomfortable that must be."

"No, you really can't."

"I'm going to take a small sample of the rash," Sarah said.

She hurried down the hall for a kit and a topical anesthetic. Back in the curtained area, she gently applied the numbing agent, then took a small sample of the rash and put it in a small container.

Sarah pulled out a prescription pad from her lab coat pocket. "I'm going to give you a prescription for an antihistamine for the itch. You can also put a zinc oxide ointment on it. If the rash doesn't go away within two to four weeks, come back and see us."

The woman's shoulders slouched forward and she appeared to melt into the bed like her bones had disintegrated on her. "I can't sleep. I can't concentrate. I can't even work from home because I can't stand the itch. The only thing that helps are cool baths. I've been having them three or four times a day."

Sarah moved closer and patted the woman's back. In her day, plague and smallpox were the killers of the time. Back then people were lucky to make it past their mid-thirties, especially when pandemics hit. She remembered the epidemic of 1721. At least with chickenpox, the rash would go away and if the patient didn't scratch, would walk away without any scars. She was tempted to remove her gloves and heal the rash to at least past the itchy stage, but she couldn't. Not without knowing exactly what the rash was.

"The antihistamine should help that. Even if you can work, you should rest. Get lots of fluids." She scribbled another prescription. "I'm also going to give you a stronger pain medication for the headache and to help bring down the fever. And try not to scratch."

Sarah filled out a requisition form for blood work. "Before you leave, please go to the lab on the second floor. I want to rule out chickenpox."

She handed over the papers. The woman hopped off the bed, pulled her coat back on, and left the curtained area.

After dropping off the sample to be sent to the lab, Sarah checked in with the nurses' station again for more patients. Another one on the list jumped out at her as being there last week with the same symptoms as Mrs. Jeffries. What the heck was going on?

"I'll take that one too." She pointed at a patient she saw last week. "Can you make sure all the rash patients are isolated? And send them to me."

All they needed was a chickenpox outbreak in the middle of an apocalypse.

After a fifteen-minute lunch from the cafeteria that consisted of a turkey sandwich with Havarti cheese and mayonnaise, Sarah ducked into the lounge to grab a quick cup of coffee. She'd eaten the sandwich on the go, instead of sitting downstairs for a proper break. She could rest later. The foremost objective in her mind was checking with the nurses' station to see if any other patients from last week had returned with a rash.

Inside the doctor's lounge, Dr. Singh and Dr. Goretti sat at the round table closest to the door. Dr. Singh laughed at something Dr. Goretti had said.

Sarah smiled at them, prepared her coffee, and took a sip as she left the room. At the nurses' station, Vanda sat looking calm as usual, even though from the looks of the waiting area, an explosion of new patients had arrived.

A door on her left, beyond the waiting area, swooshed open and Sarah's stomach churned. That door rarely opened, and when it did, it wasn't good news. She looked over to see Dr. Nabila Nejem, Chief of Emergency Medicine, sauntering down the corridor, shoulders back, her sharp brown eyes taking in every detail of her surroundings. Cataloging every patient in her mind. Her shoulder-length brown hair was down as it usually was. And her white lab coat was crisp as if she'd just put it on.

"Dr. Malak, may I speak with you for a moment?

Sarah grimaced. "I was about to take another patient."

Dr. Nejem turned to the nurse. "I'm sure Dr. Goretti can handle another patient. What do you think?"

Vanda nodded.

Dr. Nejem turned and started down the hallway. Sarah fell into step beside her but remained silent. Dr. Nejem would say nothing to her until they were alone. She didn't talk about hospital business where any patient might hear.

It felt like the corridor went on forever, yet they arrived at the Chief's office all too soon. Dr. Nejem waved a hand to usher her inside.

The office was large, with an oak desk placed in the middle of the room. A leather office chair behind the desk allowed the user to raise or lower it depending on their height. Two bookcases, one on either side of the desk, pushed flush against the wall, housed dozens of medical tomes. The blinds on the window behind the desk were raised.

Sarah took a seat at one of the two guest chairs and folded her hands in her lap. Dr. Nejem settled into her chair and leaned back, eyeing Sarah with concern.

"I'm not going to drag this out or beat around the bush. A patient at the clinic submitted a complaint toward you."

Sarah tensed, and heat burned her cheeks. "How many complaints have I had?"

"From patients? One."

"So in all the time I've worked here, you're calling me out on this." Sarah took a deep breath. "Wait. From patients?"

Dr. Nejem nodded. "Other people have complained." She shifted in her seat and picked up a file. "I've been going over your hours. You put in more time here than any other doctor."

"Because I can. I don't have a husband or children."

Sure, she had other angelic duties to think about, but it couldn't be all apocalypse all the time. Other people in her life needed her too.

"What does that leave for the people who want to pick up some extra hours?" Dr. Nejem raised an eyebrow at her.

Sarah bit her lip. Thinking. All this time, she'd thought by taking on as much as she could, she was helping her colleagues spend more time with their families. But what if they needed the shifts? The extra money? The practice that taking on more patients would give them?

Dr. Nejem shuffled papers in the file. "There's also

your volunteer work. Besides the clinic, where else do you volunteer your time?"

"The soup kitchen. But surely you can't mean it's bad to volunteer." It distinctly felt like she was being chastised for being a good person.

The chief shook her head and let out a loud sigh. "I'm suggesting you're overworked. I don't know what went on with the patient, and it's the first complaint from one we've ever received. That tells me something. There will always be lots of work. It's not feast or famine here. You don't always have to be feasting."

"So what are you saying?"

"I'm not telling you to stop. But maybe you should cut back a little. Let some of your colleagues pick up the slack."

Sarah leaned back in her chair and studied the chief's face. The woman had worked hard to get to where she was now. Not only the first chief of emergency medicine at the hospital but also the youngest. You didn't get to be the youngest at such a high-level job by letting others take up the slack. Not that Sarah wanted such a position. She was happy with being an ER physician. Once they stopped the apocalypse, she'd be going home, anyway. But she wanted to make a difference while she was here. Working herself until she was sick wasn't the best way to do that.

She'd already decided to cut back at the clinic so she wouldn't be put in the same situation again. Refusing to administer a shot to a patient, without giving them a reason, wasn't going to get easier. Maybe she should cut back on other things as well.

"You really think I should cut back?"

"Look, I get it. You feel like you have to work harder for people to see you at the same level as some of your colleagues. But you don't want to bite off more than you can chew and burn yourself out."

Her sisters had said pretty much the same thing to her. Sometimes she hated when they were right. If she cut back on her hours, she'd have more time to help her sisters with the whole end-of-the-world thing going on.

"I suggest cutting back to four days a week in the ER like most of the other doctors. Five days is too much. And I see here sometimes you've been doing six shifts. You're one of my best doctors. I don't want you to fizzle out."

Sarah nodded. "Okay. Four shifts a week. And I'll cut back at the soup kitchen and the clinic."

Dr. Nejem smiled and her brown eyes sparkled. "I have someone in mind who could use the extra hours at the clinic. Thank you, Sarah."

Sarah left the office feeling a little lighter than she had going in. Her stomach had stopped churning at some point, and a weight had been lifted from her shoulders. A tingle rushed through her wings. Maybe she had been keeping those hours from someone who truly needed them more than she wanted them.

Before she finished for the day, Sarah went through all her paperwork in the lounge to make sure she hadn't forgotten any tests, neglected to record something, or drew the wrong conclusion of someone's case. A second glance through the notes was always a good idea. Sometimes she went over the folders three and four times on the off chance she'd missed something.

By now, the specimen she'd taken from Mrs. Jeffries should be at the lab. The hospital sent all their specimens to Queen City University Group Lab for testing. It was less than a block away. Though it was in the wrong direction of home, she could make a quick visit there so she could plead her case for getting the results back faster. The bad feeling in her stomach festered like an infected wound. She was probably overreacting. If it wasn't chickenpox, it was most likely impetigo. Still better to find out sooner rather than later.

She put away her folders, making sure any doctor taking over after her would have all the information they needed. Most of her patients had been discharged. There were a few lingering cases that needed a follow-up.

It took ten minutes to walk to the lab. Cold wind nipped at her face, leaving her cheeks stinging and her nose runny. Inside, she flashed the receptionist, Delia, her hospital badge.

"I'd like to see someone about a specimen I sent earlier. Preferably the person who will be performing the tests on it."

The receptionist gave her a weary smile and flicked her eyes to the clock on the wall behind Sarah. "Dr. Althaus is gone for the day. Dr. Zach Wheatley, Isabel, and Ned are in. Dr. Wheatley might perform the test or he might let one of the technicians do it."

"I'd like to see him then."

The receptionist blew a stray lock of hair out of her eyes. A buzzer sounded and the lock mechanism on the door behind the reception switched from red to green.

"You'll have to wait in the office area. Dr. Wheatley and the technicians are still in the lab area."

Sarah nodded and proceeded through the door.

Ten minutes later, three people stepped through a door at the end of the room. Presumably a door that led to the labs and stricter biohazard protocols.

The technicians she recognized. Isabel and Ned had

been working for the lab for as long as her implanted memories went. But Dr. Wheatley was new. She expected doctors to be pictures of health, but he was pale, thin, tired-looking. Annoyance flashed across his face when he spotted her and he clutched the folder in his hand to his chest.

He touched Ned on the hand. The technician's face changed from one of light frivolity to a pinched expression. A stomach growled. Ned's hand clutched his belly.

"I was so busy I forgot to eat lunch." He raced past her, giving her a nod of hello.

"Dr. Malak, is it? Delia told me you were waiting."

He reached out a hand and she took it. The limb was cool and the shake firm. Firmer than his appearance would indicate possible.

A fleeting thought about dinner crowded into her head. And regret at giving up her shifts. She nudged them aside. Letting someone else have the hours was a good thing. And she'd be eating dinner soon.

One of his pencil-thin eyebrows rose and he looked at her hand in fascination. She pulled it away.

"About the test. I sent a specimen over a few hours ago and was hoping to get the results rushed."

He looked up and rubbed his chin with a skeletal finger. "I recall that specimen. It arrived a few hours ago. We have procedures and timelines. And other tests in front of yours."

The raising of his hand pulled his shirt sleeve up enough for her to see the bottom of a tattoo. A tattoo that looked suspiciously like the bottom of scales. Her heartbeat kicked up a thousand notches. The paperwork in his arms suddenly became a lot more interesting. She needed to know what was in the folder. Would he be so bold as to work on a virus and document everything?

Isabel hung back, looking around the room awkwardly. If she'd been doing the test, the technician would have moved it up to the top of the list. But right now, it appeared Dr. Wheatley was in charge.

"I know. And I normally wouldn't ask, but we've got something strange happening in the ER and I'd like to diagnose it definitively so we don't have a bunch of contagious people running around the city."

"Fine. I'll see what I can do."

"Thank you."

Isabel cleared her throat. "I'll be leaving for the day if there's nothing else."

"That's all. Thanks for your help today."

The young woman beamed and brushed past, but not before Sarah tossed a little magic her way. The technician stumbled into Dr. Wheatley. Papers from the folder he was carrying flew everywhere.

Sarah and Isabel bent to help him pick them up. He brushed their hands aside.

"It's okay, I can get it."

From the look of him, she was afraid he would break in two if he bent over. If he'd been a normal person anyway. The sudden hunger in Ned, the fleeting thought of dinner, and the teased scale tattoo proved to her that the doctor was Famine. It made sense he'd want to work in a lab.

Isabel got up and mumbled an apology before running through the door. A twinge of guilt bubbled in Sarah's stomach. For some reason, Isabel looked up to Dr. Wheatley or had a crush on him. And now the poor woman was embarrassed over tripping.

Sarah rummaged through the papers under the guise of picking them up and putting them in a neat pile again. Most of it was innocent. Lab results. Order requisitions for more supplies. But one of the papers stopped her cold.

On the last page she'd managed to grasp before Famine shoved everything back in the folder, snatching the papers from Sarah's hands, there was a shipping invoice and label.

Thousands of doses of the flu vaccine booster were being shipped out to clinics, pharmacies, big box stores, grocery stores with pharmacies. Tomorrow. Soon, thousands more people would be getting the booster and they still didn't know what was wrong with it.

Chapter Seven

Mind reeling after her meeting with Famine, Sarah rushed along Queen Street toward the loft. Because of her hectic day, she'd phoned Rachel earlier to let her sisters know she didn't want to cook that night. Those days were getting more and more frequent. And she suspected it would only get worse once all the horsemen were reunited. The ER was filled with people causing harm to each other, careless falls, victims of fist fights, and other crimes. Between War and Conquest, the city was more riled up than it had ever been. Even soccer moms were throwing punches these days.

She dropped her laptop bag by the door and dashed out of the loft again, making sure it was locked. Break and enters were on the rise, too. They'd installed a security system when they'd magically taken over the space, but what was the point if they left the door unlocked?

She raced down the street to Baron's, checking her watch when she pushed through the door. Becky wouldn't be there yet. In fifteen minutes, she'd be going on air for the six o'clock news. Half an hour to tell the city what was going on in Toronto, ten minutes to gather her things, and another fifteen minutes to get to Baron's meant Becky wouldn't be there until close to seven.

Sarah's stomach grumbled when the scent of a burger teased her nose. A quick glance at the bar revealed Mario was still out sick.

Rachel and Leah sat at their usual table at the back of the place, three drinks already positioned in front of the chairs. Grateful they'd ordered something already, Sarah plopped down in a seat facing the bar.

"Good timing." Rachel picked up her drink and took a sip. "We arrived about five minutes ago."

"We got appetizers to tide us over until Becky gets here," Leah said.

"I'm starving." Sarah frowned. "Or maybe I'm not."

Leah raised an eyebrow. "What?"

Sarah filled them in on meeting Famine and her sudden desire for food.

"I was worried about what the rash might be, so I went to the lab. I don't think Dr. Wheatley is going to rush my results."

Rachel nodded. "He'll probably lose the specimen."

Leah leaned forward in her chair. "Isn't that where Dr. Althaus works? Aren't reapers supposed to be impartial? Do you think Famine will try to influence her?"

"Supposed to be, yes. But are they always?" Rachel asked.

Sarah shrugged. "Hopefully, he won't even try. But it does make you wonder why he got a job there in the first place."

A waiter brought over a tray of appetizers. The fragrant smell of garlic made her mouth water. Sarah picked up a warm, cheesy piece of bread and bit into it.

Now that hunger was staved off for a minute, she put the bread down on a plate.

"It really looked like chickenpox, but now that I know Famine works at the lab where vaccines are created and tests are done, I'm not so sure."

Leah's eyes lit up. "Becky's tipster."

Rachel's brows drew together, and she shook her head. "What are you trying to say?"

"The tip she got. Follow the history. We all assumed it meant the weapons at Ralston. Maybe it has something to do with the illness. Maybe it's something old that was eradicated and we don't see anymore."

Sarah picked up her garlic bread again but paused with it halfway to her mouth. "You think even then they knew an illness would happen and they were trying to warn us?" She took a bite and garlic exploded across her tongue.

Rachel sat up straighter. "Like the plague?"

Sarah rolled her eyes, finished chewing, and swallowed. "A bacterium, not a virus caused the plague. And it doesn't look like that anyway. The problem is, so many different things cause fever, headache, aches, and pains. But now that a rash is in play, it would narrow the possible causes."

Another symptom meant she had a better chance of figuring out what was ailing her patients. The timing of the sickness bothered her. It was right on time for snow birds who traveled south for the winters. And students heading to tropical destinations for March Break.

"Maybe it's something like a plague, though, only a virus. Or maybe it is just chickenpox," Leah said.

Sarah thought about it, none of the patients' symptoms making sense to her anymore. "My one patient had chickenpox before, so logically it would be shingles. But it didn't look like shingles."

"Worry about it when you get the results back," Rachel said.

Finished with her piece of garlic bread, she reached across the table to grab another but pulled her hand away. Becky might want one. And she still wasn't sure if the hunger pangs rattling her stomach were due to her hand-shake with Famine or if she was starving. In either case, she would wait until dinner arrived before eating anything else.

Becky arrived at the table, hair and makeup still perfect from being on air. She slid into the last seat, dropped her computer bag on the floor, and picked up a piece of the garlic bread.

"What did I miss?"

They filled her in on the rash patients and meeting Famine.

"Did you call public health?" She finished the bread and licked her fingers to get the last of the garlic and butter.

Sarah shook her head. "Not yet about the rash. They kept telling me the other symptoms were because it was cold and flu season. Well, that doesn't usually bring rashes, so I want to gather more information and call them tomor-row. Three of my patients from last Thursday came back. I want to check the hospital records and see how many more there were."

While she was at it, she should check with the other hospitals in the city. She'd been too busy today to even think about that, but it would be a good indication of a pandemic. Multiple outbreaks in hospitals would spread the illness fast, to many walks of life.

"Good idea," Becky said. She took a sip of her drink and sighed. "I needed that. The news is so horrible these days, it's a miracle that people are still happy and hopeful."

Their dinners arrived. Sarah dug into hers before the waiter let go of her plate. How happy and hopeful would the city be with a mysterious new illness ravaging the city? Maybe ravaging was too strong a word right now, but she didn't know how much worse it might get. Or maybe it was chickenpox and she was worrying for nothing.

She wished she'd brought her laptop instead of stopping at home first. She wanted to get started with Leah's suggestion about looking at history. Because there was much of history she did not want people to repeat.

***

The next day, after a long shift at the hospital, Sarah yanked the loft door open so hard it bounced back. She had to stop it with her hand before it slammed closed again.

She let out a loud sigh, dropped her keys by the door, then shucked off her coat and placed that in the closet by the entrance. A coat rack might have been easier, but it was too late now. Well, not really, but why change the way the place looked now?

She trudged over to the living room and plopped down in the chair facing the TV, then gently placed her laptop bag on the floor beside her.

Rachel sat on the sofa and Leah sat cross-legged on the floor on the other side of the coffee table.

It was a quarter after six o'clock. She'd been on her feet for over ten hours. She'd gotten to work early to follow up on some cases and stayed a little longer to help out when the ER had a car accident pileup to deal with. There had been more patients with headaches, fever, and body aches. A few more patients from last Thursday were back with a rash. Still not sure what she was dealing with, she'd taken more swabs.

"The test results aren't back from the lab."

Rachel turned to look at her. "You think Famine will actually give you the results?"

Sarah shrugged. "No idea. So I sent the ones from today to a different lab. I hope they don't also have a reaper working there."

"Good thinking," Leah said. "You still think it's chickenpox?"

Sarah pursed her lips. "I'm not sure."

She reached down for her laptop. With the cases coming in so quickly today, she hadn't had time to do any more research. She opened the lid, pulled up a browser window, navigated to the medical database the doctors at the hospital liked to use, and typed in the symptoms she'd witnessed so far—fever, headache, body aches, rash—and hit the search button.

In the background, the TV was on, tuned into Becky's main station instead of the twenty-four-hour news channel. Currently cut to a commercial, her broadcast would be over in ten minutes.

Sarah looked up from her search, noticing Rachel's haggard face for the first time since she got home. "Hard day?

Rachel leaned back into the sofa. "The usual. Homicides are on the rise. If they keep increasing at this rate, we'll catch up to New York for monthly homicides."

Leah's eyes widened. "Wow, that's huge."

Rachel nodded. "As fast as we can solve a case, there are another three to take its place."

"Things will get better."

She had to believe they would, or else, why were they even here? She looked at the search results. A list of possible, but unlikely illnesses stared back at her. Meningitis, scarlet fever, Lupus, Rocky Mountain Spotted fever, shingles, chickenpox, smallpox.

When she heard the door sliding open, she realized it was almost seven. Becky dropped her things by the island and strolled into the living room, falling onto the sofa beside Rachel.

"You guys have dinner already?"

Sarah looked up from her computer. "Sorry. I got caught up in research. And it was such a long day. I'm not up to cooking."

Normally, she wouldn't let a little thing like a hectic day stop her from making dinner. But tonight, research was a better use of her time. And Rachel wanted them to train later, so research was out then.

Becky smiled. "That's okay. I can cook."

Rachel's eyes widened, and a look of horror crossed her face. "Maybe we should order."

Becky scowled at Rachel. "My cooking isn't that bad."

"It isn't that good, either." Rachel chuckled.

Leah jumped up from the floor, raced to the kitchen, grabbed her laptop from the island, and sat down again on the floor in the living room. "Pizza?"

Everyone nodded.

"Done!" Leah said.

Tension built in Sarah's shoulders and a headache teased an appearance. At this point, she needed a week-long massage, hours of meditation, a few gallons of a tropical drink, and soothing music to relax her. She was beginning to think she'd never be relaxed again. None of them would. Though Leah appeared decidedly unstressed at the moment. And every moment.

"Leah, how are you so chill all the time? Don't the students stress you out?"

Leah nodded. "Sure. I stress about report cards. That my students won't get into a good college if that's what they want. I worry about their home life. But I can't do anything except be there as a sounding board. And to teach them. I don't envy you guys. I have it easy compared to you."

A shiver went through the youngest angel, and her eyes widened with surprise. Rachel frowned. "She hasn't even done anything, and she gets power back. How is that fair?"

"I'll note that in my spreadsheet."

"We'll help you figure out your trigger," Sarah said.

Becky nodded in Sarah's direction. "What did you find?"

"Nothing good. I'm still hoping it's chickenpox. The medical database is also suggesting Rocky Mountain Spotted Fever, except we haven't had a case of that here in decades. It's not the right season, and it's not viral."

Becky frowned. "You're positive it's viral?"

"Pretty sure."

Rachel leaned closer, her eyes narrowing. "There's something else, though."

"Besides a few other long shots, like Lupus, it's never Lupus. There's one suggestion that is troubling. Because it's not possible. It brought up smallpox."

Becky gasped. Rachel and Leah let out a soft, "Whoa."

"That's not possible, though, right?" Becky asked. "Smallpox was eradicated long ago."

Sarah shrugged. "Normally, I would say yes. But we're dealing with horsemen. Who knows what could happen now."

She scrolled through the list, reading each differential, comparing them to all the patients she'd seen so far. How many more would she see? How many with the same symptoms hadn't gone to a hospital to be checked out?

There could be dozens, hundreds, or thousands of people quietly waiting it out at home, hoping it was something ordinary. Then there were the patients who went to walk-in clinics or their family doctor. She couldn't possibly know how many people in the city, or the province, had these same symptoms.

Rachel leaned back into the sofa cushions. "How long will it take the other lab to get back to you?"

"I requested a rush when I sent the specimens, but it will still probably be at least two days."

The website for the pizza pinged, indicating their pizza was in the oven. It wouldn't take long before it was undergoing a quality check and then on its way to their loft. Piping-hot, cheesy goodness. But suddenly she wasn't so hungry anymore.

Chapter Eight

A hard workout last night, courtesy of Rachel, did wonders for Sarah, leaving her tired with just enough energy for a shower before bed. Her sleep had been deep and peaceful for a change, and she slept like the innocent. At work, half an hour early to prep for the day, she sat in the hospital's doctor's lounge, sipping her second cup of coffee. The caffeine worked wonders for her.

Dr. Goretti sat opposite her. They traded stories about the ER happenings for the week so far. Her colleague had seen as many flu-like patients as she had. And also her fair share of cuts, scrapes, bruises, and violent injuries.

On her new four days a week schedule, Sarah thought about how she could fill her time for the rest of the week. If Rachel had her way, they'd all be training every spare minute they had. But they all had lives, too, sort of. Or at least they should have lives outside their work and their mission. Maybe it was for the best that they didn't really socialize with the people in their lives. Once the mission was complete, they'd go back home. Would Dr. Goretti even remember Sarah when that happened? Or would it be like she and her sisters never existed?

"Did you test for anything else besides the flu?"

Dr. Goretti nodded. "Chickenpox. Dr. Wheatley says the lab is backed up, so no idea when the results will be back."

Sarah frowned. Backed up her regained power. She was glad she'd sent the second specimen to a different lab.

"He said they were backed up? City Lab isn't usually as busy since it's closer to the border of downtown. Maybe try them next time."

Dr. Goretti nodded, then took a sip of her coffee and screwed up her face with a look of disgust. She marched over to the microwave on the counter beside the fridge and zapped it for thirty seconds. "Yes. Something about a chickenpox outbreak in one of the schools nearby. Thanks for the tip."

They finished their coffee and chatted for a few minutes as other doctors popped into the lounge for another jolt of energy. The coffee machine got a workout every day.

"Time to hit the floor." Dr. Goretti took her cup and grabbed Sarah's empty mug as well. She put them in the dishwasher, which currently had a hexagon-shaped magnet on the front with CLEAN on the top and DIRTY on the bottom with a line between the two. It was currently flipped so DIRTY was at the top.

Sarah pushed herself up from the table with a deep breath. The workout last night had helped her sleep, but it left her muscles aching and stiff. She should have done some stretches before coming into work.

Before picking up her first cases for the day, she marched down the hallway to check out the waiting area. Anyone in the seats there had already been triaged from

ER intake. It already looked like it was going to be a busy day. Two-thirds of the chairs were already occupied.

She headed to the nurses' station to get her first patient from Hui Guan. A nurse for three years, Hui Guan always had a smile for everyone. Her shoulder-length black hair with pink ends was pulled back into a ponytail, keeping it out of her face while she worked on files.

As Sarah approached the desk, Hui looked up at her and grinned.

"You're in for a busy day. I hope you had your oatmeal."

Sarah smiled. "I have plenty of energy. What have you got for me?"

Hui handed over a folder. "You saw him last Thursday. And it says in his file he came back on Saturday with a rash. Curtain one."

Sarah, intrigued, read the file, noting they didn't send a specimen of his rash to the lab.

"Thanks."

Sarah ducked behind curtain one, alarm filling her at the sight of a patient shed seen on Thursday. This rash looked painful and itchy. Round, raised marks with dimples in the center marred his face and arms. He wore a short-sleeved, loose-fitting shirt and jogging pants that looked like they belonged to someone at least double her patient's weight.

"John, I'm sorry to see you back here again. It's been a rough time."

He nodded. "I've been trying not to scratch, but it's difficult."

"How are your other symptoms?"

"Gone. Fever disappeared Sunday."

A bad feeling in the pit of her stomach had her grabbing gloves and a mask from the boxes attached to the wall. Fear crept into his eyes.

"Just a precaution." She moved closer to the bed. "I'm going to examine the lesions on your arm. Tell me if it hurts."

She touched the top of one of the sores. It was firm to the touch. Her stomach churned. Any kind of rash might be contagious. Until they knew exactly what they were dealing with, she wanted him admitted and isolated. How long had he been in the waiting room? How many people had he been in contact with?

Once she got him admitted, she would have to get someone from the hospital to do contact tracing. They needed to find out who might have been exposed to him. The hospital would say she was overreacting. But the last time she'd seen a rash similar to this, things did not turn out well.

"John, I'd like to get you admitted so we can look at this in a little more detail. Get some blood tests. Obtain a sample of the rash to send to the lab."

His eyes widened. "You think it's serious?"

She didn't want to lie, but she didn't want to alarm him, either. "It might be chickenpox." Not a lie. "There are a few other things it could be as well. I just want to rule them out."

He nodded and settled back on the bed. "Okay, Doc."

"I'll have someone come in to get you as soon as we have the admitting paperwork done and a bed available."

She hurried back out to the nurse's station to make the arrangements. Then she marched down the hallway, through the waiting room area, through the doors at the end of the corridor, and stopped in front of Dr. Nejem's office door. The chief of emergency medicine was going to be thrilled about a possible outbreak of an unknown illness in her ER.

———————

What if she was wrong? Sarah stood in front of Dr. Nejem's door, her hand hovering in the air, fingers curled, ready to knock, but what if she was wrong? It was cold and flu season. And new flus showed up every year. This might be a new strain, a flu virus that had different symptoms after the initial onset of fever and body aches. Maybe they didn't need to isolate all the rash victims in the ER rooms instead of curtains. But what if she was right?

She rapped on the door three times and waited until Dr. Nejem's voice told her to enter.

With a deep breath, she stepped into her boss's office.

Dr. Nejem sat at her desk, a folder opened in front of her, a pen in her hand. She signed the bottom of the paper with a flourish, closed the folder, and set it aside. She looked up, smiled, and gestured at one of the chairs in front of the desk.

"Dr. Malak, what can I do for you?"

Sarah bit her lip and sat down. "I think we should start quarantining everyone who comes in with the flu-like symptoms we've been getting a rush of lately."

Dr. Nejem raised an eyebrow and folded her hands on top of the desk. "That's a bit overboard, isn't it? For something that is likely a cold or the flu."

Sarah gathered her thoughts and took her time before addressing her boss. The chief of emergency medicine would listen to facts, a well thought out argument. She wouldn't respond to panic.

"Those patients are returning with rashes. And those

rash patients are coming back with pustular rashes. Antibiotics and ointments aren't helping."

"All the patients?"

"That I'm not sure about. But there are a lot of them. I sent specimens to the lab to check for chickenpox, but the results aren't back yet."

"Don't you think isolating everyone for a case of chickenpox is a little much? Considering most people have either had it or had a vaccine for it?"

Sarah sighed and sat on the edge of the chair, back rigid. "That was just one of the possible diagnoses."

She had no way of knowing how contagious this was, whatever it was. There had been nothing in the patient histories that would indicate where they picked up the virus. And that's what worried her. If they couldn't trace it, how could they eradicate it?

"What aren't you telling me?" Dr. Nejem's eyes narrowed.

"Nothing. I have a theory about what it is, but I can't say yet. I don't want to alarm anyone if I'm wrong."

She prayed she was wrong. With the way the apocalypse was going, however, she knew she was probably right. And then they'd have a panic on their hands.

"Don't you think you should tell me? So I know what to expect."

"You'll think I'm crazy."

Dr. Nejem leaned back in her chair and crossed her arms over her chest. "Try me."

"I think it is a pox, but not chickenpox."

"What then? Monkeypox? Have any of them had problems with their lymph nodes?"

Sarah shook her head, not sure how to tell Dr. Nejem what she thought. It was preposterous. What she was thinking couldn't be possible, yet she'd seen more than a few patients who were proving the impossible might be reality.

"Not that. I think it's smallpox."

Dr. Nejem gasped and leaned forward. "You know that's impossible."

"I know. It was declared eradicated decades ago by the World Health Organization. There are only two labs in the world who have any of it on hand. Yet stranger things have happened."

Dr. Nejem frowned. "I'm not convinced, but start the contact tracing. Isolate everyone with those symptoms as long as we have the rooms available in the ER. I'll talk to the triage nurse. And we'll keep them out of the curtained rooms. I'd like to stop this before it gets any worse. I hope you're wrong."

"I hope I'm wrong, too."

"I'll call the other hospitals in the area to find out how bad the situation is there with patients with the same symptoms."

"They should be getting patients with rashes soon. I called after the initial influx of flu-like symptoms to see if any of the other hospitals were seeing the same thing. They were."

"Keep me apprised of the situation."

Sarah stood and nodded. A warm feeling spread through her, knowing her boss trusted her. Having a boss who listened to your concerns and acted on them was gold as far as she was concerned. Maybe they could mitigate the damage by isolating everyone now.

She hurried back to the ER and stopped at the nurses' station. "Are there any ER rooms available?" They usually used those for the most serious cases, and in a city as large as Toronto, they filled up fast.

"Room five is open."

"Great, can you move my patient to room five? And we'll need someone to clean and sterilize curtain one right away. They need to make sure they wear the proper PPE for it."

Hui's gaze flitted around the room. "Is there something we should be worried about?"

"It's the rash patients coming in. I'm worried it's more contagious than we thought. Just taking precautions."

Sarah raced down the hall and explained to John that he was being moved to a more private location. She hoped they didn't run out of rooms. She had no idea how many more patients would need them today.

Her phone buzzed. Normally, she wouldn't answer it when she was with a patient, but she didn't want to do anything else with him until he was in room five.

"I'll be right with you in your new room."

She left the curtained area and pulled out her phone. Rachel's name flashed on the screen.

"Hey, Rach. What's up?" Her sister didn't usually call her at work.

"I'm at a call right now. Deceased female, approximately thirty years old. She has what looks like a rash covering most of her body, but they look charred and black."

Sarah squeezed her eyes shut. "Tell everyone to get out of there. Call public health and seal the scene until they get there."

Tendrils of fear slid down Sarah's back, wrapped around her stomach, and squeezed until she regretted eating breakfast that morning. If she was right about the smallpox, things had gotten a lot worse.

An hour later, Sarah stood in the hospital's morgue, located in the basement, surrounded by Dr. Padma Malani, the forensic pathologist for the city, Rachel, and Rachel's partner, Detective Michael Williams. They stood around an autopsy table, the body of Wilma Flynn lying there. Dark spots covered the woman's body, some oozing blood. Everyone wore a mask and goggles.

Dr. Malani's hair was pulled into a bun at the back of her head and she wore a crisp white lab coat that would not remain such when she continued with her autopsies. From memory, the doctor kept a few clean coats in her office in cases such as this to present to non-medical people to discuss a case.

Rachel confirmed before arriving that the apartment had been sealed, and anyone on scene was being monitored.

"This is all a precaution, of course." Dr. Malani gestured to her mask and goggles. "The rash shouldn't be contagious now."

Shouldn't, but that didn't mean it wasn't. Sarah peered at the woman's face, imagining how painful and itchy the rash must have been. Despite that, the lesions didn't look like they'd been broken by her scratching them. She admired the woman's resolve to not make the rash worse, but why had she died at home, alone?

"I'll put her autopsy at the top of my precariously balanced list since it might be a contagion."

Williams's brown eyes widened and his eyebrows shot up. "What kind of contagion?"

Sarah shrugged. "We're not sure yet. We're not even sure it is a contagion to be worried about, or one connected to some other cases I've had lately in the ER. We're just being cautious."

How many patients had they let go home? Told them

to drink fluids and get sleep. Had any of the hospitals admitted any of the flu-like symptom patients? She didn't have to call around to find out. No. They hadn't. With more serious illnesses and injuries coming into the ERs with no signs of slowing down, they couldn't use a bed for something that wasn't serious.

Dr. Malani gestured to the woman on her table. "Had the deceased traveled outside the country recently?"

Rachel moved to pull out her notepad but stopped. She shook her head. "Not that we could find. According to her neighbors, she didn't leave the apartment much. She was a bit of a recluse. No one thought anything odd about not seeing her until they noticed a foul smell emanating from her apartment."

"I'll check the hospital records to see if the woman had come into the ER for anything recently," Sarah said.

For a rash to progress to this stage, she must have been to at least one medical professional. But some people refused to go to a doctor, no matter how ill they felt. Sarah hoped the woman had been to an ER at least. Maybe that would help give them reassurance that the rash that caused her death had nothing to do with the flu-like symptoms that had been plaguing the ERs in the city.

Dr. Malani nodded. "I will send my findings to Detectives Malak and Williams, but I'm pretty sure it's not foul play. From the looks of it, she got sick, and it killed her."

"You'll request blood tests and also send samples of her lesions to the lab for testing?" Sarah asked. As soon as the words were out of her mouth, she regretted them. Dr. Malani was a fine doctor, a master in determining the cause of death, and had been used as an expert witness for the province in multiple trials.

Dr. Malani narrowed her eyes. "Of course. Not many rashes would cause death, but if they somehow got into her throat, that might have caused breathing issues. And it could be that the rash didn't kill her at all. Until I do the autopsy, I won't know the cause of death. If it was from the illness, I'll find it."

"Thanks, Dr. Malani," Sarah said. "If anyone can determine what happened to her, you can. I'm sorry if my comment implied otherwise."

Rachel frowned. "I'm worried about how she got sick."

Sarah worried about that too. If this was a natural progression of the patients she'd seen so far, would they all end up like this? Or was this stage a rare occurrence? Would the others get better before this happened? She worried about her patients. At least John had been admitted and they could monitor how he did, see if the illness got worse, and exactly when.

Williams shot a questioning glance at Rachel. "You think someone is making people sick on purpose? Your hunches are usually right, but that one sounds out there."

Sarah shot Rachel a warning look. Saying too much about her theories almost got the eldest angel into a heap of trouble when the gang war was starting due to Conquest's influence. Then, like now, they didn't have any proof of anything. The tips Becky received about the booster hadn't been proven yet. Until they got the results back on the analysis, everything was speculation. Causing a panic before there was something to panic about was irresponsible.

Rachel shot a look back and Sarah could imagine the angel sticking her tongue out at her. "I'm just thinking about all the angles. It would be a nice change of pace having a corpse that wasn't a homicide. I don't think we're that lucky, that's all."

"In this case, luck might be on your side, Detective," Dr. Malani said.

Dr. Malani covered the body with a sheet and they walked to the door of the morgue. "I should have something for you in a few days."

Rachel pushed open the heavy metal door and held it for Williams and Sarah. Her sister and her partner would go back to work, while Sarah would return to the ER and check computer records in between patients. If the woman had come in complaining of flu-like symptoms, she would find the record. Before, she'd thought it was a simple rash, probably chickenpox. Now, she worried about how many corpses this illness would cause. If it even caused this one.

Chapter Nine

Thursday, after an early morning training session with Rachel, Leah, and Becky, Sarah sat in the doctor's lounge a half hour before her shift was set to start. Despite the workout and increased energy, she still sipped on a mug of coffee. Dr. Goretti and Dr. Singh sat with her before they tackled the day.

The topics of conversation ranged from weekend plans to favorite shows, with a dash of how many rash patients have you seen?

"In the past week, I've seen at least fifty flu-like patients, and more than half of them have returned with a rash." Dr. Goretti stood to pour another cup of coffee.

She jiggled the pot. Dr. Singh declined, but Sarah thrust out her mug. After topping up the mugs, Dr. Goretti sat again.

The cream and sugar sat on the table. Sarah poured a small amount of cream and stirred in one sugar.

Dr. Singh nodded. "Same. And I've heard it's the same at all the hospitals in the province."

The TV mounted on the wall farthest from the door

was tuned into the twenty-four hours news channel. Almost every place of business, clinic, doctor's office, dentist's office with a television had set on that channel all day.

Sarah nodded to the scroll that moved across the bottom of the screen. The World Health Organization had declared a global health emergency. Outbreaks of a new pox were occurring worldwide, concentrated in Russia, major Canadian cities, Cyprus, Cairo, and vacation hot spots.

"That would explain it. But not where it came from. How it started. There's no mention of that." Dr. Goretti took a sip of her coffee.

Sarah frowned. That meant the lab results were going to come back negative for chickenpox. Whenever she finally received the results. Today was day two of a supposed two-day return time. If Famine was deliberately keeping results from her, there would be nothing in her email inbox today.

Now that the WHO confirmed a pox was going around, her stomach knotted. When chickenpox was a possibility, the illness wasn't so scary. But now that they'd declared it a new pox, she had no idea how that would play out. Was Wilma Flynn the norm or the exception?

"What's wrong?"

Sarah looked away from the television at Dr. Goretti's question. "I'm wondering about the woman found in her apartment."

She'd told the two about her when they'd first come into the lounge. It was important that they were armed with all the knowledge they could get. Keeping things from them would do no good and probably make things worse. That's why she'd gone to Dr. Nejem right away about the rash.

Dr. Singh nodded. "Norm or exception?"

"Yes. If the exception, it's not so bad. But if that's the norm, what the hell are we dealing with?"

"Time will tell. All we can do is try to keep them all contained when they come in," Dr. Goretti said.

They finished their coffees and got out on the floor.

"I'd like to take the flu-like and rash patients if that's okay."

"Sure," Dr. Goretti said.

"Fine," Dr. Singh replied. "I feel like we're getting the better deal here based on the past week."

A whiteboard of dozens of cases waited for them already. Dr. Goretti picked a slip and fall with a possible concussion. Dr. Singh chose a cut with severe bleeding requiring stitches.

Vanda handed over the folders and the doctors took off down the hall to the curtained emergency room areas to attend to their patients.

"Any of the rash or fever patients?" Sarah said.

Vanda handed over a folder for a patient presenting with a rash. "He's in room six. The triage nurse isolated him right away, but he did talk to others. And she doesn't know how long he was waiting before he approached her."

"Thanks."

Sarah turned left, taking the corridor before the curtained area, and stopped at room six. Before entering the room, she grabbed a mask from a box mounted on the wall beside the door and pulled out a pair of gloves. She put the mask on, then disinfected her hands at the hand sanitizer station under the box of masks. After pulling on her gloves, she opened the door with her elbow and stepped inside.

Her patient, a man in his mid to late thirties, sat on the bed, legs dangling over the sides. His back was straight and his gaze focused on her immediately. A rash covered his face, arms, and some of his neck. She suspected it covered his entire body. He looked vaguely familiar, but they frequently had return patients in the ER.

"Hello, Oliver Brand. I'm Dr. Malak. Is the rash painful?"

He shook his head. "Not really. Itchy, though."

"How do you feel otherwise? Did you have a headache or fever before this?"

"Otherwise okay, I guess. I did have a fever and a headache."

She scanned his information. He hadn't come into this ER for those symptoms. How many others hadn't either?

He raised an arm to scratch but lowered his hand again. The sleeve of his shirt moved slightly, revealing the bottom of an Omega tattoo.

Her heart raced. Then memories of where she'd seen him came flooding back to her. In one of the front pews of Our Lady of Amity church, listening to Father Ianetti's sermon about the apocalypse.

"I don't want to alarm you, but the WHO has declared a global health emergency related to your illness. We're going to admit you to the hospital so we can monitor you more closely. We'll also need to take blood for tests and get a specimen of one of the lesions for testing as well."

She studied his face for signs of alarm, but he smiled. "Whatever you need, Doc. I have nowhere else to be."

His lack of concern twisted the knot in her stomach. She left the room to get the equipment she needed to take the samples, half expecting him to be gone when she returned. But when she opened the door again, he still sat on the bed like he didn't have a care in the world.

When she finished gathering everything, she told him

she would check on him again later. She gathered double what she needed.

Outside the room, she wished there were locks on the doors. The smile he'd given her chilled her to the bone. She sent half the samples off to the lab, not the hospital's usual lab, because she didn't want Famine messing anything up. The remaining samples she stored in the doctor's lounge fridge with a glamour on them so no one else would see them. She knew it wasn't chickenpox now, but at least they could confirm it was the same pox as the other patients. And if the lab couldn't figure it out, she had the samples to analyze herself. All she needed to do was fake her way into a testing lab.

After a frenzy of rash patients, Sarah plopped down in a chair in the doctor's lounge to catch her breath and rehydrate. She worried about her fellow doctors, the nurses, and the sickness that was running rampant now in the hospital. It seemed as if for every one person they admitted with the rash, two more showed up. Most of them had come to the ER in the past ten days for a fever and body aches.

She poured a cup of coffee, the last of the pot, and put on another to brew. With a generous helping of cream, the liquid wasn't too hot, so she gulped it down, needing the kick of caffeine. Fortified, for the time being, she put her mug in the dishwasher, the magnet still turned to dirty. On her way out the door, she paused at the water cooler and poured water into a paper cup. After she downed that, she crumpled the cup in her palm and tossed it in the garbage.

She strolled to the nurses' station. "Vanda, what else have we got?"

The nurse nodded to the whiteboard. Relief washed over her at the absence of rash patients. At least for now. She noted there were more than five patients with flu-like symptoms.

"I'll take M. Prince. Girl, fever, headache."

There was no way she'd be able to get to them all. Dr. Goretti and Dr. Singh would have to take some.

She opened the girl's folder. "It says here she was in the ER last Thursday."

Vanda nodded. "Yes, she was. I remember her. Cute as a button."

"Would you be able to check the other flu-like symptom patients and make a note on the board if they were also here last Thursday?"

"Sure thing."

"And have them moved to an ER room instead of the waiting room or a curtain."

"That might be a little more difficult. There are only three ER rooms available right now."

"More might open up. Keep an eye on it?"

"I'll do what I can."

"Thanks. You're the best."

Vanda grinned. "I'm going to tell Hui you said that."

Sarah tucked the folder under her arm. "I tell her the same thing."

She marched down the corridor and to the left, stopping in front of room twelve. She took a deep breath and opened the door.

On the bed was the cutest little girl she'd ever seen. Despite having a fever that flushed her face, the girl smiled at her, revealing a gap in her teeth where some had fallen out. Bright blue eyes watched her as Sarah came into the room.

The girl's mother, sitting in the chair beside the bed,

hurtled out of it. "Finally. We've been waiting here for over an hour."

"I'm sorry, Mrs. Prince. We're pretty busy today."

"I know. I'm sorry. I'm just worried about her."

"That's understandable. Isn't it a parent's job to worry? And for children to just be children and oblivious to it all? It says in her chart that Melanie was here last Thursday as well."

"Yes. She fell and we were worried she broke her ankle, but it was just a sprain."

The girl nodded, stuck her leg out, and made circles with her foot. "It feels okay now."

Sarah smiled. "That's great." She turned to the girl's mother. "I don't want to alarm you, but we're going to admit her to a special ward."

She needed to see the CCTV footage of the ER waiting room area and the triage area from last Thursday. It would give her a better idea of how the illness might be spreading. If it was airborne, they were in a world of trouble.

Mrs. Prince's face turned white. "What kind of ward? We saw on the TV while we were waiting that there's a new pox. Is that what she has? It's just a fever and a headache. It's the flu. Right?"

As much as she wanted to assuage the mother's worry, Sarah had to tell her the truth. "We'll take a blood sample to confirm. But it's possible."

Melanie gasped, her eyes widened, and she pouted.

"It's okay, sweetie. It won't hurt a bit. The nurses here are the best."

Melanie nodded. "Okay."

Mrs. Prince rubbed her eyebrow and took a deep breath. She squared her shoulders and gave a quick nod. "How long will it take to find out?"

Sarah wished she knew. The results from her other requests hadn't come back yet. If they didn't come in before the end of the day, she wouldn't see them until Monday.

"Hopefully in a few days. The lab is getting a little backed up."

Sarah bent so she was eye to eye with Melanie. "How are you feeling?"

Melanie screwed up her face. "Crummy."

Mrs. Prince let out a short bark of laughter, her cheeks reddening. "She tells it like it is."

Sarah smiled. "I bet. We're going to give you something to help you feel better."

At least she hoped the medication would bring down the girl's fever and alleviate the pain. That was all she could do for her at the moment, except give her fluids.

"I'm going to talk to your mom out there, okay?" Sarah pointed to the door.

Melanie nodded. Sarah jerked her head toward the door, and Mrs. Prince followed her into the hallway.

Mrs. Prince crossed her arms over her chest. "What aren't you saying?"

"Whatever this thing is, it appears to be highly contagious. Has she been in contact with anyone else since she got sick?"

"No. I kept her home from school as soon as she spiked a fever."

"That's good."

But was it enough? Was this new illness, whatever it was, contagious when people were asymptomatic? That would increase the number of potentially infected people and make it harder to stop. A lead ball in the pit of her stomach told her the WHO wasn't revealing all they knew about the illness yet. And when they did, it was going to be bad.

"We'll want you to get a blood test as well."

Mrs. Prince nodded. "Of course. Whatever it takes."

"Try not to worry just yet. I know it's hard. You want to protect them from everything. But we'll take good care of her."

Sarah marched down the hall, through the emergency room waiting area, and stopped at Dr. Nejem's office. This was going to get a lot worse before it got better and they needed to start preparing now. She knocked three times and waited for the invitation to enter.

Dr. Nejem looked up and smiled. Sarah managed a half smile and took a seat in a chair in front of the desk.

"Based on what we saw in the emergency room last Thursday and what we're seeing now, I want to move all the flu-like patients and the patients with a rash to a separate area. We're going to run out of isolation rooms in the ER."

Dr. Nejem nodded. "I've been looking over the ER reports and I agree. Set up a ward for them. Move patients out of whatever ward you decide to use if you need more space."

"I'll get right on it," Sarah said.

Relief washed over her. She thought she'd have to argue more, convince her boss to take precautions, but Dr. Nejem was smart.

"Good. We'll need to start calling everyone who has been in the ER during the past week to see if they have symptoms. If any do, they'll need to quarantine themselves."

Sarah pursed her lips. "But will they?"

Dr. Nejem shrugged. "All we can do is tell them to. Tell them the consequences if they don't. If they care for the people in their lives, they'll listen to us. Unless they're here at the hospital, we can't enforce it."

"Counting on people to do the right thing. That's putting a lot of faith in people." Since arriving on Earth, people hadn't given her much hope that they would do the right thing. The selfishness to give in to their wants was supercharged with an apocalypse in full swing.

Dr. Nejem smiled. "It is. And I hope they don't disappoint me."

Sarah hoped so too. She'd seen people come together in the past to fight common enemies. Achieve common goals. But taking away their freedom, even if only temporarily, rarely worked out well.

"I'll get started with the ward."

Sarah left her boss's office, but instead of looking for a place to move the sick, she swung by the security office on the main floor of the hospital. At this time of day, Todd, one of the daytime security guards, sat in front of the bank of twelve monitors. They showed all floors of the hospital, switching back and forth between angles.

"Hi, Todd. How are you doing today?"

"Great. What can I do for you, Dr. Malak?"

"Is it that obvious?"

Todd grinned. "Doctors rarely come to the security office. When they do, it's usually because they need something."

Sarah sighed and stepped in when he gestured to a chair beside him.

She plopped down onto the soft leather. "I need to look at the CCTV footage of the emergency room waiting area from last Thursday. Is that possible? Do we keep footage that long?"

He put down the mug he'd been holding and rubbed his hands together. "Are we helping to solve a crime or some sort of mystery?"

"Sort of a mystery, yes."

"All of last Thursday?"

"Yes. As much of it as you can get, starting from seven thirty in the morning if you can."

While she wanted to see how many other patients before her shift might have had the symptoms, she was most curious right now about Melanie.

He pointed to a monitor separate from the bank of twelve. "I'll call it up and display it there."

When a picture came up, Sarah leaned into the screen to see it better. A lot of people came into the waiting area, sat, stood up, sat somewhere else until the waiting area became full and they had no choice but to stay where they were. Some stayed where they were, looking at their phones.

"Stop!"

He hit pause, and the screen froze. "That something important?"

"Very important." Melanie sat beside Mrs. Jeffries. The girl had shown something to Mrs. Jeffries, who had smiled and said something to her. Other than that and a brief touch of hands, there was no other contact.

The pit in her stomach grew heavier.

"Can you pull up today's footage?"

"Sure, what time frame?" The eagerness in his voice mirrored her own.

"Let's start with seven this morning and include the footage from emergency triage."

She waited a few minutes while Todd queued up the

video, tapping a finger to her lip. The screen changed and Melanie disappeared, replaced by the outer emergency room triage area. Three nurses behind Plexiglas called people to the seat in front of them, took details, gauged the seriousness of the complaint, and sent them back to wait to be called into the emergency room waiting area.

At a few minutes after eight, Oliver Brand walked into the triage area, touched every surface he could, spoke to a number of people from the security guard, to people waiting to be seen. He kept that up for at least thirty minutes before he checked in with a nurse.

"Shit."

"Not good?" Todd asked.

"No. Thanks for your help."

She dashed out of the security office before he could ask her any questions she didn't want to answer. She didn't stop until she was at Dr. Nejem's office again, explaining what she'd seen on the video footage. When she told Dr. Nejem she wanted to call public health, the chief of emergency medicine nodded.

"Do it now before you see any other patients."

Sarah hurried back to the lounge, pulled out her phone, and called public health. Based on what she'd seen, she asked for their help telling people they should quarantine.

"Yes, we think that is a good idea," the public health person said.

"You do? You didn't before."

"After the WHO's declaration of a global health emergency, we believe these precautions are wise. We will be issuing a statement shortly to the media."

When she hung up the phone, her mind raced for a solution to their problem. The hospital needed to put rash patients somewhere away from the rest of the patients.

Once the isolation rooms in the ER ran out, they ran the risk of the afflicted patients infecting others. She ran out to the nurses' station.

"Vanda, when is the dedication for the new ward?"

Felix Grundy, a multimillionaire who lost his wife to cancer, donated a ton of money to the hospital over a year ago and built a ward for state-of-the-art cancer care. The hospital was going to do a whole dedication ceremony with TV cameras, a ribbon cutting, cake and a black tie dinner afterward. Besides the equipment and budget for staff, the ward had one hundred beds.

"Two weeks, why?"

"It's perfect."

She explained why she wanted it, then coordinated to have patients moved up there. Any new patients with the same symptoms would automatically be admitted to the new ward.

On the new ward's floor, Sarah directed the porters where to put people. The hospital would have to move more equipment up there, equipment they could use for quick tests, once they had a quick test for whatever this was.

With hospital staff and patients taken care of, she wandered the halls of the ward, figuring out how long it would be until even these beds were full. Before she got to the waiting area for the floor, her phone buzzed.

She took it out of her lab coat pocket and Becky's name flashed on the screen.

"Hey, Becky. What's up?"

"That's what I was going to ask you. We received a wire from public health that people need to quarantine."

"Yes. We won't know for sure until contact tracing is done and samples are analyzed, but based on the security footage I've seen, it might be airborne."

Becky gasped. "I'm going to call Dr. Karimi and light a fire under his ass for the results of the booster analysis."

"Good. We need all the information we can get."

Maybe armed with knowledge, they could stop the illness before it affected too many people. Now that public health agreed there was a problem, they would be issuing regular reports on how many people were infected. She hoped it wasn't more than the health care system could handle. Queen City Hospital had a brand-new, never-before-used ward for the sick. Not all the hospitals in the city would be so lucky. She hoped their luck held out.

Chapter Ten

Sarah woke the next morning at her usual time for a weekday, but she lingered in bed, remembering Dr. Nejem put her on a four-day work week. She no longer worked on Friday. Three days in a row away from the hospital might be enough to do a little research, figure out a bit more about the illness, and possibly make progress in putting a stop to it.

For the first time in a long time, she would have the loft to herself while her sisters worked. That meant no interruptions when she analyzed the samples she'd brought home from the hospital yesterday.

"Sarah!"

Becky's high-pitched voice pulled Sarah out of bed. She rushed to the kitchen to see Becky staring into the fridge.

"What?"

"Why are there specimens in the fridge?" Becky wrinkled her nose.

Sarah shooed her away from the fridge, pointing to the

stools in front of the kitchen island. "Sit. I'll make breakfast. I have plenty of time now."

Rachel ambled into the kitchen and took a seat beside Becky. "What's the problem out here?"

Leah sidled behind Rachel, covering a yawn as she took a seat opposite Rachel.

"There is no problem." Sarah pulled the stuff to make breakfast out of the fridge.

"The science experiment behind the yogurt is a problem," Becky said.

"I couldn't send it to the lab at work. I wanted to check it myself." Sarah turned her back to them while she made the batter for pancakes.

Rachel stared at her. "We don't have a lab."

"We do now." Sarah grinned. "It's in the basement. And relax, the training room is still there. I just added more space."

Rachel bolted off her stool so fast, Becky had to catch it before it hit the floor. Rachel stood behind Sarah, the eldest angel's gaze unnerving. Sarah turned around, forcing Rachel to take a step back.

"All of your color is there. Plus more. How is that possible?"

Sarah shrugged. "I was expecting some of it to be gone, too."

Becky pulled out her phone and made a note. "I'll add that to the spreadsheet later."

When the pancakes were ready, Sarah piled three per plate and put the dishes on the island. She grabbed the butter and maple syrup from the fridge and set those in the center of the island too. Satisfied their hunger was taken care of, she grabbed the pot from the coffeemaker and poured everyone, herself included, a cup. Sugar already sat next to the butter, but she retrieved the cream from the fridge.

Once everything was taken care of, she finally sat on the stool next to Leah and dug into her pancakes. She didn't care if she filled up on carbs and fat. The added jolt would help her concentrate on the analysis. And she would be home all day. She'd eat healthy later.

By the time everyone finished eating, Sarah was antsy to get to work on the samples. For the first time in months, they all left the loft at the same time to go to work. Well, she was going downstairs, but it was still work and apocalypse related. Because she was sure this illness was no coincidence.

Becky looked at Sarah's empty hands. "Aren't you taking the specimens?"

Sarah laughed. "Those containers in the back of the fridge are my lunch. I forgot I didn't have to go to work today. The real samples are in the lab downstairs. I didn't know what I was dealing with, so I opted for high safety protocols."

Pink tinged Becky's cheeks, and her eyes narrowed. "That wasn't funny."

Rachel laughed. "It was kind of funny."

She walked down the stairs with them, but instead of following them out, she turned left and hurried down the steps to the basement. It was important to leave the training room the same size, so the basement was double the square feet it was yesterday. Because she didn't know what she was dealing with, she'd put in BSL 4 protocols, complete with a separate HVAC system. She was pretty sure she couldn't get sick now with the added power, but they hadn't thought they could bleed either and Rachel proved that wrong when the Esskays had shot her as she was coming out of the Grange gang's headquarters.

A number panel on the right side of the door waited for her security code before she could gain entrance. Better safe than letting a potentially hazardous biological agent get out into the world. She punched in a code and a green light flashed. The clank of locks disengaging filled the short hallway. She turned the handle and the heavy metal door that led to the lab creaked open.

Once inside, she went through the safety protocols, starting with the airlock entry, to enter the lab area proper. As a precaution, the lab was fitted for BSL 4 protocols, which meant an airtight door, a separate airflow system, and a positive pressure suit. She'd set the lab up with all the analysis equipment she'd need, plus a computer in a separate area away from the actual lab in case she needed to research anything relating to the virus. When creating the lab, she included other known viruses, currently stored properly for her to use as comparisons to the one from Oliver.

After hours of studying the virus from the hospital and comparing it to known pox viruses, she was still stumped. The new virus had characteristics of a pox, but it varied slightly. And it was not a match to chickenpox or monkeypox. The WHO said it was a pox virus. What other one could it be?

A sinking feeling in the pit of her stomach forced her to grab the edge of the lab table for support. No. It couldn't possibly be that.

The computer in the lab was voice activated with a simple voice-to-text software. She instructed the software to pull up an internet browser, navigate to a search engine, and locate pictures of the smallpox virus under a micro-scope. It took several pages before she found one she could use for comparison.

Denial crashed through her like a tsunami. It wasn't

possible, yet the sample from Oliver bore a striking resemblance to smallpox. As far as she knew, there were only two places in the world with labs that housed any smallpox samples, and Canada wasn't one of them. So how did it get into at least one person in Toronto? Based on the progression of the illness, all the patients with flu-like symptoms would test positive for smallpox. And if it wasn't smallpox, it was pretty close.

Pain in her jaw from clenching her teeth urged her to loosen up a little. She took a deep breath, did a few jaw exercises to ease the pain away, then turned back to the samples. She needed more information. Cursing her oversight in bringing the earbuds for her phone, she walked through the disinfectant shower, took off her protective suit, then cycled out of the lab and into the research area. At least she'd had the foresight to outfit the lab with four positive pressure suits. She'd need to use a new one when returning to the lab.

She pulled her phone out of her pocket and called Becky to find out what they were shipping out of Ralston. Was it more than just weapons? It was still early enough that she wouldn't be on air. Most likely Sarah would catch her in the office or out following up on interviews.

Becky answered on the fourth ring and confirmed weapons were shipped out to be destroyed. At least that's what it said on paper. They knew now those weapons had actually been fired at Russia and made to look like they came from the United States of America.

"What else did they have?" Sarah asked. "Did they have smallpox?"

Becky gasped. "No. They couldn't. Could they? I'll do some digging and will call you back."

"Thanks."

Sarah ended the call. Not knowing how much longer

she would be in the lab looking at samples, she jogged up the stairs to the loft and found her earbuds on the table beside her bed. On her way back down to the basement, she connected the earbuds to the phone, put the buds in her ears, and made sure voice activation was turned on in case Becky called back while she was still looking at slides under the microscope.

After donning her protective equipment again and cycling back into the lab, Sarah looked at more samples. If it wasn't smallpox, it was pretty damn close and that thought was terrifying. A shiver went through her, and not the good shiver that meant she was getting some power back. A bad shiver at the memory of how the disease had devastated Boston in 1776. The stench of the decaying bodies filled her nostrils like she was there again.

To run more tests on the samples, she would need more equipment, more scrubs, more slides. When she set up the lab, she hadn't thought the illness would turn out to be something so devastating, so the supplies had been lacking.

Becky called her back over an hour later, confirming that what they were storing at CFB Ralston was moved to Queen City University Research Group. And it was smallpox samples.

"I'm sending over records. I had to use some power to get them because we needed them fast. Don't tell Rachel."

"Thanks. I won't. The WHO said it was new, and it does look a little different to smallpox, but it looks the same too. And based on the movement of the illness I've seen, it's airborne."

"That's not good," Becky said.

"No, it's not." When humans had eradicated the disease by 1980, she'd done a little happy dance from her cloud. Progress, no matter how small, was progress. Humans had a lot more research to do on other illnesses and diseases, but they'd triumphed over one that was devastating.

When she was more sure of her findings, she would forward what she had to the World Health Organization, public health, and the Pan American Health Organization. The news didn't have much on the illness except infrequent updates that people presenting with flu-like symptoms had increased this year. All the reports chalked it up to the subpar vaccine for that year and reiterated the need to get the booster.

Once she was out of the lab, she'd go over the documents Becky sent over. Probably upstairs in the living room where it would be more comfortable and not so claustrophobia inducing. When she'd been alive, she hadn't minded small places, but being in the suit induced a suffocating feeling.

"I dug a little deeper. The prime minister at the time wanted to keep some of the virus for testing and defensive purposes after the agreements were signed to destroy them because he wanted Canada to be prepared by continuing research," Becky said. "On paper, the samples were destroyed. But it looks like he did keep them."

"Great. What could have gone wrong with that?" There was a reason it was agreed only two labs in the world would keep the virus on hand.

"It gets worse. He was and probably still is in the doomsday cult."

Sarah's hands shook and she took a deep breath. "They kept it so smallpox would come back when they decided to reintroduce it."

Friday evening, after spending most of the day in the home lab, Sarah stood in the kitchen, making dinner. Being out of the suit was a nice change of pace for the day. Working with the thick, protective gloves made detail work tricky and she was happy to be rid of them. While she chopped vegetables for their meal, Rachel, Becky, and Leah sat in the living room, watching TV. Now that a global health emergency had been declared, most people were glued to their television sets to watch the numbers of the infected rise in breaking news reports. Almost every channel was airing something related to the health crisis, even specialty channels that didn't normally air news.

A gasp from Becky almost caused the knife to slip as Sarah julienned some bell peppers. She put the knife down.

"What is it?"

Becky bolted off the sofa and raced to the kitchen. Rachel and Leah followed close behind her, exchanging bewildered looks. Becky shoved her phone at Sarah, rocking it back and forth so fast Sarah couldn't read anything. Sarah wiped her hands on her apron and grabbed the phone before it made her dizzy.

An email from Dr. Karimi was open. Sarah scanned the message and gasped.

"Okay, that's two gasps and no explanation. What the fuck is going on?" Rachel asked.

Sarah handed the phone back to Becky and nodded.

"Dr. Karimi got back to me about the booster. It's not a vaccine. It's the virus. The variant of smallpox that's going around."

Rachel slumped onto a stool in front of the kitchen island. "Shit."

Glad she'd put the knife down, Sarah sank onto the nearest stool in the kitchen. "We definitely can't give out the booster now, but how do I destroy what the hospital has left without getting arrested and fired? Probably in that order."

Leah nodded. "You can at least stall, but there are other places giving out the booster. Even spa-type clinics are offering it."

Sarah stood and returned to chopping her vegetables. "I'll have to tell my boss. And public health needs to know. They have to stop all the ads about getting the booster."

"What are you going to say when she asks how you know?" Becky asked.

Sarah shrugged mid-chop, then continued preparing the vegetables. "I'll figure that out when she asks. Maybe this will get her to pester the labs to get results back to us. Famine will be able to delay only so long before people question why it's taking so long. We'll have to retest those patients for smallpox now. If that's truly what this is. There are differences, but it's close enough that the smallpox test might help identify people."

She didn't have actual smallpox samples to check against the specimens taken from the patients at the hospital, but if the virus was in the booster and that was made at Queen City University Research Group, they must have samples on file that they shouldn't. Without using magic, there was no way to get in there to test her specimens or get a smallpox sample to test in her home lab. Even with magic, the reaper and horseman would not be fooled. Isolating the virus in the booster would be difficult without more knowledge and expertise or a little more magic.

Sarah drizzled oil over the vegetables and popped them in the oven. Her mind reeled with events of the past few days. Pandemic, smallpox, the Omega sect spreading illness through hospitals. Where else were they congregating to spread the virus?

While dinner cooked, Sarah made calls to the WHO headquarters in Geneva, leaving a message about the boosters. She also called the Pan American Health Organization in Washington D.C. to let them know what was going on if they didn't already know. Her next call was to Health Canada. The Toronto public health department knew some of what was going on already, but the rest of the health units in the country needed information about what they were facing. Lastly, she called Canada's version of the Centers for Disease Control, the National Microbiology Laboratory in Winnipeg. They would need to do testing. For a vaccine as important as this one would be for the new strain of smallpox, NML would be the place to develop it. Once developed, it might be farmed out to laboratories like Queen City University Research Group to mass create the vaccines to send across the country.

A churning in the pit of her stomach momentarily took her appetite away. She needed to make sure the development of a vaccine wasn't interfered with. There was no telling how many reapers were on Earth. How many were in positions that could throw a wrench into the plans to cure this illness.

She was getting ahead of herself. Maybe there was already a vaccine ready to go. She knew the United States kept some on hand for this very scenario. Humans had eradicated smallpox before. They could do it again. But how much worse was this variant than the original?

Chapter Eleven

Saturday afternoon, after a morning filled with research and talking to her boss, Sarah slumped into the chair facing the television, dread crawling up her arms like a cluster of quick, skittering spiders. She shook her arms to dispel the sensation and shivered. No matter what channel they tuned into, there would be coverage of the health emergency. While she wanted to know everything she could about what was happening, the speed with which the virus spread was disheartening. How could they come up with a vaccine to stop it before it killed half the planet?

Becky sat on the sofa closest to the television, remote in hand. Until now, they'd kept it off, focusing on searching for answers online. But now, commentary from officials might give them the information they needed.

Leah sat on the floor beside the coffee table, laptop open. While Sarah had been talking to Dr. Nejem, Leah had been tracking down the final ingredients to send Famine back to limbo. All the occult shops were still out of limestone from Mt. Hermon.

The loft door swished open. Sarah turned, the frown on Rachel's face not boding well for the fate of Toronto so far. The early morning call in due to lack of coverage hadn't been a surprise.

"Busy?"

Rachel plopped onto the sofa with a huff. "Half the detectives are out sick."

"Detective Williams?"

"He's fine. He didn't have time to get the booster. I think the whole family was going to go next week."

"That's a bit of good news at least," Leah said.

Rachel nodded. "It is." A second wind bolted her off the sofa and she paced in front of the floor-to-ceiling windows behind the television. "I think we should train. We know what this virus is and we can't do much about it. At least not right now. We need to ready ourselves for when we summon Famine."

Rachel gave Leah a pointed look. Leah shrugged. "It's not my fault they ran out of limestone. Father Ianetti probably bought all they had. When it comes in again, we'll buy everything they have again. We won't need it to summon Death because I'd rather the priest do that anyway. It's going to be draining. More so than summoning the others."

"I know it's not your fault. I'm tired of all the violence, the increase in homicides. I want to do something."

"Won't the ingredients to break Death away from his reapers be harder to get?" Sarah asked.

Leah nodded. "We'll worry about that later. I'm planning the teachers' March break trip around that."

"Yes. Let's concentrate on Famine and this health crisis for now. If the priest ends up summoning Death, we'll deal with that when it happens," Becky said.

Rachel stood in front of the television so they could

only see the sides of the screen. Hands on her hips, she pinned each of them with a stare. "Training. Ten minutes, downstairs."

Grudging mumbles of acceptance filled the room. Leah was the first to stand, stretching her arms over her head and bending at the sides to work the kinks out from sitting on the floor. Sarah didn't know how the floor was comfortable for the youngest angel, but that had been her spot of choice since arriving on Earth.

Sarah pushed herself up from the armchair, holding up a finger when her phone buzzed. She swiped to answer, her lips pursing as Vanda spoke. She listened for a few minutes, nodded, and said, "I'll be right there."

Rachel frowned. "It's your day off."

"It is, but I left instructions with the nurses to call me if any more people came into the ER with a rash who had been there last Thursday."

"Okay, you go. We'll train," Rachel said.

"You might want to come too. The patient is Richard Black."

"He wasn't in the ER waiting area that long." A frown marred Rachel's face.

"No, but this thing is persistent and quick. By the time we get there, hospital staff will have moved him to the quarantine ward."

Rachel grabbed her badge and weapon from the safe under the coffee table, then plucked her coat from the rack beside the door and shrugged into it. "Training will have to wait."

"I thought that guy was in jail," Becky said.

Rachel spun around, her lips open to comment, but she snapped them shut and took a deep breath. Most likely swallowing a comment on Becky's chosen profession and having a scoop.

Instead, the eldest angel shook her head. "He's out on bail. It was a pretty steep price too. My team is still gathering evidence for his murder trial."

Becky nodded. "Thanks for telling me that. I won't use any of it in a story unless you say it's okay."

Rachel smiled. "Thanks."

The drive to the hospital seemed to take forever. Though it was Saturday afternoon and a global health emergency had been declared, people milled around the sidewalks and cars cluttered the road. Long honks and short beeps reflected the agitation of the drivers.

When they arrived at the ER, Sarah waited while Rachel signed in with the desk so the hospital knew a detective was there. Then they took the hallway to the new ward.

Since she'd last been there on Thursday, according to the intake sheet, the ward had swelled with fifty more patients in the immediate quarantine room. Other rooms, for the more severe patients, were separated from the main quarantine room, with separate entrances of their own and safety protocols to follow.

Before being allowed in, Sarah and Rachel donned the proper protective gear, making sure they were covered from head to toe. Their street clothes neatly piled in a locker, they wore hospital scrubs under the gear. They walked into the room, through the heavy plastic curtain, into a sealed room. Once through the chemical shower, they proceeded through a door into another small sealed area. A green light displayed on the panel beside the door and a lock clicked. They passed through more heavy hanging plastic into the room.

Beds, propped in every available space, littered the ward. There was barely enough room between them for hospital staff to walk. The number of beds with sick patients saddened her.

Rachel pointed to a bed at the far side of the room, near the window.

They weaved their way through the maze of patients. Each person sported a rash. If many more patients showed up with the same symptoms, they would have nowhere to put them. Already, the rooms were overflowing. The hospital would have to be prepared to discharge patients who could be released early. And in the coming days, she suspected elective surgeries would have to be postponed. They needed the beds.

At the side of the bed, Rachel frowned at Richard Black. "Don't think this is going to get you out of a trial."

His hands were wrapped to prevent him from scratching his rash. "I was the victim."

"Yes, this time, but that's because you killed Mrs. Denton's husband."

He snorted, rubbing his hands against his chest. "You can't prove that."

Rachel leaned closer to him. "Don't bet on that. Get well soon because I want to see you in court." She turned to Sarah. "I'll wait outside. I'm sure you're going to check on some other patients while you're here."

Disheartened to have so many patients to check, Sarah followed Rachel's retreat until the eldest angel slipped past the heavy plastic curtain. Hopefully, these patients were put here before they could infect anyone else. Some of the flu-like patients now attempted to scratch their new rashes with hands wrapped in gauze. Absent were some of her other patients who presented with a rash. She hoped that meant they were better and had been discharged, but she doubted that was the case. They'd probably been moved to make more room in the main quarantine area.

Not seeing Oliver Brand in the current room, she asked a nurse about his location.

"He was moved to the room next door." She pointed to another plastic-curtained doorway to her left.

A sinking feeling in her stomach propelled Sarah through the maze of beds. She cycled through the safety procedures to get into the new room, which were less than to get from a safe area into the quarantine zone. She was still going into a quarantined area.

Oliver occupied the first bed closest to the door she'd come through. On the opposite side of the room, there was another door, similarly curtained. His bed, unlike the ones in the main room, was also curtained with plastic. When she got closer to the bed, she understood why. Like the woman who had been found dead in her apartment, Oliver's rash had turned flat and dark. Blood pooled under the skin of all his scabs. His hands were fastened to the bed so he couldn't scratch, not even with gauze-wrapped hands. Any kind of friction against the wounds might break them open. At this point of a virus, the scabs would be one hundred percent contagious.

Being from the Omega sect, that had been his plan all along. How many had he infected while waiting in the ER? How many more had he infected before then? Contact tracing for him might not yield anything if he wasn't truthful with his answers. She checked his chart. The staff was doing everything they could for him, but he wasn't responding to any antivirals. Now that they knew it was smallpox or a variation of it, nothing would work except a vaccine.

She pulled herself away from his bed and walked the floor, peering in on the other patients. Of the ten people in the room, all had presented with rashes, and now half of them had turned hemorrhagic. They would need a wider sample to verify the likelihood of that happening, but these numbers didn't bode well for them. In smallpox, only two percent turned hemorrhagic. On a grand scale, that wasn't a horrible number, until you took into account once it reached that stage, it was one hundred percent fatal.

In the doctor's lounge an hour later, Sarah pulled out her phone and called Becky while she poured a cup of coffee. Keeping the phone to her ear, she added cream and sugar, grabbed her cup, and sank into a chair facing the television. Infected counts, information from the WHO, and other virus-related news replaced the frivolous *news* that normally scrolled along the bottom. The lounge was empty save for her but would receive visits later when doctors had a minute to spare.

When Becky answered, Sarah filled her in on what was happening at the hospital and that Rachel had gone back into the police station.

Becky sighed. "So you're going to stay?"

After taking a sip of coffee, Sarah said, "Yes."

For the same reason, Rachel had gone back to the station. They needed her. With more of the detectives out sick, Rachel wanted to see if she could help the ones still standing. And so far, doctors and nurses had remained healthy, but how long would that last? She was pretty sure she would be okay due to her angel status, but the rest of the staff were mere mortals. Before they realized what the virus was, they hadn't been isolating or taken any extraordinary measures. The regular hand washing and sanitizing of hands and instruments had been the most they'd done because it worked. For most things.

Becky cleared her throat. "I've been analyzing my

spreadsheet and you get power back when you don't do extra work. Or when you don't finish all your food."

Sarah sighed. "Maybe that was true when I was hoarding the hours for myself and preventing someone else from working, but right now all hands are on deck. And they need more hands."

Looking back, a twinge of guilt ruffled her feathers for taking all those hours away from other people. She'd thought she was doing them a favor. And she had to admit, it was nice having some downtime to look into all things apocalypse. But right now, even if it meant losing some power, she needed to be at the hospital.

"Okay. I'll make dinner. And by that, I mean going to the burger joint and picking it up when I know you and Rachel are on your way home."

"Great. Thanks for that. I shouldn't be too much longer. I want to make sure the ER isn't bursting at the seams before I leave."

After she'd finished checking on the quarantine patients and getting out of her protective gear, she'd taken a few patients waiting in the ER. It was a relief to treat a broken bone, a cut, and sore stomach for a change. How long would the hospital be able to handle such cases if the infected continued to rise at the current levels?

She downed the rest of her coffee and movement on the left side of the TV screen caught her attention. A press conference was being set up. According to the new information scrolling along the bottom, it was with the WHO, live from their headquarters in Switzerland.

Groups of people stood on both sides of the screen, huddled in conversation, waiting for the press conference to start. Sarah leaped out of her chair, scanning the room for the remote control. The television was never off, so the location of the device to turn it up was a mystery. She checked the table under the television, in between the cushions on the sofa against the back wall. Nothing. Next, she pulled out the drawers in the kitchen area. Not really a kitchen area, but it had a sink, there was a fridge, and some counter space. Drawers beside the sink, rarely used, might hold the remote. When she yanked out the bottom drawer, a rectangular, black device slid to the front. She snatched it up and pointed it at the television until she could hear the commentator say the press conference was about to start.

She sat facing the television again, hands folded on the table, her stomach churning. It would not be good news. At the beginning of a pandemic, it was never good news. And that's what she thought they were dealing with now.

A somber-looking man in his late fifties took his place behind the microphones. He waited for the room to quiet down.

"The WHO is now declaring a global pandemic. We have confirmed this new virus is a variant of smallpox, variola virus, and it travels through micro droplets produced by speech or sneezes, or through direct contact with a surface that holds those droplets. While we are still investigating the virus and its origins, we can tell you it has been seen in all continents with the exception of Antarctica. We are asking that health care professionals quarantine the sick and anyone who has been in contact with the sick. Public Health departments around the world will be receiving more information to help them fight this. With the current infection rate, we are estimating an R0 of 10 for this illness. But with a shorter incubation period than the normal smallpox virus. The contagious period also appears to be longer."

He talked a little more about the measures that needed to be taken, which the hospital was already doing. Then he stopped to take questions from the reporters present. They fired off their queries without mercy, fear fueling their desire for answers, not just because they needed to file a story. The pandemic would affect everyone.

The door to the lounge burst open so hard it hit the wall. Sarah jumped and turned around. Dr. Nejemi stood in the threshold, a frown on her face. "I'm glad you're here today. Emergency meeting, my office."

Sarah turned the volume down again, put the remote back in the drawer, and followed her boss out of the lounge. Dr. Nejemi had a television in her office, a small one that fit onto a shelf of her bookcase. It was there for something just like this. Being able to watch the press conferences in private enabled her to process the information without the world watching her.

A crowd of emergency room staff members milled around Dr. Nejemi's office. It looked like half the staff were present, while the other half continued to look after patients. Sarah suspected she would have the same meeting with the other half of the personnel when this meeting was finished.

Dr. Nejemi moved through the crowd and stopped at her office door. "Everyone, I need your attention. With the WHO's announcement today, the hospital is announcing the intention to hire more staff. Public Health, working with ER departments across the province, will be doing the contact tracing of everyone who has visited the ER over the past two weeks. We will continue to isolate anyone with flu-like symptoms. Priority is to rule out or confirm this new variant of smallpox so they can be quarantined properly."

She went on to talk about their safety protocols, the isolation suits for examining patients, and other PPE equipment that would be needed to treat people safely.

"I'm not technically on shift. I can do a count of the

PPE and isolation suits. Do a bed count to see how many are available, check our antiviral situation."

Sarah doubted the antivirals would be needed because they'd tried them already and they didn't work on those patients. It was best to save them for something they did work on, but if there was a chance an antiviral might put the tiniest dent in the illness, she wanted to make sure they had enough on hand.

"Great. Thank you. Everyone, be safe out there. And tell anyone currently on the floor to come see me."

Sarah started with the beds in the ER, the isolation rooms for the more serious cases that were brought in, then went to the quarantine floor. Instead of donning the PPE to enter the quarantine area, she did her count from the outside. Next, she checked the remaining floors. When she had all the numbers, she cross-checked them with the hospital's computer to see if they matched, and if not how far off they were. The computer said they had 125 free beds. But her count said 130. It was possible some of the discharges entered into the computer hadn't been executed yet. The bed count was dwindling. Fast. If the rate of infection kept up, they would need to start cancelling non-urgent surgeries to save bed space.

After turning in her findings to Dr. Nejemi, she grabbed her stuff from her locker and left the hospital. Now that the pandemic was global, all hell was going to break loose.

Expecting a rest when she got home, Sarah groaned at the sight of Rachel, Becky, and Leah donned in workout garb, standing in the living room. At the sound of the door to the loft closing, Rachel whirled around and smiled. Where did she get her energy from? It wasn't angel power because she was still sorely lacking in that area compared to the rest of them.

"Get dressed for a workout. We're training before dinner." Rachel turned off the television and tossed the remote on the sofa.

The mention of a meal caused Sarah's stomach to grumble. It had been hours since she'd eaten anything and now her body wanted all the food it could handle. She should have known better than to think the trip to the hospital was more than a small reprieve. Rachel had been determined that morning to have them all work out and she wasn't going to give up.

"You go. I'll rest and do double tomorrow." Sarah's body screamed at her to sit. She walked past Rachel and dropped onto the sofa.

A frown appeared on Rachel's face. She put her hands on both hips and shook her head. "We can't get soft. We need to be prepared. Conquest almost killed Leah and we were only dealing with one horseman."

War had almost killed Leah too, but by then three horsemen might have been on Earth. They were more powerful together, even if not in the room or space. Rachel's argument was sound, and Sarah grudgingly acknowledged the eldest angel was right. They could not afford to be weak. The more they could physically tire out the horsemen, the less magic they would need to use. As God's warriors, it was up to them to roll back the apocalypse as much as possible.

"I'll go first so you can rest a little," Becky said.

Leah stepped forward. "And I'll go next. You can observe from the benches until we're done."

Rachel raised an eyebrow in question, daring her to come up with another excuse she could refute. Grumbling, Sarah pushed herself off the sofa. "Fine. I'll go change."

She ambled to her bedroom, then did a quick change into the most comfortable clothes she owned. There was a slight chance she would fall asleep on the benches while watching Leah and Becky spar with Rachel. It would be Rachel's fault for not letting her nap before dinner. Detouring through the kitchen, she grabbed a bottle of water from the fridge, hoping the cool liquid would give her a burst of energy.

The last to exit the loft, she yanked the door shut, then followed her sisters down the stairs to the basement. Rachel frowned as they walked by the lab.

"I'm still annoyed you didn't lose any power for that."

Sarah gave her an incredulous stare. "Would you prefer I had?"

Rachel's shoulders slumped forward. "No. That's not what I mean."

Becky patted Rachel on the shoulder, garnering her a withering look. "We know you're frustrated. We'll figure out how you get your power back."

Sarah hoped it was sooner rather than later. Once all the horsemen were here, it would help if she and her sisters were at full angelic capacity. Becky was already there. Leah gained more each day when she was genuinely not envious of something or someone. And now that Becky had cracked how Sarah gained her power back, Sarah would do what it took to fill the well again. But with Rachel, they were all stumped.

In the training room, Sarah took a middle bench to watch Becky and Rachel spar. Well, trying to kill each other with rubber-tipped swords. Leah sat on the bottom bench, gaze focused, back straight, her head darting back and forth like she was watching a tennis match. Sarah smothered a yawn and took a gulp of her water. If she faltered while Rachel leaned in for a slice, the eldest angel would never let her live it down. Which was why she'd wanted to wait until she'd had a nap, or at least been able to unwind from the hectic ER setting.

When it was her turn, she stretched her arms and legs, then did a few twists to prepare her stomach muscles. She took another sip of water, then tossed the bottle on the bench. It rolled a few centimeters and stopped before falling off the bench.

"I'll take it easy on you." Rachel smiled. "No swords today. Hand to hand."

Thankful for the light training, Sarah relaxed. The fatigue she was feeling, though not profound, would make lifting a sword interesting.

Before she took her place in the center of the mat, Rachel's fist sailed through the air. Sarah barely blocked it, the force of the blow causing her to stumble backward a few steps. Sarah shook her head, rolled her shoulders, bent her knees. When the next blow came, she was ready. Blocking it easily, she punched back, landing a jab to Rachel's ribs.

The adrenaline rush of a workout gave her a second wind. Blocking Rachel's punches became second nature, and by the time they were finished, Sarah's arms were tender from the contact. When Rachel let her guard down, Sarah went in with a sweep of her legs, knocking Rachel onto her ass.

Rachel picked herself up and wiped imaginary dirt from her slacks. "I think that's enough for today. But you need some extra time so we can go over sword work again."

Back in the loft, Sarah sat slumped in the chair, facing the television. Leah was in her usual spot on the floor beside the coffee table, with Becky and Rachel on the sofa. They'd agreed to order dinner and were waiting for it to be ready so Becky could pick it up. Since she regained power when she did something active, it was a chance for her to get more power back.

Now that Sarah knew how to get her own back, she would start doing whatever it took to get the white back in her wings. Even if it meant not taking on as much. But she'd given up her volunteer work at the soup kitchen and scaled back her days in the ER to a normal shift. She didn't know what else she could do, but somehow, she would figure it out. This pandemic needed all the angel power they could get.

Chapter Twelve

Sunday morning, her body still stiff from the workout the night before, Sarah had breakfast at the kitchen island by six. Despite it being the weekend, she and her sisters rarely slept past seven. She'd been up for an hour, getting ready for work and making breakfast. On her second cup of coffee, she sat on one of the stools facing the living room. The TV was on, set to mute, with closed captioning on so she could read what the people were saying. The scroll across the bottom relayed more of the same information about the newly announced pandemic. This was the first one most people had encountered in their lives and chaos, worry, and panic were high.

Becky padded into the kitchen, still wearing the shorts and T-shirt she usually wore to bed. The reporter gave Sarah an exasperated look and frowned. "You're going into work."

Sarah nodded, taking a sip of her coffee. "Eat breakfast before it gets cold."

Becky huffed, grumbling under her breath while she piled a plate with scrambled eggs, bacon, and home fries.

"We went over this yesterday. The spreadsheet clearly indicates if you do less, you get power back. When you don't take hours from others, or food from others, you get a power boost."

Sarah, about to snatch a home-fry from Becky's plate, yanked her hand back. Instead of taking more food from the platters on the island, she took her empty plate to the dishwasher. Proving Becky's point, a shiver skittered through her wings.

"See! You have a new, small patch of white."

She turned back to the island. "Yes, but I'm not taking hours from others in this case. The ER needs everyone there and I'm not clocking in. They don't need to pay me for being there today."

She would get an argument from her boss about that, but she would insist. And if they did end up paying her, she would give the money back or donate it where it was needed most. With all of them working, they didn't need an extra day of her pay to keep the loft running smoothly. The hospital was the best place for her right now.

Becky took a forkful of egg and made delighted sounds. "Okay, if you say so." She used her fork to point at her food. "This is so good. What does the news say about the pandemic this morning?"

"Public health is urging people to stay away from the ER and clinics if they can. There's speculation on how the virus started, with rumors ranging from it being found in the ice melt near Antarctica to terrorists engineering it."

"They aren't far off with the terrorist angle," Becky said.

Sarah nodded. "You won't be able to keep the Omega sect connection out of the news for long. They'll be stepping up their game."

"Which is why you should stay here and get more power back," Becky argued.

Leah walked in with a yawn. Her eyes widened as she took a deep breath.

Sarah sat on her stool again. "I may be the only one not affected by the illness."

Leah, settled onto a stool beside Becky, added another two strips of bacon to her already full plate. A questioning look crossed her face. "But we know we can get hurt. Rachel was shot. What makes you think you can't get this illness?"

It was a good question and one she'd thought about a lot before falling asleep last night. After the workout and dinner, and a short research session that led to more dead ends for the items needed to send Famine back, she'd stared at her ceiling for at least an hour, contemplating the possibilities of getting sick. Other medical staff, especially the doctors and nurses, were likely to catch this. The safety measures were put in place too late to prevent all medical staff from getting sick.

She put her hands around her mug, the coffee inside now cool. "Rachel didn't have a lot of power back when she was shot." She pointed at Leah. "You were thrown off the roof and didn't die because you still had angel power. With the safety precautions and my angel status I'm sure I'll be okay."

Rachel sauntered into the kitchen dressed in a pantsuit. Becky frowned at her. "You're going into work, too?"

Settling onto the stool beside Sarah, Rachel grabbed a piece of toast. "I just got off the phone with Reyes. More people called in sick. Murders don't stop because of a virus."

They finished eating. Everyone helped clear the dishes away and load the dishwasher. Soon, it looked like nothing had been cooked in the kitchen that morning. Since Becky and Leah were staying at home, they would try to track down the ingredients they needed to deal with Famine and Death. On their way to the living room, they absently waved goodbye when Sarah and Rachel headed for the door.

By the time Sarah arrived at the hospital a little before 7:30 a.m., chaos already consumed the ER. Filled to capacity, it was standing room only, and even those spots were scarce. A sick person took up every space where someone could stand. The second a chair became available, someone beelined for it. It was survival of the quickest. The less sick they felt, the faster they moved. Some of the standing patients had given up trying to stand and slid down the wall to slump on the floor until they were called. It was going to be a long day.

Dr. Nejem's glassy-eyed stare greeted Sarah when she walked into the ER, away from the sardine can of the waiting area. Her boss looked heavenward, and a slow smile curled her lips. Dr. Nejem let out a big breath and some light returned to her eyes.

"I am so glad to see you here. After our talk about taking on too much, I was sure you would stay away until Monday."

"I couldn't stay away. Not when the hospital is this busy."

"Thank you for that. Let me know if you need anything. We have requests in to hire more physicians, but all the ERs in the city have been hit hard. There's no telling if or when we'll get more help."

Sarah waited until Dr. Nejem had retreated down the

hall and turned down the corridor to her office before sidling up to the nurses' station to see what cases were on the whiteboard. Unsurprisingly, the majority of cases fit the early symptoms of the new smallpox virus. Another handful of cases fell in line with worsening of the illness, with the patients presenting with rashes. There were only a few that fell in with the usual ER cases before the pandemic hit. A couple cuts and scrapes. Suspected heart attack that Dr. Goretti was already handling.

Sarah grabbed the files for three of the suspected smallpox cases from Hui.

"Jumping in feet first, huh?" the nurse asked.

"We've got to get them tested as soon as possible."

"They were all triaged as soon as they came in and they're up on the quarantine floor."

A niggling feeling in the pit of her stomach said that wasn't enough. They'd still been in the waiting area long enough to infect other people. The hospital needed a secondary emergency room set aside for suspected smallpox patients. Once she finished with some of the cases, she would tell Dr. Nejem. Her boss had asked if there was anything she needed. No matter what they were doing, they could do more to halt the spread of this thing.

On her way back down from the isolation floor, a flash of dark blue ink on a porter's arm caught her attention. Most of the tattoo remained hidden under the long sleeves, but the material was pushed up enough that she recognized it as the bottom of the omega tattoo she'd seen on other sect members. A fist in her stomach clenched. He was pushing a gurney toward the elevator that a teen-aged girl occupied.

She held up a hand to stop him and leaned closer to read his name tag. "You must be Egon, the new porter. I'm Dr. Malak."

He clenched his jaw but smiled. "Started this morning. If you don't mind, I have to get her up to X-ray." He nodded down at the patient.

"All hospital staff are being tested for the new virus." She glanced at the folder she held. It was a patient folder, but he didn't know that. "You're not on the list of those who have had a blood test."

"I can't right now. She needs to be in X-ray."

As if to emphasize his point, the teenager shifted a fraction on the bed and grimaced in pain. Her eyes squeezed shut and she drew in large gulps of air.

A porter she recognized came around the corner, stopped short, and swerved to get around them. She picked up the patient's file from the end of the gurney.

"Hey, Mitra, can you take this patient up to X-ray?"

"Sure thing, Dr. Malak." He shot a questioning glance at Egon.

Egon stepped back and let the newcomer take over. Once the patient was down the hall and waiting in front of the elevator, she turned back to Egon. "Follow me."

She marched him down another hallway to a stairwell they were using for ambulatory staff and patients. She guided him past the stairwell to another corridor that led to the quarantine ward. A separate elevator car had also been designated for anyone sick or suspected of being sick with the new smallpox virus. At the elevators, she pushed the call button and when the designated car arrived, she ushered him inside and pressed the button for the sixth floor where the blood tests were being done.

In the quarantine ward, garbed in more protective gear, she took his blood, labeled it, and placed it with the samples that would be transported to the lab. Every hour, on the hour new samples were sent. She marked this one a rush. Then she escorted him to a chair in the isolated area of the floor to wait.

"I have to get back to work," he insisted.

Back to what work? Infecting more people? While she believed he did actually work there, hospital security was strict about who walked around with badges, she did not believe he had the patients' best interests at heart. "You'll do that once we get the results back from the blood test. Until then, you're staying put."

Before she left the area, she informed the staff to watch out for him.

"Why is he here?" Dr. Singh asked. "He doesn't look sick. Is he showing any symptoms?"

"A precaution." She sighed. It wasn't like she could tell him she had a feeling. And it was more than that. If he was in the sect, he was most definitely carrying the virus. Maybe he'd just been infected and wasn't showing symptoms. What worried her the most was the thought he might be asymptomatic. He could be carrying the virus and not show any symptoms at all. That made it a lot easier to spread when you didn't look or act sick.

"We need to keep the beds for the actual sick."

"He doesn't need a bed. Leave him in the chairs. Just keep him in here at least until after his blood work comes back."

Dr. Singh wrote something in a chart and nodded. "Fine. Let us know as soon as his results come back."

"Thank you. I promise."

Since they'd started using the other lab, the one that didn't employ a reaper and a horseman, results were coming back quicker. By the end of the day, she would know if she was being overly cautious with Egon or if her angelic intuition was back to full force. She took off the quarantine protective gear, made sure she went through the decontamination shower twice, then donned fresh personal protective equipment.

The ER waiting area was still packed tighter than an '80s rave. A buzz from her pocket pulled her attention away from the whiteboard. Though she didn't have time for idle chitchat, she needed to speak to her sisters if they called. At this point, they wouldn't be calling to talk about the weather or gossip about the neighborhood.

She answered the call with a sigh. "What's up, Becky?" She walked to the doctor's lounge, where it was quieter.

Crinkling sounds of paper filtered through the phone. "Public Health is going to do a news conference to provide updates on the pandemic. And they're going to advise to stop administering the booster. WHO is issuing a recall order of all the boosters remaining."

Sarah slumped into a chair. "That's good. It's a start, anyway."

"There's more. The prime minister made a statement that we're in talks with the US to acquire smallpox vaccines they have stored there. They have enough to vaccinate every person in the US, but since they haven't been affected as much, the prime minister is hoping they'll spare some. Canada has some smallpox vaccine, but not nearly enough for everyone who has become ill already."

Frowning, Sarah shifted in her chair to see the television. The replay of public health's press conference appeared on the screen. "It won't help. It was created from a less harmful version of smallpox. This strain has been altered too much for the old vaccine to do any good. And I'm sure more than a few of those doses are expired."

Becky sighed. "That's all we've got right now. He's sending funds to labs across the country to start working on a new vaccine that will work against this version."

Sarah got up and poured a cup of coffee, gave it a

dollop of cream, and three sugars. "At least they'll have a starting point. We still have the formulation. They can use the current smallpox vaccine as a base for the new one. I need to get in on the research. The problem will be convincing a lab to let me help."

"But you gave yourself that training when you created the lab in the basement."

At the table again, Sarah took a fortifying sip of caffeine. "Yes, but I didn't put it into my planted history. Everyone at the hospital still thinks I'm an ER physician. I'll try normal channels and try to convince a lab to pair me with a clinical research study at least. Or I can work alongside a research associate to help them out. I can analyze the data while they do the experiments."

"Do what you can. Will you be home for dinner?"

Becky's conclusions about how Sarah earned her power back crashed through Sarah's mind. Giving up hours that weren't really hers might not help, but it couldn't hurt either.

"I'll see a few more patients and then come home."

She would need to unwind, have a good meal, and get a lot of rest. After the WHO recall, and the public health announcement, tomorrow would only be worse with panicked people showing up at the ER.

Chapter Thirteen

After Dr. Nejem insisted Sarah get some rest, she sat on the chair in the living room Monday, watching Becky deliver the six o'clock news, a laptop open for research. Dinner simmered in the kitchen, waiting for the reporter to get home so they could eat together. Since the pandemic had been declared, most businesses were closed or working under reduced hours. Due to more than half the staff being out sick and patronage down, Baron's was closed for the week.

Despite a heavy workload, Rachel was also home, sitting on the sofa, shuffling through paperwork. The fewer people congregating in close proximity, the better, so detectives were putting in their shifts and then bringing work home with them.

Leah sat in her usual spot, cross-legged on the floor, her computer open on the coffee table.

Rachel turned the sound up on the television. Shuffling papers on the table, Becky looked into the camera, her face impassive. She delivered the news about violence in the city on the rise, food shortages, and infection rates. Almost extinct were the light, humanitarian pieces, special interest stories that ended the news most other nights. Those had disappeared a week ago. The pandemic, on everyone's mind right now, was the only thing the viewers cared about. Before signing off, Becky said the WHO would be issuing another statement in the morning. And public health wanted to remind everyone with symptoms to quarantine, and they wanted everyone to wear a mask. With the virus being airborne, the mask was a given, but was it too little too late now?

When Becky began her sign off, Rachel turned the volume down again and put the remote on the coffee table. A splash of liquid on the burner prompted Sarah to jump out of her seat. She stirred the sauce, turned the heat down, and put the lid back on. She plopped into her seat again in the living room.

"The mask mandate should have started earlier," Rachel said.

Sarah nodded. "I agree, but they did what they could with the information they had. They didn't know right away that it was airborne, and by then, the damage was done."

Leah half closed her laptop's lid and worry lines marred her forehead. "Half my class is out sick. A handful of the teachers are too."

"It will be a matter of time until you have to teach remotely to reduce the risk. The hospital has established a separate ER for those with initial symptoms. And I'm sorry to report that Darla and two of her friends were admitted today. I saw her after I talked to Becky."

Rachel gasped. "She's worked so hard to get into a better place."

Sarah shook her head, a wave of panic crashing in her stomach. "It doesn't look good. We're still seeing a trend of fifty percent turning into hemorrhagic smallpox. That means at least a fifty percent fatality rate. With regular smallpox, if it turned hemorrhagic, it was one hundred percent fatal."

"Can the hospital handle that? Can any of the hospitals in the province handle that?" Rachel asked.

"No. The morgue only holds ten cadavers. The city is looking at gyms, university dorms, parking lots with freezers for the piling body count."

Leah huffed out a breath. "We know what we need to send Famine back. It's frustrating that most of the ingredients are still on back order."

Rachel nodded. "Father Ianetti was smart. He grabbed up all the occult stores had to make it harder for us to interfere because he doesn't need that stuff for summoning the horsemen."

As usual, Rachel was right. Sarah leaned back in her chair, letting her head rest against the back. They had all they needed to summon Famine, but without the ingredients for the vanquishing spell, they were stuck. "I wish we could send them all back at the same time."

Leah's glance darted to Rachel, then she lifted the lid of her laptop again, focusing on the keyboard. "But we can't…"

Rachel scowled. "You can say it. We can't because I don't have enough power yet. Sending even one back is draining enough. Three would do us in."

"Even if we were all at full power, we don't know if we'd be able to send all three back at once. We'll concentrate on Famine for now. Partly because we can't get all the items to separate Death from his reapers back until Leah goes on her March Break trip. And partly because we need to strengthen ourselves both physically and spiritually."

"Is the trip still a go?" Rachel asked.

Leah shrugged. "Maybe. They're on the fence. If it's allowed, they'll probably limit the number of teachers who can go. I'll get myself on the list, even if I have to use angelic power. The flos vitae only blooms on Mt. Hermon."

Rachel raised an eyebrow. "How are you going to get the flower? Let alone bring it back?"

Sarah leaned forward, curious about Leah's strategy. Bringing back plants from other countries wasn't exactly allowed, and she was sure that picking the flos vitae was against the law as well. Regardless of any laws, they needed the flower to complete the spell to separate Death from his reapers, assuming they couldn't stop Father Ianetti from recombining them in the first place.

Leah shrugged. "Wing it. Same with how to convince the Pope to give us holy oil and holy water blessed by himself."

"I'm sure you'll think of something when the time comes," Sarah said.

Either that or the youngest angel would use magic to get what she needed. The Pope might be the hardest to convince. But once angelic power was unleashed, he would have no choice but to believe.

Rachel stood. "Becky will be home soon. We should eat dinner, then train. We need to be ready as soon as the ingredients we need come in. I'd feel better if the Canadian National Microbiology Laboratory and the labs were studying the virus and trying to come up with a vaccine that worked without Famine hanging around on Earth."

After a long day at the lab, Famine settled into one of the plush high-backed chairs surrounding War's dining room table. This time there was a veritable feast of beer and snacks like regular folk liked to eat when meeting with colleagues. He swirled the amber liquid in his glass and took a large gulp. The hoppiness of the beer danced on his tongue. Too bad when he was finished, there wouldn't be enough hops to make beer or rye to make most alcohols.

He reached out a thin arm, his spindly fingers snagging a few potato chips. He popped them in his mouth, enjoying the sting of salt on his lips and over his tongue. His lips turned up into an amused grin as Conquest and War fought over who was in charge. Red-faced with pinched features, spittle flew out of Conquest's mouth, his voice growing louder with each insistence he should be in control.

War's face was calm, controlled, as the horseman watched Conquest's antics. War steepled his fingers under his chin, waiting for Conquest to run out of breath. Conquest finally sagged back into his chair.

"Are you done?" War asked. "We all know I should be the one in charge."

"I was here first, got the ball rolling, causing chaos in the city. So much so that it's bleeding into neighboring cities." Conquest's face had returned to its normal color and his features relaxed. "Now people are choosing bad over good because it's freeing."

War leaned back in his chair. "That's great. I'm still in charge." He looked at Famine. "What have you done?"

What had he done to help famine run amok following the pestilence that was upon them? Famine leaned forward to grab another chip. "My seeds have gone out to most farms in the area. Plus farms around the world. A lot of seeds have been sent to China and the United States. Also, packed with the seeds at no additional cost, is an airborne fungus designed to destroy any seeds they already have. It's a hardy fungus, easily spread, and should wipe out any crops they currently have in the fields as well. Even in climates where the farmland is currently blanketed by snow."

War tipped a bottle of beer into his mouth and took a long drink. He wiped his mouth with the back of his hand as he swallowed. "Good. Father Ianetti is almost ready to summon Death."

Famine tapped his foot. "Why doesn't he summon him now?"

War rolled his eyes. "He's an old man. He needs to recover longer after each summoning."

"What about the angels?" Conquest asked.

"They'll be hard to kill, so stay clear of them if you can. If they send any of us back to limbo, it will delay the final countdown. It's already taking the priest over a week to regain his strength after summoning just one of us."

Conquest puffed out his chest. "I'll stay clear, but what about sending my gang after them?"

From Conquest's bragging, one would think he'd single-handedly put the gang together and propelled them on a path of chaos and destruction. All he did was give them a little push in a direction they were already headed.

Famine shook his head. "It's not your gang anymore."

It was time credit was recognized where credit was due. War, along with Famine and the ensuing pestilence, brought in more deaths than Conquest. There was a reason Conquest was the first horseman summoned. You didn't bring out the big guns right away and give away your strategy.

Conquest's fingers tapped the table. "True, but I'm sure Caleb could be persuaded in a way he doesn't know I'm still here."

While it was true the glamours they could affect would

fool even the most discerning scrutiny, they couldn't risk Conquest's continued involvement with the gang. There were more important items on the agenda to take care of. Chaos in the city was on the rise, as was violence of all kinds. But recruitment to their side, especially of the souled, would help usher in the final days of the apocalypse.

War shook his head. "Steer clear. I don't want either of you doing anything that will tip them off or get their backs up."

Conquest crossed his arms over his chest. "Fine."

War grinned. "Not to worry, brothers. The end will soon be nigh."

Chapter Fourteen

Tuesday morning, Sarah sat in the doctor's lounge, taking a five-minute break to catch her breath and recaffeinate. She took the opportunity to eat a power bar and banana as well, to keep her energy up. Caffeine could only do so much. It helped that she'd had a good night's sleep, for once not tossing and turning due to dreams plagued with images of a burning city. That's how she pictured Toronto most of the time now that three horsemen were here. Death would soon follow.

The scroll across the bottom of the channel announced a breaking announcement at 10:00 a.m. In the top right corner of the twenty-four-hour news station, the time ticked closer, with five minutes until the press conference. Already off the floor for five minutes, Sarah weighed the consequences of staying in the lounge to hear the announcement. Arming herself with more knowledge would mean being able to better treat her patients. She settled back in the chair and waited.

As with most press conferences in the city, this one did not start on time. Ten minutes late, Dr. Monica Antonini, the public health representative and Prime Minister Olaf Becke took the floor. They stood in front of a podium, somber expressions on their faces. Like they were going to be telling the country they had bad news.

The door to the lounge burst open as Dr. Goretti and Dr. Singh rushed into the room. Dr. Goretti plopped into a chair facing the television. Dr. Singh leaned against the counter in front of the sink.

"Did we miss it?" Dr. Goretti asked.

Sarah shook her head. "It's about to start."

For fifteen minutes, the public health doctor talked about the severity of the outbreaks, what the province was doing to fight the virus, and steps they would be implementing over the next few days to stop the spread. When the prime minister took the podium, his face grim, a fist tightened in her stomach.

After the statements were finished Dr. Antonini and Olaf took questions to clarify what they'd just said. Someone from Becky's television station was probably there. One of the questions might have even been from them. Everyone had heard correctly. As of Friday, the government was issuing stay-at-home orders for everyone except for essential services. People could go out for food and healthcare. Utilities companies would operate with skeleton crews and all office work would be conducted from home, where possible. And they strongly urged companies to make it possible.

Along with the stay-at-home orders the government issued, the public health authority detailed the stages of the illness. In typical smallpox, the incubation period was between seven and seventeen days, followed by the early onset symptoms of fever, aches, sometimes vomiting. After four days of that, the rash set in. Once the rash appeared, it could turn hemorrhagic at any time. All symptoms might be accelerated if the patient already had underlying conditions that affected their immune system. That explained why some of her patients were getting sicker than others with the same length of exposure.

Sarah grabbed the remote and turned the volume on the television down. She didn't need to hear the question-and-answer phase. She had patients to attend to.

The hospital had a rhythm going now for the smallpox patients. There had been so many of them that the routine was ingrained in everyone who worked there now. All patients were screened for the virus and if variola virus, smallpox, was present, they were quarantined right away. Then they were monitored until they got better or died. So far regular antivirals didn't work, but the prime minister had requested Tecovirimat, an antiviral stockpiled for smallpox preparedness from the United States. Even patients who didn't develop the hemorrhagic strain were dying at a ten percent rate. For variola minor, it should hover around one percent.

Before checking the ER for new cases, she hurried through the corridor to the new quarantine ward to check on some of her quarantine patients. Once she was immersed in the ER turnover, it would be difficult to get away. After going through the safety protocols and fully clad in her PPE suit, she pushed the heavy plastic curtain aside, walked through the door, and waited in the airlock area for a nurse on the other side to open the other door.

Once inside the quarantine area, the number of beds crowded into the space staggered her. Some patients looked healthy except for the flush in their cheeks, presumably suffering from the initial symptoms of the illness. Others had progressed to the rash stage based on the parts of their body she could see. With only enough room between beds for a person to stand, the floor had twenty more beds than it normally would. Every patient was a confirmed case of the new smallpox variant, so proximity to another patient didn't matter much. What mattered was keeping them all in the quarantine ward, away from the rest of the hospital patients.

She did a circuit of the floor, checking charts, noting the decline of most of the people. Only twenty people appeared to be on the mend. That confirmed the WHO's fatality estimations.

Once she finished the main area, she checked the quarantine room where the sickest of the rash patients were. Oliver was nowhere to be found. Neither was Doreen Jeffries, one of the first patients.

Finished with her check, she stopped at the quarantine nurses' station before going downstairs to ask about Oliver.

The nurse glanced at the computer. "I'm sorry, Dr. Malak. He died yesterday. One of the fifteen who passed."

She thanked the nurse, moved through the safety protocols as quickly but thoroughly as she could, then headed for the elevator. Not being able to heal any of them was frustrating. What good was the power she'd received back if she couldn't help people? She needed to do more for them.

She stopped at the ER nurses' station and told them she had an errand to run and to page her if they needed her. There were plenty of doctors on the floor now, so a short errand wouldn't hurt.

The lab on University Avenue was unusually busy for normal circumstances. But this wasn't normal. A receptionist sat as gatekeeper at an oak desk, answering calls, transferring people, accepting deliveries. Five minutes into her visit, five batches of samples had arrived while she sat on one of two chairs in a waiting area. The receptionist had said there was no one available to talk to her, but she needed to be part of the solution. She could do the most good helping to come up with a vaccine. There wasn't much she could do in the ER for any of the smallpox patients. Because there was no cure for the virus, patients had to wait it out and see if it went away. Or if it killed them. Far too many people suffered the latter and she refused to let it continue if she had anything to say about it.

Her small errand turned into a lengthy one. Half an hour after she arrived, a manager came out of the lab area and gave her a terse nod. The man appeared to be about forty, with dark unruly hair that looked like it hadn't seen a comb in weeks. Soft gray smudges under his brown eyes were evidence the lab was as busy as the receptionist said.

"Dr. Malak, is it? Dr. Richardson. I'm sure Faye already told you how busy we are. We're going through samples and sending back results as quickly as we can. Like every other lab in the world, we're working around the clock."

"I'm sorry. I'm not here for that."

Dr. Richardson's face softened. "Then what did you come here for?"

Sarah shrugged, not knowing herself. Helplessness washed over her. "I guess I just feel a little useless over in the ER and I wanted to do something more."

"You can help by finding us more people to work on this. Isolating the virus strain, running tests, analyzing the data, testing various components to fight the virus all take time. Having the original smallpox virus has helped, but this strain is quite different."

"Thank you, Dr. Richardson. I'm sorry to have bothered you."

What did she think her visit would accomplish? She left

the lab no better off than when she'd arrived. Why did she even try? Was it possible to stop this virus?

Adrenaline kicked in the moment she stepped back into the bustle of the ER. It washed away the melancholy and allowed her to focus on treating the patients. Dr. Singh and Dr. Goretti were taking care of the makeshift quarantine ER, so she checked the nurses' station for regular patients in need of care.

Before lunch, she set a broken bone, diagnosed a heart attack, and sent three people for X-rays. The manager's words from the lab still gnawed at her. By the end of the day, his words played on repeat, like an ear worm you couldn't get out of your head. She marched down the hall to her boss's office and knocked on the open door.

Dr. Nejem looked up from her desk and smiled, waving her in.

Sarah plopped down on the chair in front of Dr. Nejem's desk and blew out a breath.

"What's wrong, Dr. Malak?"

"I've been thinking about research. They need all the help they can get at University Lab."

"You're right, they do. But you're an ER doctor, not a researcher."

"I guess."

"You've had a long day. Go home and get some rest."

Sarah pushed herself out of the chair and dragged herself back to the door. "See you tomorrow."

Despite her boss stating the obvious, Sarah couldn't let the manager's words go. Somehow, she would find a way to do more to help.

A light snow dusting the city in a soft blanket of white didn't stop the citizens from wreaking havoc in the streets. Sarah and her sisters, after a quick dinner, patrolled the downtown streets to gauge how the government's order affected their neighborhood. Parking lots at every store, regardless of what they sold, were full. Customers lumbered out of shops weighed down with bags and bags of items, most of which they probably didn't need. At the grocery store, a glimpse inside made her cringe at the selfishness of the people fighting over rolls of toilet paper.

A crash to their right focused their attention in that direction. Across from the bar, coming out of a store, two men argued over a bag of flour. When it came to blows, Rachel jogged across the street and forcibly pushed them away from each other. Her hand rested on the taller man's shoulder, her other arm outstretched in front of the shorter man.

"Don't make me arrest you." She looked at the bag. "Who bought that?"

The taller man, his hand gripping the handle until his fingers turned white, puffed out his chest. "Me."

Rachel raised an eyebrow. "Receipt?"

The man grumbled, jerking his shoulder out of Rachel's grasp. "Nah, forget it."

He stalked away, his head turning left and right. Sarah suspected he was looking for other store customers to harass.

"I guess we can be thankful there's been no looting so far. No broken windows."

Rachel pierced her with a glare that sent shivers down her back. "You had to say it, didn't you?"

Sarah rolled her eyes and shrugged. "If those things were going to happen, they were going to happen whether I mentioned them or not. And if they weren't going to happen, me saying something about them won't bring them forth."

"Despair is palpable. More detectives are out sick. At the regular divisions almost half the constables are out."

"Williams?" Becky asked.

"He's still fine. As soon as the announcement was made, they started protocols in his house to make sure no one brought it with them. And they're careful when they have to go out."

"That's a relief," Leah said. "Half my students are out too. A few more of the teachers. If what they're saying is true, then most of them won't be back."

The deadliness of the virus sickened Sarah. Her stomach churned, thinking about all those needless deaths. Though they started safety measures relatively early, the damage was done. Whoever had tweaked the smallpox virus made it more likely to spread as well as twice as deadly.

"Lockdown starts Friday. It's going to get a lot worse before then." Rachel sighed.

Another scuffle to their right pulled Rachel's attention away. She took off to break it up. Becky pulled out her phone and called her producer to send her cameraman to cover the incidents.

"What's wrong?" Sarah asked.

Becky shoved her phone back in her purse with a sigh. "They're sending Patrick. Henry is out sick. We haven't done field pieces for over a week, and I didn't even think…"

"Maybe it's not this virus. He could have a cold," Leah said.

"I don't think it's a cold." She turned to Sarah. "He's not going to be okay, is he?"

Sarah shook her head sadly. "Chances aren't good. But

don't lose hope. What about Laura? She should be better off at home now that she was released from the hospital after her attack."

"She's still okay. The interns transitioned to working from home the moment the pandemic was declared. Most of the office staff have been. It's mostly on-air talent, cameramen, producers in the building."

Becky waited for the new cameraman to arrive, while the rest of them broke up fights and treated minor cuts as they walked toward Baron's. The place was deserted with two tables occupied by regulars. The rest of the seats were empty. Mario was still out sick, probably not coming back if the trends for the new smallpox variant continued. Sarah shook her head, arms wrapped around her body to keep from falling apart.

Nothing was happening inside that needed their attention, so they turned back the way they'd come. By the time they reached Becky again, the cameraman was there. She was finishing off her sound bite, with more fighting behind her, this time over hand sanitizers.

It was only Tuesday and Sarah felt like she'd worked double shifts for an entire week already. They headed back to the loft. They'd need all the energy they could get to make it through the rest of the week. Lockdown didn't mean nothing would happen in the city, but hopefully, it would slow down the violent crimes.

Chapter Fifteen

Wednesday morning, Dr. Nejem called a staff meeting for all doctors and nurses on the day shift while the night shift still worked through cases. They sat in one of the offices at the far end of the building that held enough chairs to seat forty people comfortably. A whiteboard at the front of the room still had black streaks across it from a previous meeting.

Sarah took a sip of her coffee, thankful she'd come in early. Everyone in the hospital arrived at least fifteen minutes before their shift, but most pushed that to half an hour. When everyone was seated, Dr. Nejem, standing behind a podium in front of the whiteboard, plopped a thick folder down and cleared her throat.

The cacophony of voices died to a whisper, then fell silent. Those there early enough to grab a chair sat, while others stood at the back of the room, one foot pointed toward the door.

"A delivery of smallpox vaccine and an antiviral for smallpox arrived at area hospitals today. Each hospital received two thousand doses of the vaccine and three thousand doses of the antiviral. Now it is up to us to decide where they will do the most good. Those in quarantine, especially those in the advanced stages of the disease, are not eligible. Unfortunately, there isn't much we can do for them if the antiviral doesn't work."

It was a horrible position to be in, deciding who would receive the antiviral, who would receive the vaccine. There was no guarantee that either would work, but they were the best shot at slowing the virus down. Ultimately, Dr. Nejem, as Chief of Emergency Medicine, would decide and for that Sarah was grateful.

"The vaccine will be given to people who don't have the virus." She looked down at the folder she'd placed on the podium. "I can confirm that everyone who came into the ER two weeks ago when the first flu-like patients were here are now back with the same symptoms. In some cases, it has already progressed to the rash stage. Some of those flu-like symptom patients will be getting the antiviral."

A murmur of assent filtered through the room.

Dr. Nejem called for quiet. She flipped a page in the folder. "Half of the patients with a rash in quarantine have had it develop into hemorrhagic smallpox. This confirms the WHO estimations about it being at least fifty percent fatal."

Sarah raised her hand. "None of the hemorrhagic patients have survived?"

Dr. Nejem shook her head. "Some of the rash patients have improved, so it never reached that state."

A flutter of hope settled in Sarah's stomach. Once it got to the hemorrhagic phase, it was one hundred percent fatal. But at least not all rash patients suffered the final phase. There was hope that some patients currently in quarantine would get better.

"I want all staff, especially doctors and nurses dealing with the quarantine patients, to have the vaccine." She pinned Sarah with a stare. "No exceptions."

It amazed Sarah how well her boss knew her, even though all those memories were planted. She understood the reasoning behind Dr. Nejem's orders. Doctors couldn't treat patients if they got sick. And they needed all the doctors and nurses they could get. But she didn't want a dose wasted on her. Sure, when she didn't have much of her power back, it was possible to physically hurt her. They'd seen that when Rachel got shot. But with almost a full angel charge, she was confident she couldn't get the virus even if she was exposed.

"What about the police, firefighters, EMTs?" Sarah asked.

Dr. Nejem nodded. "They also received doses and they are getting protective gear. My main concern is my staff. Get the shots, today."

If the United States sent more doses, the vaccine would become available for more people, triaged into the most needy and at risk first. That meant Becky and Leah weren't likely to get one soon. Rachel would and might actually need it until she got more power back.

Dr. Nejem ended the meeting with another order to go to the sixth floor to get their vaccine. Sarah followed Dr. Singh and Dr. Goretti out of the room and to the elevator. Once in the room handling the injections, she used a dose of magic on the doctors and the nurse doing the vaccinations to make them think she got one.

Band-Aid as proof in place, Sarah printed a copy of the list of patients due to get the vaccine and the list to get the antiviral. The last time she'd checked on Darla, she met the criteria put in place that morning to get the medicine. Sarah scanned the lists and smiled at seeing the woman's name halfway through. The sex worker had worked so hard to make her life safer, it would have been awful to miss out on potentially lifesaving treatment because there wasn't enough to go around.

Darla could use some good news. "I'll handle telling these patients they're getting the antiviral." Sarah held up a few pages of the list and handed the rest of it to Dr. Goretti and Dr. Singh.

All the patients on the list were in the quarantine ward. Most of them in stage one, an area marked by beds lacking a plastic curtain. While still contagious, at least the WHO believed they were contagious at the fever and headache stage, they weren't as likely to spread the disease as those with rashes.

Sarah weaved her way through the floor to Darla's bed. The woman's eyes were closed. Bruises she'd sustained weeks ago had faded, but new ones took their place. Sarah's heart twisted. Though she tried to be safer on the streets, there was still the occasional customer who thought he could live out his wife-beating fantasies on sex workers.

Not wanting to disturb her, Sarah turned away from the bed. There would be time later to let Darla know. But a soft whisper stopped her.

"Bad news, Dr. Malak?"

Sarah's hearted twisted. All Darla expected was for the world to let her down. Sarah spun around and smiled. "Good news. We received some antiviral medication that should help make you feel better."

Always should. Never will. There was no telling how well the medication would work since it was designed to treat the original smallpox virus, not this twisted variant.

Darla smiled. "That is good. Thanks."

Sarah squeezed her hand gently. "Get some rest now. A nurse will be by later to give you the injection."

Darla nodded, her eyes already closing.

After checking on a few other less severe patients, Sarah stopped at the heavy plastic curtain that led to the extreme cases. A curtain of plastic had been erected over Rachel's murder suspect's bed. Sarah peered in at him. Flat, dark marks covered his body.

Sarah left the quarantine area, following all the safety protocols, then took the short route back to the ER. As she stepped into the corridor, she pulled out her phone to tell Rachel her suspect would never stand trial. He would be dead in a few days.

Pre power, a stressful day in the ER would have left Sarah exhausted, bone-weary. But on her way home from the hospital, none of the usual aches and pains afflicted her. Chalk one up for angel power. Almost at full capacity, it was like having a proper eight hours of sleep and an espresso shot. Energy hummed through her. This sensation, the vigor was why she'd hoarded her magic when they first arrived. Every little bit she gained back made the exhaustion of being human a little lighter.

The streets still teemed with people gathering supplies before the city's mandated lockdown. Police presence was thin, with a few constables patrolling the area. More were probably out sick. They needed to be vaccinated as quickly as possible. Special clinics to issue the injections would be set up to accommodate law enforcement, firefighters, nurses, and doctors. And if the antivirals worked on those with initial symptoms, there was hope the death toll wouldn't remain at fifty percent.

She stopped at a grocery store on the way to the loft to pick up a few items for dinners for the rest of the week.

Though she'd promised to cut back her time, she wanted to do more. Making dinners for the week on the weekend and freezing them would free up a lot of her time during the week.

More crowded than she'd ever seen it, Sarah managed to get an empty cart from a woman who was leaving. Sarah trundled along the aisles, frowning at the absence of fresh fruit and vegetables. At least there weren't any she'd buy to feed to people. The ones left in the aisles were past their ripeness. Shelves in the baking aisle had been emptied of the most common household staples. The toilet paper and paper towel aisle had suffered a similar fate. And the pharmacy shelves had also been picked clean. Even though the government had assured the public food and medication would still be able to cross the border, people panicked.

Healthier options, whole wheat, for flour and pasta were all that was left, so she put those in her cart. Fresh fruits weren't an option, so she picked up canned and frozen. For sweetener, she opted for honey. They still had some sugar at the loft that would have to tide them over until she could shop again. Granola and oatmeal were still available and those went into her cart. At the meat counter, she picked up what they needed to get them through until the following Monday. She stocked up on powdered milk and eggs since the dairy fridges were almost empty. For fresh vegetables, she avoided the ones that were rotting, picking up the forgotten veggies. The ones no one liked. Beets, turnip, kale, Brussels sprouts. Though every instinct told her to get everything left on the shelves, she picked up only what they needed. Not just because Becky told her if she left food on her plate, or didn't eat the leftovers, she'd get power back. But because others might need it more.

On her way to the checkout, she assessed what she had

in her cart, running through recipes in her head. If they kept getting power back, she wouldn't need to cook much longer, but she'd want to cook. She enjoyed the activity and the food was delicious. As full angels, they might not need the nutrition it provided, but that didn't mean they couldn't enjoy a meal every once in a while anyway.

The pregnant woman in front of her in line grasped her hands together until the knuckles were white. She glanced over her shoulder toward the cereal aisle, her face contorted in despair, mumbling about no oatmeal.

"Is everything okay?" Sarah asked.

The woman started, eyes wide. "I wanted to get oatmeal for the little ones at home, but there is none. I grabbed something else. I don't think my kids will eat it, though. They're so fussy sometimes and everything going on right now is stressful for them."

Sarah glanced in her cart at the two bags of slow oats. They'd been the last two on the shelf. Guilt stabbed at her for taking both of them. She picked up both bags and offered them to the woman.

She shook her head. "I couldn't."

Sarah walked around her cart and placed them in the woman's cart beside a bag of flour. "I insist. I was going to use them for baking. Your children need it more."

The woman continued to thank her until she pushed her cart, now filled with her bagged groceries, out the sliding door of the store. A tingle of energy settled in her wings. Another spot had gained back power. It wasn't the reason she'd given the oats to the woman, but she was glad for the bonus energy boost. They needed all they could get right now.

She pushed her cart up, pulled items out of her cart, and placed them on the belt that continued to move items toward the cashier. Once her groceries were paid for and bagged, she followed the path of the pregnant woman out of the store. With all she'd been able to buy, she still needed to figure out what she could make for dinner.

Chapter Sixteen

The next morning, Sarah cleared the clean dinner dishes out of the dishwasher to make room for the Thursday set. Despite limited ingredients, she'd made a decent goulash, with whole wheat pasta. Up early, though, she dreaded another day watching people in quarantine die. She made breakfast for her sisters, then set the coffeemaker's timer to brew a fresh pot in half an hour when Rachel would be up. If the food got cold, they could always heat it up in the microwave. She finished setting the syrup and butter on the table.

She gulped down the rest of her coffee from the pot she'd brewed when she woke up. She put her empty mug and her plate in the dishwasher. No interest in the waffles she'd made for everyone else, she'd wolfed down toast with peanut butter. Once she started rounds and needed a boost, she'd grab fruit from the cafeteria.

Leaving for work early had the added bonus of light traffic, both street and pedestrian. The regular ER offered patients with cuts, deep wounds, trauma caused from accidents, heart attacks, suspected strokes. Anything that indicated even the slightest chance of being smallpox had been diverted to the alternate ER entrance to be assessed and moved.

Sarah put her winter coat in her locker, no reason to cause questions about why she didn't need a coat in the frigid January weather. She pulled out her crisp white lab coat, put it on, then checked the pockets for debris. Next, she grabbed her stethoscope, draping it around the back of her neck. Before starting rounds to check on the patients still there from the overnight shift, she took the elevator up to quarantine to see how the antiviral had done.

At the nurses' station, she smiled at Vanda, checked some of the charts, and made note of the new cases on the whiteboard that had come in overnight. Notes on most of the charts indicated no change in the patients who had received the antiviral. Not a surprise, since it was a modified strain of smallpox, but she'd had hope. It had been less than twenty-four hours, so hope might win out.

Vanda frowned. "I can let you know if there's a change in a particular patient if you like."

Sarah put the charts back and nodded. "That would be great, thanks. Could you let me know if there's any change in Darla Baxter's condition?"

Vanda made a note on a pad of paper beside the phone. "Will do." She looked up and said, "There's another patient you might want to check."

Intrigued, Sarah leaned closer. "Who?"

"She just came in. They are brining her up now."

Vanda pulled up a record on the computer and Sarah's heart sank. Laura. Flu-like symptoms and being admitted to the quarantine ward. Becky would be devastated.

"Thank you. Yes, please let me know if there is a change in her condition as well."

Sarah pulled out her phone and called Becky.

"What's up, Sis?" Becky asked.

"It's not good, Beck. Laura has been admitted."

Silence on the other end lasted for thirty seconds. "Thanks for letting me know. Please reassure me we're going to fix this."

"We are going to fix this." After a few more updates, Sarah ended the call and dropped the phone back in her pocket.

Wanting to do more to help solve the problem instead of just treating the symptoms, Sarah bypassed the ER and went to the hospital's research lab on the second floor. Major breakthroughs in surgery, cancer treatments, and medicine occurred regularly at the hospital. If she couldn't help in an outside lab, maybe the internal one needed assistance.

Unlike Queen University Research Group, the hospital lab had a BSL of 2, which meant she didn't have to go through extreme safety protocols. A technician sat at a desk next to the door, and she looked up when Sarah entered.

"Hey, Doc. Get turned around? We don't usually see you guys here."

Some of the lab tests for the hospital were done in the lab next door to the research lab, but it was rare for any of the doctors or nurses to pop in to research.

Sarah gave her a wide smile. "I came down to see if you guys were studying the new virus."

Heavy metal doors with windows five feet up from the ground closed off the lab area from the outer waiting area. The windows weren't big enough to give a full view of the room, so she couldn't tell how many researchers worked away on the various computers and microscopes. From what she could see, it wasn't many. It wasn't enough.

"Not here. That's being done over at the satellite office for Canadian National Microbiology Laboratory on

Gerard Street West." She nodded toward the wall behind Sarah. "A few of our doctors are over there. They put out a call last week."

"Thanks. How many went?"

"Most. Only a handful stayed here. I guess cancer research moved to the back burner when smallpox came back."

Sarah marched over to the board on the wall with notices, the latest safety report, fire alarm protocols. In the center, a bright yellow notice requested researchers to help combat the latest virus crisis.

She pointed to the notice. "This is where I need to be."

The technician raised an eyebrow. "Aren't you an ER doctor?"

"Right now I am."

Sarah took a picture of the notice, then shoved her phone back in the pocket of her lab coat. Back on the ER floor, she dashed into a bathroom and checked all the stalls to make sure she was alone. Research was going to fix this pandemic. Before famine could be defeated, disease needed to be cured. It was a vicious circle. Famine caused disease, but disease could cause famine. The shelves at the grocery store were proof of that. And with the actual horseman here, working in a lab no less, she shuddered at what havoc he might have wrought.

Tapping into her power, she gave herself the knowledge she would need to help in a lab setting. Not so much that she'd be a researcher—that would take too much magic—but enough that the doctors at the CNML satellite office would let her help with the testing. She kept an eye on her wings so she didn't drain too much of the power. Rachel would never forgive her if she lost it all. But the white didn't disappear. Instead, it spread, replacing black feathers.

Images of training in a lab, helping doctors prepare slides, looking at viruses under a microscope flashed in her mind. Anyone who needed to know of her magically gained knowledge would remember her doing those things when she turned up at the lab. But first, there was one more hurdle. Dr. Nejem.

Satisfied the information should have filtered through, Sarah bypassed the ER check-in station, marched down the hallway leading to the offices, and knocked on Dr. Nejem's open door. Her boss looked up and waved her in.

Sarah took the chair closest to the door, perching on the edge of the seat, hands folded in her lap. "I want to help more." She pulled out her phone and showed Dr. Nejem the picture calling for volunteers at the CNML office on Gerrard. "I would just be on loan to them for a few weeks. Maybe a few months until we can get this thing under control."

Dr. Nejem leaned back in her chair, steepling her fingers under her chin. Had the new information reached her? The magic shouldn't take that long to work. Sarah raised her hand, prepared to use a little more magic to make Dr. Nejem agree with her, but she rested it on her lap instead. Free will meant angels, demons, God, Lucifer, couldn't force humans to do anything. All they could do was offer choices and point to the right direction. Would her boss see the right course of action or force her to stay in the ER, working on heart attacks, broken bones, stab wounds, gunshots, and the myriad of other cases they received every day?

Hands tingling to make one small exception to free will, Sarah forced herself to lean back in her chair and take a few deep breaths. The concentration on Dr. Nejem's face indicated she was thinking about her request. Hopefully, the new history Sarah had created for herself had reached her boss.

Dr. Nejem sighed, moving her chair closer to the desk. "Okay. But this is only temporary. You're needed in the ER."

Sarah smiled, her heart racing. "Temporary. Got it."

"I mean it, Dr. Malak. I'll make the arrangements with CNML to expect you tomorrow. No more than a month. Got it?"

Sarah nodded, thanked her boss again, and raced out of the woman's office before she could change her mind. Now she might be able to make a contribution to stopping this pandemic.

Father Ianetti finished his sermon, and instead of walking to the front of the church to speak to his flock as they left, he ambled back to the office and sagged into his chair. Summoning two horsemen, with little time to recuperate between them, left him weak. The assistant priest and his secretary insisted he go to a hospital, but he knew it would pass. There was nothing modern medicine could do for him. Time. That's what he needed. Time to gather his strength so he could join Death with his reapers and put the apocalypse on the final lap.

"Mrs. Edwards," he called toward the side door of the office.

She poked her head through the door, a concerned smile on her face. "Yes, Father."

"I need to run an errand before my afternoon confessions. I'll be back in a couple of hours."

If he was late getting back, Father McGrady could start the confessions. With the cold weather and blustery winds, his aging body wouldn't be as quick on his walk. It was too bad there wasn't one occult shop that had everything he needed. Instead, he had to make trips to three different stores.

In his room, he shoved his feet into his boots and bundled into his coat. Making sure he had some reusable cloth bags, he exited the church through the back door. Thick wool gloves protected his hands from the nip in the air.

First on his list was College Street Occult Supplies where he picked up more holy basil. He grabbed everything on the shelves and asked for any stock they had in the back. He also picked up the black candles. He chose to get those closest to the last minute in case Father McGrady went through his things and found them. Not that the assistant priest had a habit of going through anyone else's belongings, but he tended to forget his own relics and had to borrow from others.

Before leaving, he asked the clerk if anyone had purchased the same things he had. She said only the holy basil. But it was a popular item.

A gust of wind hit him as he left the store. He clutched the neck of his coat tighter and fought the wind to exit the shop. On the street again, he ambled around pedestrians and managed to get to the next store before it started to snow.

The first of the huge, fluffy flakes descended while he browsed the shelves for the rest of his items. He watched snow meander through the air. Soon, the entire city would be ablaze. But before that happened, he needed to combine Death with his reapers. There would be mass casualties, more than the city had ever seen at one time, and the horseman had to be ready.

Time was counting down on a clock in his head. If the

rest of the horsemen had done their assigned jobs, the event would be here in a little over a month. There were a lot of moving parts. Everyone had to be ready. With Death, beasts, demons, and Satan would also arrive.

It was imperative that he get his strength back. Some of the items worked for healing. He grabbed as many herbs and plants from the shelf as possible. A soothing tea with a little bit of magic thrown in might help him recuperate faster.

After rushing through the check-out process, asking about someone buying similar items and getting another no, he waved at the clerk absently and ambled out of the store. One more stop to make and he would have everything he needed.

He arrived at the third store during an afternoon rush. Navigating the crowded narrow aisles, it took longer to find the items he needed. As he walked down the aisles, he wished he'd read more of the ancient texts to see what was needed to break Death apart from his reapers, besides the completion of the apocalypse, the arrival of Satan and beasts from hell, and the burning Hell Fire that would sweep the land. Survivors would be few, but there would be enough to start the Earth's population all over again. Maybe they would do it right the second time.

Not that it mattered what anyone needed to separate him. The angels wouldn't be able to accomplish such a task. Breaking him apart from his reapers would be harder and more dangerous than combining them.

Though he believed in his mission, he wished he would be able to see the result of all his hard work. From the beginning, he knew he'd only see it partly done. He had to trust the horsemen to accomplish their task of bringing about a mass casualty event. One big enough to summon

Death himself away from war-torn areas of the world where he usually frequented.

He gathered the remaining ingredients and waited in the long lineup to pay, tapping his foot on the floor. When a till opened up, he shuffled forward, releasing all the items piled in his arms in a huff. Arm muscles burned from holding them up for so long.

He paid for his purchase, making small talk with the clerk before leaving the store. The snow had accumulated on the roads and sidewalk while he'd been shopping. Fluffy flakes still tumbled down from the sky. He stepped carefully, shuffling along the pavement. The last thing he needed was a slip and fall, resulting in a broken hip. That would throw off everything. Though he understood the city's mandate to not plow the roads or clear sidewalks until two centimeters had fallen and it stopped snowing, his heart pounded with every footfall.

It took double the time it should have, but he arrived back at the church winded but safe. Late for afternoon confessions, he hustled to the back of the church, nodding a quick apology to the members of his flock patiently waiting beside the confessionals. Once he put away his items, he would be ready to hear confession. Maybe, before summoning Death, he should confess. Get absolved of all sins. It wouldn't do any good. Nothing could completely absolve him now. Saving mankind would mean losing his soul to Hell and he was fine with that.

Chapter Seventeen

On what would have been her day off, Sarah pushed through the double doors of the CNML satellite office on Gerrard Street. Despite the snow the day before, the streets and sidewalks were clear. The snow plow workers had been working all night to get the streets and sidewalks ready for Friday morning.

Inside the main door was a small reception area used for deliveries that consisted of a desk, chair, a four-drawer filing cabinet, and a computer. There were only two chairs in the quaint space. They didn't expect people to stay long. Behind the plexiglassed reception area, the muffled chug of a printer grew louder the closer she got to the desk.

The woman sitting behind the desk looked up and smiled. "Can I help you?"

"I'm here to help Dr. Cooke. On loan from Queen City Hospital. I'm Dr. Sarah Malak."

The receptionist puffed out a big breath, blowing the light brown bangs out of her brown eyes. "Thank you for volunteering. I know they welcome all the help they can get right now."

She picked up the phone and told Dr. Cooke there was a doctor here to see him.

Halfway to a chair, the door beside reception buzzed, a click sounded, and the heavy metal door hissed open. Sarah spun around. A middle-aged man wearing a white lab coat, light blue shirt, and dark trousers emerged. She half expected dry ice smoke to puff out behind him. The clothes hung loosely on him and Sarah wondered when he'd eaten last. Dark circles under his eyes emphasized his pale complexion.

He extended a hand to her. "Dr. Malak. Thank you for joining us for as long as your hospital is willing to spare you. I'm Dr. Cooke. I'll show you around the lab, introduce you to the researcher you'll be helping, then you can jump right in if that's okay. Based on the information your hospital sent over, you already have a background in research."

Sarah nodded, thankful that her magic had traveled to him and presumably the rest of the people in the building. All of her knowledge lay in pockets of planted memory in her brain. All she had to do was tap into it while in the lab, almost like a computer retrieving files. And she would be almost as fast.

She fell into step beside him after he swiped his card and walked through the door leading to the lab area. "Yes, I worked extensively in research, but then decided to go into trauma medicine."

"The ER's loss is our gain." He waved his hand to the right, indicating a long corridor. "At the end of the hallway, we'll be going through our BSL4 protocols. You need to decontaminate going in and going out of the main lab. You'll have your own positive pressure suit. Check it for leaks before you put it on every time."

His card opened the door at the end of the hall. They

stepped through and went through all the protocols. Once in their suits, he took her through another door into the lab, and pointed at a woman in front of a station with specialized microscopes and a PCR machine for DNA amplification.

The woman took her time, peering through an electron microscope and making notes on a pad beside the scientific equipment. When she finished, she looked up and smiled.

"Dr. Belle, this is Dr. Malak from Queen City Hospital. She's here to help you with your research."

Dr. Belle nodded. "Nice to meet you. In the nick of time. We have a lot of testing to do and not a lot of time to do it if we want to stop the spread of this virus."

Sarah pointed to the microscope. "Is that it?"

Dr. Belle stepped aside and waved at the sample. "Care to take a look? You won't get a lot of opportunities to see it close up."

Sarah filed that away for now. When the time was right, she would assert her power again so she could be a researcher, not an assistant.

She looked through the viewfinder. A brick-shaped virus appeared on the slide. It fascinated and terrified her that something so small could cause so much destruction. Though she wanted to use the virologist knowledge she'd magically acquired, the people at the lab didn't know how much she actually knew about viruses and vaccines. While the power to plant memories in the heads of her coworkers made it easy for them to believe she could help solve this, her magic didn't extend as deep with the CNML. The employees here saw her as an ER doctor with extensive training in research with the qualifications to assist a researcher compile data.

She stepped back, allowing Dr. Belle to resume her

position. "Has anyone explained what you'll be doing here, Dr. Malak?"

"Not yet."

"I will be examining the virus under various conditions, introducing it to a number of agents to attempt to kill it, and I will be writing notes of the outcomes. You will compile all the data, do some modeling, and present it in a way that helps us determine the best course of action."

Sarah rocked her head from shoulder to shoulder, like a prizefighter limbering up to get into the ring. "I can do that. I can do much more if you need another set of eyes on the experiments."

"Data compiling will be fine for now. There are four other research assistants in the lab." Dr. Belle pointed to the other lab stations.

Everyone's heads were down, viewing the virus, or taking notes. The assistants typed on laptops, displaying charts, diagrams, and figures. Eager to make a difference, Sarah took a position in front of the computer at Dr. Belle's station.

"I'm ready."

Later, once she'd been there for a few days, she would look into gathering all the data. There must be other work the assistants could do. As an angel, with a good deal of power back, she would be able to get through the research data faster. And the world needed them to be faster. Before smallpox 2.0 took over the entire planet.

Before enjoying almost full power back in her wings, all day standing caused sore feet, an aching lower back, and sometimes a headache that started at the base of Sarah's neck. Now, she had the energy to continue for another eight hours doing research, or at least compiling it for Dr. Belle. She wouldn't stop trying to get behind an electron microscope.

Still, she wanted to blend in, so she huffed out a breath, touched her hand to her lower back, and plopped down on the stool in front of the laptop.

"Are the days always like this? No progress?"

Dr. Belle frowned. "Right now, we're working with the vaccine the United States had on hand."

"But that doesn't work."

"We know. But it's still all we have until Queen City University Research Group creates the vaccine based on the formulation on file. Maybe this one didn't work because it expired early. When we get vaccines that were created recently, we'll test those."

Sarah didn't like their odds. Old vaccines might be part of the problem, but it wasn't the only problem. The virus had been altered to make it more contagious and more deadly, and probably harder to eradicate.

"Go home, have a relaxing weekend and come back here fresh on Monday," Dr. Belle said.

"Does anyone work on weekends?"

Though pushing herself too much might prevent the return of even more magic to her wings, Sarah refused to stop working on a vaccine. She didn't need as much sleep or food as when she'd first arrived back on Earth. She hadn't eaten all day except for breakfast and she wasn't hungry.

"There will be researchers here on the weekend, but not me." Dr. Belle held up a hand to stay any comments. "You were assigned to me. I want you fresh and on the ball. That means rest, relaxation. Spend time with family or friends. We might be farther along by Monday and have some real interesting stuff to check."

"I think we're going to have to get creative."

"Like what?"

If Sarah could keep her talking, keep her interested, maybe they could continue working. "Combining the current formulation for the smallpox vaccine with ones to inoculate against hemorrhagic viruses like Ebola."

A low whistle escaped Dr. Belle's lips. "It's not a hemorrhagic virus."

"I'd say it is now. Based on current infections, it has a fifty percent chance of turning into hemorrhagic smallpox, or whatever they're going to call it, since it's smallpox on steroids. And hemorrhagic smallpox so far is proving to be one hundred percent fatal."

Dr. Belle jerked her head in the direction of the airlock they needed to go through to start the exit protocol for the lab. Sarah fell into step beside her.

Inside the locker room, Dr. Belle sighed. "I'll get the Ebola vaccine and samples from storage first thing Monday morning."

Sarah eyed the door. If she went back into the lab after Dr. Belle left security cameras or a helpful assistant might alert Dr. Belle. And the woman wasn't wrong. Despite having almost full power, a little sleep and relaxation would make for a clearer head on Monday. Barring breaking into the lab, there was no other option but to acquiesce to the researcher's instructions.

Sarah reached into the metal locker and pulled out her purse and coat. "I'll see you Monday morning then."

Forcing herself to walk out the door, Sarah paused at the entrance to the lab. A little magic, and she could be at the research station again. Unsupervised, there was a chance her research would progress faster. A shadow fell on the door, blending with her own. She glanced over her shoulder, gave Dr. Belle a quick smile, then hurried out.

The work would still be waiting for her after the weekend.

Becky sat at her desk at the television station, halfway through dialing Laura's desk. Tightness squeezed her chest. She put the receiver back in the cradle. Another intern would help her if she asked, but Laura was her favorite. Maybe she shouldn't have favorites. All the interns worked their asses off for the reporters, but Laura went far beyond anything asked of her and with a smile on her face. The office was less bright since she'd been sick.

Becky moved some figures around in her piece about the pandemic. Temptation sat on her shoulder, urging her to use inside knowledge about the illness and what was being done about it. But she stuck to information gleaned from official sources. Not that it mattered. Her piece would drown in the myriad stories already floating around on television and online. Sometimes she wondered if anyone was listening anymore. People hit panic mode, and with this pandemic, panic was understandable. But by not thinking logically, they were causing some of the problems they were initially worried about.

She had no doubts Famine was digging his fingers into the food supply, but the masses panic buying things they rarely bought before made things worse. Before the pandemic, no one at the station, save three ladies in marketing, made homemade bread. Now everyone was a master baker in need of vast quantities of flour, butter, and yeast.

The shrill ring of her phone made her jump, her hand flung out, knocking over her travel mug. She jumped off the chair and righted the mug before the dregs of coffee left in the bottom could spill onto her desk. An almost empty floor amplified the ring of the phone shriller than normal.

A quick glance at the call display told her the call was coming from the hospital. But it wasn't from Sarah. She would just use her mobile phone. And she was at the CNML satellite office. She snatched up the receiver before the phone could ring again.

A cold fist of dread seeped through her body until her fingers, freezing, hurt to grip the phone tight enough. It slipped, but she caught it, pressing the device to her ear and whispering a greeting.

"Becky Malak?"

The crisp voice of Dr. Goretti sapped the energy out of Becky. She slumped back into her chair. "Yes."

"Dr. Malak told me I should call you if Laura Kendrick's condition worsened."

"How bad is it?"

"I'm only telling you this because Laura said it was okay. She's not as bad as others with the same amount of exposure, but she's getting worse. The rash has started to form pustules."

Becky listened in stunned silence to the rest of the details. A knot coiled in Becky's stomach, tightening with each horrible symptom Dr. Goretti chimed off. Why would the doomsday cult help engineer something so awful? If you wanted to wipe out half the planet, there were other ways, less horrible ways, to accomplish your goal.

When the doctor stopped talking, Becky said, "I'll be right there."

She grabbed her purse and made a dash to the elevators at the end of the row of cubicles. On the way down, she called Sarah. It went to voice mail. No doubt she was arms deep in research.

The quarantine ward at the hospital had tripled in size, pushing out diagnostic equipment originally purchased for the ward's intended cancer research to accommodate the increasing numbers. Becky donned protective gear and walked through the thick plastic curtain separating the rest of the ward from the sick. At the end of a long row of patients, a figure caught her attention. He sat covered in protective gear, head down, his hand touching the bed. Mark, Laura's fiancé.

Becky's heart twisted at the devastated expression on his face. They were so young. She remembered her first love from her first time on the planet. That life had been taken from her too soon, leaving her to guide others. What good was she as an angel if she couldn't help Laura?

He looked up as she approached, unshed tears glistening in his eyes. "She's getting worse."

Becky stood beside him, peering down at Laura. Her face pale, angry red welts covering her face and what was visible of her body. A machine helped her breathe.

"Hang in there, Laura. We're doing all we can."

A tear escaped her intern's eye, sliding into her ear. The hospital kept the patients heavily sedated to alleviate the discomfort of being on the ventilator. But she could still hear what was going on around her. It gave Becky some comfort knowing Laura was aware of visitors.

Becky put her hand on Mark's shoulder. "Don't give up hope."

Outside the quarantine area again, free of most of the protective equipment, Becky took a deep breath, pulling the paper of the surgical mask she still wore to her nostrils. There was no doubt the apocalypse was underway, but she was more determined than ever to halt it, and hopefully wind it back before half the population was gone.

Chapter Eighteen

Saturday morning, Sarah dashed through the new quarantine area ER doors, hoping Dr. Nejem wouldn't notice she was there. With Laura getting worse, and more patients admitted in daily, she couldn't stay away. Now that she had more power in her wings, she required less sleep to keep herself refreshed.

Chaos greeted her. The new makeshift ER burst at the seams with patients in various stages of the disease. Those with visible rashes were whisked through to the quarantine area up on the fifth floor of the isolation ward. There was standing room only and even those spots were hard to come by. By her estimation, based on the waiting area, the hospital was almost out of beds.

Tempted to use a little angel magic to cloak herself while she walked to the quarantine area, she peeked around the corner to see who sat at the nurses' station. Some nurses knew her better than others, but Vanda sat typing something into the computer. Would Vanda tell Dr. Nejem about Sarah being there?

Instead of using power, she zoomed past before Vanda

looked up from the computer. Someone in the hospital would recognize her anyway. It was only a matter of time before word got back to her boss. Hopefully, by the time that happened, she'd be at home again with her sisters.

At the quarantine area, she donned protective gear and slipped through to the first area. Too many people took up too many beds. In the early stages of the disease, their chances weren't good. Without a proven treatment, they would get worse like all the others.

She paused to check a few patients, confirming her initial guess. These masses would soon move to the next quarantine area. And at least half of them would progress to the third area when it turned hemorrhagic, the guarantee of death.

At the entrance to the second level protected area, she took a deep breath, pushed through the heavy plastic, and stopped. She already knew Laura was at the far end of the ward, but there were patients Sarah wanted to check on first. Too many of them had already been moved to either the third level or the morgue since the last time she'd been there.

She walked past the man struggling to breathe to the woman who quietly endured the fiery ache of the rash. By the time she reached Laura's bed, Sarah's heart ached. The intern was resting as comfortably as possible, given her condition.

Sarah picked up the chart at the end of the bed. Numerous medications had been tried, with none working. If the research on creating a vaccine wasn't fruitful, soon thousands, maybe hundreds of thousands, would die.

Now that she'd completed her check of the two wards, she squared her shoulders, took a deep breath, and mentally prepared herself for the third ward. Abandon all hope and all that.

Despite the mask and PPE she wore, the scent of death still permeated the air. Without the protective barriers, the smell would be unbearable for most civilians. Before she was an angel, the sickly sweet scent of decay would have her doubled over, tossing her cookies into a bucket. But now, it went with the job. Thankfully, up until the pandemic hit, she'd saved more people than she lost.

She started at the front of the ward, checking the charts of the dying. Those who'd turned hemorrhagic five days ago had little time left. They were in the back of the room. Newer admissions took up the front, to be gradually moved to make room for more patients as the ones at the back passed away.

At the halfway mark in the room, a little girl cringed as she moved her arm to get more comfortable. Sarah raced to her bed, grabbed her chart, quickly skimming through it. The girl had turned hemorrhagic two days ago. She lay alone, her eyes welling with tears. Due to new pandemic protocols issued that morning, not even her parents were there to say goodbye to her. Or hold her hand through the worst of the pain. Maybe her parents were in the ward somewhere, too. The new strain of smallpox was far more contagious than any strain in history.

Sarah looked down at her hands as she put the girl's chart back. How many cameras watched the sick? Moving closer to the bed, she glanced around. Half the patients didn't know she was there, the other half were too weak to do or say anything about her presence.

She maneuvered herself between the bed and one of the cameras. Sure an angel couldn't get the disease, she yanked off her gloves. Without her power, she could get hurt and possibly die, but she'd gained most of her strength back. Maybe it would be enough.

She put her hand on the girl's arm, her heart breaking

when the girl winced at the contact. Golden light emanated from her hand where she touched the girl. Focused on killing the smallpox virus, turning the pustules to scabs, she blocked out everything around her. The sound of the monitors faded away. She no longer heard the whimpers and groans and labored breathing of the sick. Her world consisted of this girl.

Tapping into her magic, fear that she would use it all to save one person tugged at her conscience. But what was the point of having her power back if she couldn't help anyone with it?

Light glowed up the girl's arm, across her face, down the rest of her body. Slowly, the pustules scabbed over. The girl's breathing changed to deep and even. The grimace slid from her face like toppings on an ice cream sundae.

Before her small patient could open her eyes, Sarah walked away from the bed, pulling her gloves back on as she walked. At the door to the ward, power surged through her. Without looking in a mirror, she knew more of her abilities were back. Becky was right.

Outside the room, she took off her heavy-duty protective gear, leaving the minimum PPE needed for the rest of the quarantine ward. She stopped at the nurses' station.

"You should check on Melanie. She might need to move out of the ward now. She seems to be doing better."

The nurse gasped and ran down the hall.

Rachel sat at the breakfast island across from Becky and Leah, glaring at Sarah as their resident cook whipped up dinner. Sarah did an excellent job being a doctor and a chef, but Rachel missed Baron's. No matter how hard Sarah tried, she couldn't recreate the bar's burger.

Still simmering after Sarah informed them of her miracle cure in the quarantine ward, Rachel shifted in her seat. The scents of the burgers frying made her mouth water. Her stomach grumbled. It would be months before restaurants went back to normal operations. If that. With the severity of the pandemic, it might be a year or more. That didn't bode well for anyone.

Sarah plunked a plate of burgers on the kitchen island, followed by a plate of buns. The condiments were already sitting there. A special sauce in a medium-sized bowl perfectly matched the red color of Baron's house sauce. Maybe this would be the time Sarah got it exactly right.

As soon as Sarah sat, all the angels assembled their burgers. Rachel slathered on the sauce, put on the perfect amount of lettuce and onions, and topped it with a small dollop of mayonnaise. She took a big bite, closing her eyes as she savored the flavors. If not for the quiet of the room, she could believe she was eating a Baron's burger.

"I think you got it this time," Becky said.

Rachel put her burger down and glared at Sarah. "You can't put your hand on everyone in the world who is sick and heal them."

Sarah sighed. "I know. But I couldn't do nothing. It was a little girl. Besides, I get power back when I do that."

Rachel folded her arms over her chest. They were kicked out of Heaven because of a sin they committed. Sarah's was gluttony. Becky's had to be sloth because every time she did something instead of delegating, she got power back. Leah's was envy. Of that, Rachel was convinced.

But what about her? Sometimes the doctor got power back when she used her power to help someone. Other times when she jumped in and worked overtime, helping out colleagues by taking their shifts, Sarah didn't get anything back.

And being a detective, Rachel expected to get the most back because she helped people all the time. But so far, it had been like pulling teeth to get even a minuscule amount of power back.

Rachel sighed. "I know it's hard to do nothing. But you don't know how long it will last. What if the next time you do it, you lose power? We need all the power we can get to fight Famine."

Sarah took a few more fries from the communal plate. "I'll try not to do it again."

Rachel gave her a side-eye. She noticed she didn't say she wouldn't do it again. Trying was a whole different story and didn't require strict adherence.

"I have almost full power now. That should be enough for us." Becky took a sip of her water.

Rachel took another bite of her burger, nodding as she chewed. "I need to figure out what I did. Becky can get power back at will now. It's still random for me, it seems."

Becky shook her head. "Not random, but we do need to figure out what sin you committed."

Leah sat up straighter, waving a fry in the air. "Assuming we each committed a different one. That leaves lust, greed, wrath, and pride."

Rachel huffed. "I don't think I committed any of those. I was a fucking angel. I hung out on a cloud all day, watching my charges to make sure they stayed on track. Every once in a while flinging a bit of angel dust down on them to guide them in the right direction."

Sarah looked Rachel in the eyes. "It has to be one of them."

Becky fixed Rachel with a glare. "I'm betting on wrath or pride."

Leah's eyes widened. "I hope it's not pride. That is the hardest to get rid of."

Rachel's heart pounded. "The way I feel right now, it's probably wrath. Definitely wrath."

Father Ianetti sat in his room, a pile of items beside him on the bed. The last of his flock had left over an hour ago. For the other horsemen, he'd rushed to perform the ritual to call them as soon as the church was empty. For this one, he hesitated. Summoning Famine had taken a lot out of him. And then the angels had thrown a wrench into the plans by sending War back. Having to summon him again had taken its toll too.

Would he survive joining Death with his reapers? None of the texts he'd read mentioned anyone attempting this before. But the spells existed for a reason. Someone must have performed them. Of course, the only way to know for sure was to try.

The cleansing of the Earth had to take place. He pushed himself off the bed, feeling every one of his seventy-five years. He pulled the robe out of the drawer and placed it on the bed with the other things he needed. First, he had to cleanse himself, wash away the sins of his flock that he willingly absorbed every time they came to confession. Since the apocalypse began, the horrible nature of man bared its soul to him in the confessional, on television, in the streets. He hadn't noticed it as much before. But it was there, before this end of the world had been set in motion.

Now, with his good deeds, man would be born again, without the burdens of over population, stretched resources, thinking of only oneself. This apocalypse would teach them to care for one another. At least that was his hope. Sad that he might not be around to witness it.

He entered the bathroom, disrobed, and stuck a foot into the tub of cool water. The rest of his body followed. Once submerged, he enjoyed the coarseness of the salt against his skin. Taking a deep breath and holding it, he ducked his head under the water, the saline solution stinging his eyes. An insistent pounding in his head from lack of oxygen forced him to surface. He gasped, sucking in air.

Bath over, he left the tub and pulled the stopper so it would drain. Who would take over his congregation when he was gone? The cleaning lady would still clean the church, including the humble quarters he called home. Someone else would call it home if he did his job right. Maybe Father McGrady.

Using the threadbare towel, he dried himself as best he could. The black robe flowed over him, sticking in spots. He pulled them away from his body until the robe hung loose around him. He gathered the bowl, sigil, candles, and other items and hurried out to the backyard.

At the altar, he placed the candles in a circle around him. The athame lay on the stone, waiting for him. A soft breeze pulled a shiver through his body, making him yearn for the comforts of his bed. The warmth of the blankets. But that was being selfish. Sacrifice was a noble calling.

He carefully placed items in the pewter bowl, ending with the limestone from Mt. Hermon. Any old limestone wouldn't have worked. It had to be from a holy place. It had been a blessing in disguise that the occult shop had it on back order. Until yesterday he hadn't felt strong enough to attempt reuniting Death with his reapers.

He took the athame, pricked his finger, and squeezed five drops of blood into the bowl. Next, he lit the sigil of

Death on fire and dropped it in the bowl. Unlike the other summonings, a spiral of smoke trailed upward from the bowl.

Anticipation made his hands sweat, his stomach to churn. The air around him turned hot, suffocating. Struggling to breathe, his heart beat faster. Hoof beats filled the night air. But the thick, suffocating air didn't subside.

Life drained out of his body. He wanted to be there for the fresh slate he was giving mankind. But he was dying for a noble cause. From the beginning, he knew it might come to this, and he was prepared. His will waited in the middle drawer of his desk. Upon finding his body, there would be an eventual search of the church, of his meager possessions. He didn't have much, but everything he did have was going to the church. To help his congregation, what was left of them, move on after the apocalypse.

Gasping for air, he fell to his knees. He tried, in vain, to take even a shallow breath.

The hoof beats grew louder. A wisp of a figure appeared, slowly turning solid in front of him. While the others arrived naked and had to conjure appropriate attire, Death arrived fully clothed in an ensemble of black trousers, black shirt, black robe. A skeletal hand wrapped around the pole of a tall scythe. The slash of lips and flashing eyes rebuked him for having the nerve to summon Death. But he didn't just summon the horseman.

Streams of ghostly smoke rushed into the horseman. His whole body glowed for a moment, then went dark again. Death raised a hand, releasing the air.

Father Ianetti sucked in gasps of air like a thirsty man chugging water at an oasis. The last of the smoke slammed into Death.

The horseman glared at him. "What year is this?"

Father Ianetti stood on shaky legs. "It's 2025."

"This was not the timetable I was expecting."

"We started early. The Earth needs to be cleansed."

"The others?" Death held up a hand. "Never mind. I found them."

In a wisp of smoke, Death disappeared.

After dinner, with the dishwasher whirring in the background, Sarah sat in the living room, flipping through channels, having taken the remote control away from Becky, who insisted on keeping the television tuned to the twenty-four hours news station. Every news channel reported worsening news about the pandemic and the state of the world in general. The twenty-four hours news station hadn't shown a "fluff" piece to lighten the mood in at least a week.

Bright colors and a laugh track made her pause on a sitcom. At least the inane daily life of the main characters might let the angels think of something else. Let her own mind wander away from the death and violence going on around them. For thirty minutes, they could forget about the world.

Leah sat on the floor as usual, her laptop on the table, with enough browser windows open to stall a super computer. Becky, lounging in the chair directly across from the television, frowned at Sarah's selection of show. Rachel sat beside Sarah on the sofa, closest to the television, making it easy for her to change the channel manually if she wanted to get up.

Sarah set the remote control on the table, peering out of the corner of her eye as Becky leaned forward. Sarah snatched the device back, placing it beside her leg on the sofa. They'd had enough of Becky's station hogging the screen.

Outside, a metal screech filled the air, a huge crash following shortly after. Sarah shot off the sofa and dashed to the kitchen to grab the first aid kit. Without a word, the rest of the angels followed her out the door and down the stairs.

Two mangled cars littered the snow-covered street. A small blue car, dented, side doors crushed inward, blocked part of the sidewalk. On lookers, eyes wide, gasped. A dark green car, halfway through the intersection, fared slightly better, with a crumpled hood.

Sarah pointed at Rachel and Becky. "Check on the green car. I'll take the blue car."

Rachel was already jogging toward the car in the intersection. Becky nodded and pulled out her phone. The brief conversation with her producer to request a camera man on scene boiled Sarah's blood. Usually, she defended Becky, but this wasn't the time for reporting the news.

From her vantage point, halfway between both cars, Sarah noted a child in the green car, with a man who looked dazed, but otherwise appeared okay. Of course, there could be internal damage. But the woman in the blue car needed her attention more. That car looked like it had been crushed, rolled up like a piece of paper, and thrown into the street.

Sarah dashed over to the woman, but the blank stare told her everything. She couldn't help the dead.

She rushed over to the green car to assist Rachel.

"Good, check on the kid," Rachel said as she pulled out her phone.

"This is detective Rachel Malak. I need an ambulance on Queen Street near Baron's Jazz and Blues Bar."

"Patrick will be here soon," Becky said.

Rachel's nostrils flared and muscles clenched in her jaw. "Why does the city need to know about this crash?"

Becky shrugged. "To let people know to stay away from the area. Maybe there are factors involved, like road conditions."

Rachel rolled her eyes. Sarah hid a knowing smile. In this instance, she agreed with Rachel's eye roll.

Sarah reached into the car to check the man's pulse. She assumed he was the child's father.

"Sir, can you hear me?"

He nodded and cringed. "Yes. Check on my daughter, please."

The man had strong vitals, though a slightly elevated heart rate. Understandable considering the collision he'd been involved in. Sarah hurried around to the back seat, passenger side door to check on the girl. Tears streamed down the girl's face.

"How are you, sweetie?"

"Yvette," the man said.

"Yvette, are you hurt anywhere?"

The girl shook her head. "I don't think so."

"I'm going to do a quick check to see if you're hurt, okay?"

The girl nodded. Sarah proceeded to do a standard check to make sure the girl hadn't cut anything, broken anything, or bruised anything. Every area she checked resulted in no sounds from the girl. Nothing appeared to be broken or bruised. And Sarah saw no blood.

"Uh, guys," Leah said.

Sarah looked up to see what caused the youngest angel concern. Leah pointed at the car with the woman driver. A wispy, skeletal, ghostly apparition floated out of the car. It flew over to the green car, sniffed the man, sneered at Sarah, and then sniffed the girl. A thin frown turned its lips downward. Without a word, it took off through the intersection and then disappeared.

Sarah straightened and huffed out a breath. "That's not good."

Leah shook her head. "Death and his roaming reapers have already combined. So more reapers need to be created to handle one-off deaths like this."

"We need to make the horsemen weaker by sending Famine back," Becky said.

Rachel frowned. "Yes, and if we can, send War and Conquest, too."

Leah wrinkled her brow. "It took too much out of us for just one, but we can try. The Mt. Hermon limestone is still on back order."

"At least one would help," Sarah said.

The angels nodded.

Sarah turned back to the girl and her father to make sure they remained stable. Ten minutes later, an ambulance pulled up to the scene. Cora, an EMT she'd seen around the hospital emerged, gear at the ready as she rushed over to the scene.

"Hey, Doc. What have you got for me?"

Sarah filled her in about hearing the crash, the death of the woman in the blue car, vitals and observations for the man and his daughter.

"We'll take it from here."

She backed away from the scene, hugging herself in the cold January air. They all looked on until the man and his daughter were loaded into the ambulance. Now that Death had been combined with his reapers, things were going to go downhill fast.

Chapter Nineteen

Sunday morning, after dealing with the crash the night before, Rachel sat on the sofa half listening to the television, forcing herself to stay away from the police station. On her days off, she would normally go in anyway, but with the apocalypse heating up she needed to stay close to her sisters. But that meant she wasn't around to protect Detective Williams. So far, he'd managed to avoid getting sick.

She picked up her phone and shot off a quick text message to her partner to make sure everyone was still okay. A few seconds later, a soft ping sounded from her phone.

We're still good. How are you and your sisters?

MW

So far so healthy.

RM

With the three of them at almost full power, Rachel suspected the healthy part would continue no matter how bad the pandemic got. But she still didn't get power back as quickly as she wanted to. Pleased her partner and his family remained in good health, she put her phone on the table.

From the floor, Leah blew out a breath and shoved her laptop away. "The limestone is still on back order."

Becky sauntered into the living room area carrying a tray of mugs. She put a tea down in front of everyone, then settled in the chair facing the television.

"Why don't we send Conquest and War back while we're waiting?" Becky took a sip of her tea.

Rachel picked up her mug and took a sip. "We don't want to risk running out of the ingredients to call the horsemen."

Rachel hated to admit it, but Becky had a point. Why weren't they? If they sent Conquest and War back, that would put a huge crimp in the priest's plans for ending the world. Even with Death combined with his reapers, the absence of two horsemen had to put things back to normal. At least seminormal. It would buy them some more time.

Even if they did send two of them back now, while waiting for the rest of the ingredients to send Famine back, the priest would summon them again. The ritual to banish them to limbo took a lot out of them. It made sense to conserve their energy.

Did Becky get more power back in her wings for asking the question? Since her sin was sloth, wanting to take action was not slothful. Or did Becky have to actually take action to be rewarded?

Second-guessing how to get power back did her no

good. She would continue to tell Becky anytime a power surge happened and hope that the reporter would be able to figure out the trigger.

A buzz from the table startled her. And she almost laughed when the other angels also jumped. It was a different buzz from the text messages. Rachel grabbed the phone, the number of the hospital on her screen. She swiped to answer, her heart hammering in her chest. The only person she'd get a call about, who didn't live with her, was Williams. But he'd just said he was fine.

"Detective Malak," she said.

"Detective, this is Dr. Sharp. There is a woman here with your business card and she wanted us to call you."

If she hadn't already been sitting, she would have collapsed into the sofa. "I'll be right there." Before the doctor could explain more, Rachel ended the call and shoved the phone in her pocket.

"What's wrong?" Sarah asked.

"Darla's worse."

She reached the door and stopped. In hot pursuit, the other angels bumped into her. At her questioning look, Sarah shrugged. "We're coming too. We all care about her."

With a curt nod, she moved out of the way, ushering them out the door with a wave of her hand.

Ten minutes later, in the middle of the quarantine ward, Rachel's heart shattered. Reports littered the news channels about the pandemic, droning on about the symptoms, the reality of smallpox taking over again. But she'd avoided the hospital because she didn't want to see this. The death that lingered in the air. And she wasn't even in the worst of it yet. The hemorrhagic ward lay beyond the simple quarantine ward.

Becky hurried past her and stopped at Laura's side. Becky's face crumpled. Rachel walked past Laura's bed, glancing at the sick as she passed, wishing she had more power to help them. She stopped at Darla's bed. The woman looked up at her.

"Sorry. Even in a pandemic, we have to work. The online work wasn't bringing in enough money."

Darla turned her head and nodded to her left. Rachel peered over to see another sex worker. How many more of them would end up in this ward? Or worse? Linger in this ward for a few days only to be moved to the certain death ward?

Rachel glanced over at Sarah, who was doing rounds since she was at the hospital. Sarah looked up at her, then hurried over to Darla's side.

Sarah's face scrunched up at the rash on Darla's face. "I can't tell yet which way it will go."

"We can't let this happen." Helplessness settled in the pit of Rachel's stomach.

"I can't put my hands on everyone and heal them, remember?"

Becky abandoned Laura's beside to huddle beside Darla's. She glanced over at Laura. "Not all. But some."

Rachel couldn't believe she was about to agree with Becky. It was rare for them to see eye to eye, but in this case, Rachel couldn't argue. She gave Sarah an imploring look. "You get power back when you don't hoard it."

Sarah sighed. "We'll need Leah."

Leah stopped speaking to a patient and rushed over. "I'm here."

"Use your combined power to disrupt the camera feeds," Sarah said.

Rachel, Becky, and Leah held hands, concentrating their efforts on blurring the cameras. Sarah put her hands on Darla, the doctor's face impassive, focused. Color returned to the sex worker's cheeks. The rash and sores faded. Once finished healing Darla, Sarah made her way through the ward, healing Darla's fellow sex worker, then to Laura's bed.

Rachel smiled down at Darla. "How do you feel?"

Wonder rushed into Darla's eyes, and she took a deep breath. "I feel amazing."

"You'll still need to rest, but you should be able to leave the hospital soon," Rachel said. "Sarah, is that correct?"

Sarah stopped at the bedside of a man who looked to be in his fifties. "Yes, lots of rest. Once another test is done to confirm the virus is gone, she'll be able to go home."

The tension in Rachel's shoulders loosened and the churning in her stomach subsided. She watched Sarah move from bed to bed, healing as she went. So many people would get to go home. That had to be a good thing, right? At another bed, Sarah put her hands on the patient and the glow from her fingers healed the young woman. A patch of white in Sarah's wings turned to black.

Rachel broke the connection with Becky and Leah, pulling her hand out of theirs, and yelled. "Stop!"

Sarah jumped, spinning around. "Why? There's still so many more. And I haven't even started on the most sick patients."

"Because you had been getting power back, but the one you just started healing drained some away."

"I should have started in there." Sarah nodded her head toward the hemorrhagic ward.

Rachel sighed. "I guess you really can't go through the hospital ward and heal them all."

"But maybe if we weaken the horsemen, Sarah won't have to heal them all," Becky said.

Rachel nodded, but didn't think that would make a

difference. Vanquishing the horsemen wouldn't kill the disease, would it? If the apocalypse was accelerated with artificial means, did that mean everything associated with it would fix itself once the horsemen were defeated? She didn't think it would be as easy as that.

At least Sarah had been able to heal some people. Exhausted, with nothing more they could do, they said their farewells to Darla and Laura and headed home.

Becky's fingers danced over the keyboard as she dove headfirst into her research. The hum of the computer and the soft glow of the screen illuminated her features, casting a halo around her red hair. Why did she always delegate this to the interns? Doing the work herself helped with understanding what she was uncovering. She found herself craving the satisfaction that only came with uncovering the truth herself.

"Guys, listen to this," Becky said, her eyes still glued to the screen. "I found articles about these miracle seeds that can grow in almost any condition, providing much-needed food during times of crisis."

"Sounds promising," Leah said.

"Maybe," Becky admitted, narrowing her eyes as she scrolled further down the page. "But there's a catch. These seeds produce food that is less nutritious than their regular counterparts, and they deplete the soil of its nutrients at an alarming rate. Who knows what other issues the seeds will cause."

Rachel crossed her arms over her chest. "Let me guess. Famine's behind this?"

"Very likely," Sarah said. "The lab he worked at did testing on seeds, too. I think his plan is to make people insatiable and dependent on these seeds. He's creating food that leaves you hungry and malnourished."

Becky nodded in agreement. "It's a vicious cycle. People will keep eating more and more, but they'll never feel full. And the land will be left barren, unable to support any life."

Leah shuddered. "What kind of future will my students have if we don't stop him? If everyone is constantly hungry and desperate for more, society will crumble."

"At least we're uncovering his plans bit by bit," Becky said, her fingers still tapping away. "The more we know, the better equipped we'll be to stop him."

"True," Sarah said. "But we need to act fast. We can't afford to let Famine get the upper hand."

"Agreed," Leah said. "We have a responsibility to protect the world from this sinister plan. And I, for one, am not backing down without a fight."

With each piece of the puzzle that fell into place, they grew stronger, more resolute. The horsemen and Father Ianetti would not win.

"All right," Becky said, turning to face her sisters. "As soon as we have everything we need to summon him, let's stop Famine and save the world."

"Great," Rachel said. "I hate this waiting for a fucking ingredient, so we can finally summon his ass and send him back where he belongs."

"Patience is a virtue," Becky said. She knew her sister's impatience all too well, but it was important to stay focused and not let frustration cloud their judgment.

Rachel gave her a look that could only be described as an annoyed glare. Becky shrugged, knowing Rachel would eventually understand the importance of patience in their mission.

"All right, let's shift gears for a moment," Leah said.

"What about the ongoing pandemic? It's already weakened humanity, making them more susceptible to Famine's plan."

"True," Sarah said, her expression somber. "The world's resources are stretched thin, and people are scared. It's like the perfect storm for someone like Famine to step in and take advantage."

Becky nodded, her thoughts turning inward. She couldn't help but feel responsible for informing the public about these issues, but how much could she reveal without exposing their true identity? And without causing a panic. Another panic. The pandemic took care of the first panic.

"Maybe we can use this situation to our advantage," Becky said. "I mean, I'm a TV reporter. I have access to the media, and I can inform the masses about the dangers of these miracle seeds. We could encourage people to be cautious and to rely on more traditional sources of food."

"Every little bit helps," Leah said. "The more awareness we create, the better chance we have of stopping Famine before his plan takes root and spreads even further."

"Let's do what we can with the tools we have," Sarah added. "We may be fallen angels, but we still have a responsibility to protect humanity from harm."

"Right," Rachel said, her tone softening slightly. "But we have to conserve our power for the showdown with Famine. No sense using it all up before we even face him."

"Agreed," the sisters said in unison.

Becky went back to the digital newspaper article, a sinking feeling growing in her chest. The words seemed to blur together as she focused on the implications of Famine's plan for humanity. The room fell silent for a moment as each sister mulled over their thoughts.

"Speaking of seeds," Leah said, breaking the silence,

"Okay, maybe not seeds, but flowers, the high school gave the teacher's learning conference the green light." She glanced around at her sisters, who were now staring at her with interest. "Part of my mission is to get the flower from Mt. Hermon and retrieve water from an ancient pool in the holy land. It could be vital to our fight against Famine."

"Wait," Rachel said, brow furrowed. "You're going on a trip during the pandemic? That sounds risky, especially with all the quarantine rules and potential exposure to the virus."

Leah nodded. "I understand the danger, but we need that flower. Plus, the ancient water might boost our spells for sending the horsemen back to limbo. And as an angel, my chances of getting infected should be pretty low."

Becky bit her lip, her mind racing. "Sarah, what if we used our regained powers to protect ourselves and others from the virus while we investigate Famine's plan? I mean, it's not like we don't have some measure of influence over the elements, right?"

"Interesting idea, but no," Rachel said firmly, her gaze locked on Becky. "We need to conserve our powers for the showdown with Famine. We can't afford to waste them on other endeavors."

Becky's shoulders slumped, but she understood Rachel's point. They were walking a tightrope between saving humanity and preserving their own abilities for the final battle.

"Fine," she said, her fingers drumming on the table. "But we can't sit idly by while Famine continues his plans. We need to be proactive, gather information, and do everything in our power to prevent further damage to humanity."

"Agreed," Rachel said.

They knew the stakes had never been higher, and the road ahead would be fraught with danger and uncertainty.

Becky glanced at Leah, who had been deep in thought, her eyes narrowed in concern. "Leah," she said, breaking the tense silence that had settled over the room, "I know you're worried about your students, but we need to focus on the bigger picture."

Leah looked up, her brown eyes filled with a mix of worry and determination. "You're right, Becky. We can't afford to lose sight of what's truly at stake here. I'll keep a close watch on my students, monitoring their behavior and health for any signs that Famine's seeds are affecting them." She ran a hand through her dark hair, her teacher instincts kicking in. "I'll do everything I can to protect them from harm."

"Good," Rachel said, nodding her approval. "We need all the information we can gather to understand Famine's plan and how to stop it. But we must act quickly—every day that passes brings us closer to his endgame."

The weight of responsibility settled on Becky's shoulders, pressing down like an invisible anchor. Her fingers twitched as she fought the urge to reach for her phone and start digging for more information on the so-called miracle seeds. Instead, she took a deep breath and concentrated on the conversation at hand.

"Okay, sisters," she said, trying to exude confidence despite the knot of fear twisting in her stomach. "We know what we have to do. Let's keep our training on point so we'll be ready to face Famine when we have all the ingredients we need."

"Let's do this," Sarah said.

"Agreed," Leah said, her eyes shining with a fierce light that mirrored her sisters' unwavering determination.

"Then let's get to work," Becky said, her voice steady and resolute. She knew they had no time to waste—Famine was already several steps ahead of them, and they would need every ounce of cunning and courage to outmaneuver him and save the world from his plan.

Chapter Twenty

Sarah stood in the lab at the satellite office of CNML. The overhead lights cast a harsh glow on the white walls and countertops, reflecting off the various state-of-the-art machines that hummed and whirred around her. The lab was working tirelessly on a vaccine for the new form of smallpox that had emerged, but progress was agonizingly slow, and she couldn't shake the worry that gnawed at her. After the researchers left, she stayed to continue work on her own. A little angel magic gave her more research experience.

Despair settled in her stomach as yet another experiment failed to yield results. The weight of her responsibility pressed down on her, countless lives hanging in the balance. The memory of healing people at the hospital yesterday lingered in her mind, along with the knowledge that she had temporarily lost some of her power in doing so. But giving her lunch to Dr. Cooke earlier had helped her regain that lost strength. The CNML researcher had forgotten hers, and though Sarah didn't really get hungry with most of her power back, she enjoyed the taste of food.

As she worked, she couldn't help but reflect on her fallen angel status and her mission to stop the apocalypse. With each failed attempt at creating a vaccine, the weight of her responsibility grew heavier. She paused for a moment, looking into a microscope, as her thoughts drifted to Famine. If only they could recall enough of the tainted seeds through Becky's broadcast tonight, perhaps they could still mitigate the danger. It was a slim hope, but it was all she had to cling to in these desperate times.

Sarah's frustration grew as she leaned back from the microscope. Another dead end, another wasted effort. She shook her head, trying to clear her thoughts and refocus. Time was running out, and every minute spent without a viable solution weighed on her conscience. She pushed herself to carry on, knowing that the lives of so many people were in her hands.

As she busied herself with sample preparations and data analysis, Sarah couldn't shake the feeling of guilt that came with being unable to fulfill her divine duties. A fallen angel, tasked with the monumental mission of preventing the end of days, yet here she was, struggling to find a cure for this devastating disease.

Despite her need to focus on the task at hand, Famine continued to occupy her thoughts. How had he managed to infiltrate the global food supply so insidiously? And how could they stop him from spreading further destruction?

Her mind raced as she considered the implications of their failure. With each passing day, more lives would be lost, and the world would inch closer to the brink of collapse. The reality of their situation was overwhelming, but she refused to give in to despair.

Maybe there's still time. She gritted her teeth as she refocused on her work. If she could just unlock the secrets of this new strain of smallpox, perhaps they could avert the catastrophe. As Sarah peered into the microscope, she hoped that this time, she'd find the answers she sought.

The minutes ticked by, and still, no breakthrough presented itself. Her frustration grew, but she persisted. What other choice did she have? She couldn't afford to fail, not when the fate of humanity hung in the balance.

With a heavy sigh, Sarah pulled yet another test result from the screen, her heart sinking as it revealed no promising leads. The sterile whir of machinery filled the air, the occasional beep of equipment monitoring the smallpox samples punctuating it. As much as she wished she could be at the hospital, laying hands on the afflicted and easing their pain, she knew the key to saving more lives was here, in the lab, developing a vaccine.

Her gloved fingers danced across the keyboard, inputting commands that would run another round of tests on the samples before her. She glanced up at the clock, noting the hours that had passed since she began her work.

In her mind's eye, she couldn't help but picture the quarantine ward, filled with suffering people. She pictured the astonishment on the doctors' faces when they witnessed what they would call a miracle: dozens of patients recovering simultaneously after she had secretly used her healing abilities. That thought fueled her determination; she needed to find a way to bring that same sense of hope to everyone this terrible disease affected.

Before coming into the lab, she'd detoured to the hospital to gather various blood samples from the patients she'd healed. She'd arrived at the lab early and created numerous sample slides. It was a long shot, but if there was even a chance that there were antibodies present, then it was worth a try. Sarah opened the refrigerator, retrieved the samples, and placed them under the microscope, her brow furrowing as she examined each one in turn.

She prayed silently, knowing full well that her own miraculous healing wouldn't leave traces in the form of mere antibodies. Yet, she couldn't shake the feeling that there might be some hidden clue within these vials, something that would lead her to the solution she so desperately sought.

As she continued her examination, her thoughts raced between the patients she had left behind and the responsibility that weighed heavily on her shoulders. Their only hope was a vaccine that worked against smallpox 2.0. But as the microscope revealed no useful findings within the blood samples, Sarah couldn't shake the nagging feeling that time was running out. The clock continued to tick, each second bringing them closer to catastrophe.

Sarah's eyes burned with the strain of peering into the microscope for hours, her vision blurred and unfocused. She needed a break. With a sigh, she pushed herself away from the lab bench and rose from her seat, stretching her stiff limbs. As she paced the sterile, white-tiled room, her thoughts churned just as restlessly as her body.

Her phone rang, shattering the silence, and Sarah issued a voice command to answer it. The sound of Leah's voice on the other end brought both comfort and urgency.

"Hey, Sarah, have you used any limestone recently?" her sister asked without preamble.

"Limestone? No, why?"

Leah hesitated before continuing. "It looks like the small amount of limestone we had and a few other ingredients to summon the horsemen are missing. I just want to make sure we're not running low."

Sarah furrowed her brow, concern creeping in. "I haven't touched any of it, but what about our plan to summon Famine when the last ingredient, mandrake root, arrives?"

"Everything's still in place for that," Leah reassured her. "The sigil for Famine is untouched. Maybe we just didn't have as much as we thought."

"Perhaps," Sarah said, though she couldn't shake the feeling that Leah wasn't entirely convinced. "Well, try not to worry about it too much. I'll be home soon to make dinner, okay?"

"All right," Leah said, her voice a little more relaxed.

She issued a voice command to end the call.

As she turned back to her work, Sarah's determination surged anew. One more hour, she vowed silently. One more hour, and then she would return home to tend to her sisters and prepare for whatever challenges lay ahead. For now, though, her focus remained on the task at hand: developing a vaccine against the deadly new strain of smallpox that threatened to push humanity ever closer to the brink.

Rachel wedged a brick in the threshold to keep the rooftop door from locking her out. The cityscape spread out below her, a chaos of light and shadow that mirrored her own turmoil.

Why hadn't they focused on vanquishing another horseman while waiting for the final ingredient to summon Famine? She hated to admit Becky had been right. Her confidence, once again, had gotten in the way of reason. But now, with her sword, a pewter bowl, and the stolen ingredients at hand, Rachel would make things right. If she could weaken the other horsemen by sending Conquest back, it would give her and her sisters a fighting chance of defeating them all.

Rachel kneeled on the rooftop, arranging the ingredients in front of her. The wind danced through her hair as she took a deep breath to steady herself. Her sword gleamed in the moonlight, a reminder of the power she once wielded effortlessly.

It was now or never. She steeled herself for what was to come.

With careful precision, Rachel placed the ingredients in the pewter bowl. Her fingers trembled slightly as she held her sword aloft, the tip hovering just above her index finger. She hesitated for a moment, feeling the weight of what she was about to do. But hesitation wouldn't save the world. It was time for action.

She pressed the sword into her fingertip. A small bead of blood welled up, crimson and bright against her pale skin. She clenched her jaw against the stinging pain, watching as five drops of blood fell into the bowl, mingling with the other ingredients. The mixture hissed and bubbled, its contents reacting to her essence.

Taking the sigil of Conquest in hand, she held it above the bowl. The parchment trembled slightly as she struck a match, the flame casting flickering shadows across the sigil. With a deep breath, Rachel set the sigil alight and dropped it into the bowl, watching as the flames consumed the parchment, turning it to ash. Her heart pounded in her chest, each beat echoing with anticipation and fear.

As the last remnants of the sigil burned away, Rachel stirred the ashes into the mixture with her sword. The wind picked up around her, howling like a chorus of lost souls. In that moment, she felt both powerful and terrified, knowing that she was playing with forces beyond her comprehension.

"I'm waiting for you, Conquest," she said, the words barely audible over the gusts swirling around her. "Face me, you bastard."

The air crackled with energy, the atmosphere thickening as if charged with electricity. Rachel's eyes never wavered from the bowl, watching as the ingredients began to shift and transform before her.

She clenched her fists, hating to admit that Becky was right. They should have been working together to vanquish the Horsemen, not waiting for the final ingredient to summon Famine. But Rachel couldn't help herself; she needed to prove that she was strong enough to face them on her own.

As the ritual neared its completion, the wind intensified, whipping around her like a tempest. Her hair flew wildly about her face, stinging her cheeks and obscuring her vision. She squinted against the onslaught, her grip on the sword tightening.

Rachel had to act quickly before Conquest could gather his strength. She would send him back, weakening the other Horsemen in the process. If she succeeded, it would give her and her sisters a fighting chance to defeat the rest of the apocalyptic riders. And if she failed...

No. Failure was not an option. With a fierce determination burning within her, Rachel prepared to face Conquest and whatever may come.

The cacophony of hooves echoed through the rooftop garden as Conquest materialized before Rachel, his form wisping into existence like tendrils of smoke coalescing into a solid figure. Rachel wasted no time, her voice ringing out over the din. *"Circulus defensionis!"* A protective circle shimmered into existence around the roof, an ethereal barrier designed to keep her from plummeting off the edge.

Conquest watched her closely, a predatory glint in his eyes as he took in her every move. His lips twisted into a knowing smile, as if privy to a secret she was not yet aware of. It unnerved her, but Rachel refused to let him see her falter. She was an angel, a warrior, and she had faced much worse than this.

"Is that all you've got?" Rachel taunted, summoning light charges in her palms that she hoped didn't drain too much of her power. She'd admonished her sisters for using power indiscriminately, but they at least knew how to get power back.

"Ah, a show of power," Conquest said, his tone dripping with mock admiration. "Very well, let's see what you can do."

With a defiant cry, Rachel hurled the light charges at Conquest, using more of her power than she'd intended. But it would be worth it if she succeeded in banishing him. Conquest charged her in response, moving with unnatural speed.

The impact sent Rachel flying through the air like a rag doll, her breath stolen from her lungs as she careened toward the edge of the rooftop. She braced for the bone-shattering fall, but instead collided with the protective barrier she had conjured. The force of the collision reverberated through her body, leaving her disoriented and gasping for air.

Conquest laughed, the sound cruel and mocking. "Is that really the best you can do? I expected more from a second round."

Rachel gritted her teeth, rage and humiliation fueling her determination. She would not let Conquest win. She would prove herself worthy of redemption, even if it killed her.

Rachel's heart pounded in her chest as she reached for the sword lying on the rooftop, gripping the hilt with determination. Her muscles tensed, the weight of the weapon familiar and comforting in her hand.

"Let's see how you fare against this," she said, brandishing the blade before her.

Conquest grinned, his eyes gleaming with malice. "A sword? How quaint." He raised his bow, nocking an arrow with unnerving precision.

Rachel had been training relentlessly, but now, faced with this deadly foe, she worried it wouldn't be enough. She forced the fear from her mind, focusing on the task at hand. As Conquest loosed his arrow, she tried to dodge, but her movements were sluggish, a half-second too slow. The arrow grazed her arm, pain searing through her flesh like white-hot fire.

"Pathetic," Conquest sneered, already nocking another arrow. "You'll die here, Rachel, alone and forgotten."

Panic clawed at her insides, threatening to choke her. She couldn't die here—not like this. But she refused to let Conquest see her fear. With a defiant roar, she charged him, sword raised.

The battle was brutal and unforgiving. Conquest seemed to dance around her, his laughter echoing in her ears as he tossed her about like a rag doll. Each collision with the rooftop sent shockwaves of pain through her battered body, and soon, every breath felt like a struggle.

Rachel landed hard on a ceramic planter, the impact shattering it beneath her. The shards dug into her skin, drawing fresh blood that mixed with the dirt and grime coating her wounds. For a moment, she lay there, gasping, the agony coursing through her veins consuming her thoughts.

But she couldn't give up—not yet. With a surge of desperation, Rachel mustered what remained of her strength and power. She thrust her hand toward Conquest, who was stalking closer, his arrow aimed at her heart.

"Get back!" she yelled, releasing a wave of force that sent him flying away from her.

As Conquest slammed into the far end of the rooftop, Rachel struggled to catch her breath, her chest heaving with the effort. Pain wracked her body with each inhale, but she couldn't afford to rest. She had to keep fighting, had to survive—for herself, for her sisters, and for all those who depended on her.

Through the haze of her pain, Rachel became aware of a commotion at the rooftop door. It burst open, revealing the worried faces of her sisters.

"Rachel!" Sarah's voice cut through the air like a sharpened blade, laced with fear and concern.

As Conquest grinned maliciously, the air around them turned hot, suffocating. The heat intensified as Famine and War wisped onto the rooftop, their sinister presence adding to the oppressive atmosphere.

"Get down!" Becky yelled, raising her hands and forming a protective barrier around Rachel as Sarah and Leah rushed to help.

"Guys, there's already a barrier up," Rachel managed to choke out, grimacing at the throbbing pain coursing through her body.

"Thanks for the heads-up," Leah said as she surveyed the scene, her eyes narrowing in determination. "All right, let's send these horsemen back to where they came from."

Together, the sisters removed the initial protective barrier around the roof, pooling their powers into a unified force. They struck with precision, sending the horsemen flying off the edge of the rooftop with an explosion of energy.

"Guys, we need warding, now!" Leah shouted, sprinting toward the edge of the roof to watch the horsemen plummet to the ground.

"Right!" Becky said, quickly beginning the incantation that would protect them from any retaliation.

"Keep your guard up," Sarah said, even as she focused on healing Rachel's injuries. "They won't go down without a fight."

Rachel gritted her teeth, trying to push aside her lingering fears of dying at the hands of the horsemen. Her pride had led her here, and it was her responsibility to help her sisters see this through. With every ounce of her strength, she vowed to herself that she would not let her loved ones down.

"Sarah, you've got to be quicker," Rachel said, her voice tense. "We can't afford to give them any more time."

"Almost there," Sarah replied, her hands glowing with healing energy as she worked on Rachel's wounds. The pain began to recede, giving way to a renewed resolve.

"Rachel, I know you're strong," Leah said, glancing at her sister with a mix of concern and admiration. "But we need to work together. You can't do this alone."

Nodding in agreement, Rachel took a deep breath, preparing herself for the battle that lay ahead. They faced the greatest threat they had ever known, but together, they would find a way to prevail.

"All right," she said, gritting her teeth. "Let's finish this."

As they gazed down at the fallen horsemen, who were already beginning to stir and regroup, the sisters knew their fight was far from over.

"Are we ready for what comes next?" Sarah asked.

The dim lights of the loft flickered as Sarah and Leah, each supporting an arm, guided a battered Rachel toward the worn, inviting sofa. Becky dropped into the chair that faced the television, her eyes glazed over from exhaustion, while Leah settled herself on the sofa beside Rachel.

With the four of them gathered together, their weariness from battling the horsemen was palpable. Despite their celestial lineage, the physical toll had left them all feeling quite mortal. Sarah, ever the caregiver, sat delicately on the edge of the coffee table, facing Rachel. She extended a hand to continue healing her sister, but Rachel flinched away, shaking her head vehemently.

"No," she said through gritted teeth. "The last time you healed a patient in the hospital, it drained your power. You used so much to save me on the roof already."

Rachel glanced at Leah and Becky, concern etched onto her bruised face. "You all used a lot of your power to save me."

Sarah's hand wavered in the air before she reluctantly withdrew it, settling back on the table. Her brow furrowed, worry emanating from her as she asked, "Are you sure you don't want my help with healing?"

"Positive," Rachel said, stifling a moan of pain as she shifted on the cushions.

"What were you thinking?" Sarah asked, unable to mask her frustration.

"Thought I could weaken them while we waited for the ancient grains to banish Famine," Rachel said, her voice heavy with regret.

"It's pride," Becky said, her tone devoid of judgment yet holding a note of accusation.

Rachel's silence hung heavy in the loft, her thoughts a whirlwind of guilt and anger. She stared down at her bruised hands, clenching them into fists as she fought to find the words that could justify her actions.

"It's not pride," she finally said, her voice strained and defensive. "I am the strongest. A protector. It's my job."

Leah, her eyes filled with concern, asked gently, "Why didn't you ask for help, Rachel?"

"I thought I could do it on my own," Rachel said, her voice barely above a whisper. "He caught us off guard last time, sending you over the roof. I had that covered this time."

"Sounds like pride to me," Becky said, her words sharp, but not unkind.

Rachel clenched her jaw, her blue eyes flashing with defiance. "It wasn't pride," she insisted, though doubt gnawed at her heart.

Becky leaned forward, her gaze steady and unwavering. "What would you think of a human who acted like that?" she challenged.

Rachel hesitated, wincing as she leaned back against the couch. She sifted through her thoughts, replaying the events that led them to this moment, the pain they'd endured, the risks they'd taken. And as she analyzed her actions, the truth hit her like a wave, washing away the remnants of her denial.

"Huh," she said, a rueful smile tugging at the corner of her lips. "So, it is pride."

The dim light cast from the loft windows bathed Sarah's face as she spoke, her eyes alight with conviction. "We are a team," she said, her voice unwavering. "The four horsemen of the apocalypse are known as a group because they work as a group."

Becky nodded, her expression resolute. "This has to be a team effort." She fixed Rachel with a penetrating gaze, her words heavy with the weight of experience. "We need to rely on each other's strengths to succeed."

Rachel stared at her sisters, their words settling like

stones in her stomach. All around her, the loft seemed to grow smaller, the air thick with tension and unspoken fears for the battle that lay ahead. She shifted her weight gingerly, biting back a hiss of pain as her injuries flared in protest.

Leah's hand rested on her knee, her touch gentle and comforting. "Now even if the ancient grains come in tomorrow," she said softly, her eyes filled with empathy, "we have to wait for you to heal. And all of us to power up again."

It was then that the truth of what her sisters were saying flooded into Rachel, filling her with an icy clarity. In that moment, she remembered every instance when she had regained her power; every time she had swallowed her pride and allowed herself to be humble.

She looked at each of her sisters in turn, their faces etched with concern and love. "I'm sorry," she said, her voice barely audible, the words tasting bitter on her tongue.

A pang of fear stabbed through her as she imagined facing Detective Williams at work the next day, her appearance a testament to her recklessness and pride. What would he think? How would she explain the bruises and cuts that marred her skin, the pain that hid behind her carefully constructed facade?

"Rachel?" Sarah's voice cut through her thoughts, a lifeline in the storm of her mind.

"Williams," Rachel breathed, her eyes wide with panic. "How am I going to explain this to him tomorrow?"

***

Tuesday morning, the cacophony of ringing phones, clacking keyboards, and hushed conversations engulfed

Rachel as she stepped into the police station. She held her head high despite the bruises and cuts peppering her face, remnants of her harrowing battle against the horsemen. She strode past her fellow officers, ignoring their questioning looks and whispered speculations.

As she arrived at her desk, which faced Williams's, he glanced up from his paperwork, taking in her appearance with a wince. "Let me guess," Williams said, a hint of concern breaking through his usual joviality. "I should see the other guy."

Rachel attempted to laugh, but the motion sent a jolt of pain through her side, causing her to wince instead. She touched the tender area gingerly. "Actually, it was a car accident. But I'm fine." Lying didn't come naturally to her, but there was no way she could reveal the truth—that she had fought three of the four horsemen and lost.

Williams raised an eyebrow, obviously unconvinced. "You don't look fine."

"Malak!" a stern voice called out. Their boss, Detective Sergeant Diego Reyes, strode over to their desks, his brow furrowed. He nodded in agreement with Williams, surveying Rachel's battered face. "Desk work for the next few days."

"Sir, I can handle leg work," Rachel protested, her pride flaring at the idea of being relegated to the sidelines. But deep down, she knew she was in no condition for field-work. And pride had gotten her into this mess.

Reyes crossed his arms, unmoved by her objection. "No, you're on desk work." His tone left no room for argument.

Rachel clenched her jaw, swallowing her indignation. With a curt nod, she acquiesced, knowing that she'd have to focus on healing and regaining her strength. She couldn't afford to let her pride get in the way of their ultimate goal—stopping the apocalypse.

Rachel forced herself to ease into her chair, a wince accompanying each movement. "Fine," she said, "desk work for the day." She tried to ignore the nagging feeling that she was letting her pride dictate her decisions. After all, there was a mountain of paperwork waiting for her.

The pandemic hadn't halted crime; in fact, it seemed to have fueled it. Homicides were down slightly, but people were still killing each other at an alarming rate. Among her three ongoing cases was the death of Caleb's father. Her gut told her Caleb was involved, but so far, no evidence supported her suspicion. And she suspected there would be no evidence. Caleb had Conquest on his side.

As she dug into her paperwork, Rachel's focus began to dwindle. Two hours in, and the pain from sitting too long brought her thoughts back to her injuries. Shifting in her chair, she let out a small gasp.

"Everything all right?" Williams asked, genuine concern etched on his face.

"Fine," she muttered through gritted teeth, pushing herself up from the chair. "Just need a bathroom break."

Inside the restroom, Rachel winced at her reflection. Her bruised and battered face stared back at her, a reminder of her failure against the horsemen. A pang of regret surged through her as she thought of Sarah's offer to heal her. They couldn't risk their doctor angel losing any more power, but staring at the damage now, she wondered if maybe they should have.

Rachel shook off the doubt, forcing herself to focus on the present. One thing was certain: she needed help, even if it meant swallowing her pride. Together with her sisters, they could stop the apocalypse.

Rachel took a deep, steadying breath and raised her

eyes to the dimly lit bathroom ceiling. She sent up a silent prayer, an apology for her stubbornness and her inability to face her own limitations. She couldn't afford to let her pride stand in their way any longer.

"Please," she whispered, "I know I can't do this alone."

As if answering her plea, Rachel felt a familiar tingle at her back, where her wings were hidden from human eyes. The sensation spread like wildfire across her bruised face, and she looked up in astonishment as her reflection transformed before her. Her battered skin healed, regaining its previous smoothness, and the pain that had plagued her all morning vanished.

She spun around, peering over her shoulder, and caught sight of a small, white patch blooming among the dark feathers of her wings. It was as if Heaven itself had acknowledged her humility and granted her a measure of grace.

"Thank you," she said, awed by the sudden change. She stretched her arms and flexed her wings, bracing herself for lingering discomfort, but found none.

Rachel strode back to her desk with renewed purpose, her steps light and her heart filled with determination. Williams looked up from his paperwork, his eyebrows shooting up in surprise when he saw her seemingly unblemished face.

"Rachel... what happened to your injuries?"

"Makeup," she said with a small, confident smile. "It works miracles. Let's go out there and catch bad guys. Don't tell Reyes."

Williams stared at her for a moment, clearly dubious, but then shook his head and chuckled. "All right, Malak. Whatever you say."

Together, they left the building with renewed energy, ready to tackle the challenges ahead. Rachel knew that her sisters would be doing the same, each playing their part in the grand scheme to save humanity. Bolstered by the knowledge that they were all in this fight together, she felt a surge of hope that the apocalypse might yet be averted.

"Let's do this," Rachel said, her voice steady and strong, as they climbed into their unmarked police car. "Let's catch bad guys."

As the engine roared to life and they sped off toward the dark heart of the city, Rachel knew that her newfound unity with her sisters would make all the difference in the world.

Chapter Twenty-One

A month after the botched attempt to dispatch the three horsemen, Sarah entered the loft, exhaustion etched on her face as she removed her lab coat. During that time, she'd magically given herself a promotion at CNML to researcher.

"I'm sorry for coming home so late," she said, her voice barely above a whisper. "And not being able to make dinner."

Moonlight flooded the loft through the floor-to-ceiling windows, casting eerie shadows upon the concrete walls. The cityscape outside seemed to have lost its usual vibrant hues, replaced by a monochrome palette that mirrored the somber atmosphere within the apartment.

The angels were in their usual spots at the loft. Rachel lounged on the sofa, her eyes betraying the weariness she tried so hard to conceal. Becky sat in the chair facing the TV, her gaze distant as if deep in thought. Leah was sprawled out on the floor, facing the sofa and a stack of papers on the coffee table in front of her.

"Your work is important, Sarah. We all understand," Becky said, offering a supportive smile.

"Besides," Leah said, "we ordered burgers. Yours is in the microwave." She gestured toward the kitchen with her pen.

Grateful for her sisters' understanding, Sarah retrieved the lukewarm burger from the microwave without bothering to heat it. She plopped down beside Rachel on the sofa, taking a bite of the cold, greasy meal.

Rachel turned to face her, concern etched on her features. "How's the vaccine progressing?"

Swallowing a french fry, Sarah sighed. "We're making progress. Since it's a smallpox variant, I combined components of other hemorrhagic diseases and applied them to the virus."

Her mind replayed countless hours spent hunched over microscopes and test tubes, scrutinizing every detail. If she were still human or hadn't regained all her angelic power, her eyes would be fatigued beyond belief.

Leah sat up straighter. "Ingenious."

Sarah smiled. "We've finally had a breakthrough. We want to start clinical trials next week." She couldn't help but feel proud of her accomplishment, even though she didn't take credit for the breakthrough. Delegating tasks and sharing the workload, now that she was a researcher, had helped her regain her power, and she noticed that Becky and Leah's wings were fully white once more.

"Congratulations," Rachel said, suppressing a yawn. "We all knew you could do it."

"Thanks," Sarah said, feeling the weight of responsibility on her shoulders. With each step closer to a vaccine, the stakes became higher—and time was running out.

Becky's genuine smile lit up her face as she leaned

forward in her chair, her eyes shining with pride. "That's fantastic news."

"It is," Sarah said, nodding in agreement. But an uneasiness gnawed in the pit of her stomach. Even if the vaccine worked, it would only prevent those who had been exposed to the disease from contracting it. The people already afflicted were doomed to wait it out, unsure whether they'd recover or succumb.

As she chewed on another cold fry, her thoughts churned relentlessly. She wanted to work on a cure desperately, but it wasn't feasible right now. Preventing the spread was their best defense at the moment. A heavy sigh escaped her lips.

Rachel's brow furrowed and she shifted her weight on the sofa, angling her body toward Sarah. "I'm worried about the increase in violence since Death recombined with his reapers. It's not just here; it's happening all over the world." Her voice wavered as she spoke, exhaustion evident in every word. "Places with little to no crime have had murders and assaults. I'm run ragged."

Sarah studied Rachel's face, noticing the dark circles under her eyes and the weariness etched into her features. Even with half of her power restored, Rachel looked spent. Her heart ached for her sister, understanding the immense burden she carried.

"Is Williams still okay?" Becky asked, her voice laced with worry.

Rachel nodded, a flicker of relief crossing her face. "He is, but a lot of other detectives are out sick. And with the severity of the disease, I know at least half of them won't get better." A heaviness settled over the room as the gravity of their situation pressed down on them.

Sarah clenched her fists, determination igniting within her. They couldn't afford to be complacent; the stakes were too high. She resolved to work even harder on the vaccine, knowing that every moment counted.

As the sisters sat in somber silence, contemplating the immense task before them, Sarah's mind raced with ideas and strategies. The weight of their responsibility was immense, but together they would face it head-on. And as the night wore on, the flickering city lights outside the floor-to-ceiling windows seemed to whisper a promise that they would never give up, no matter how dark the world became.

The room's energy shifted as Leah leaned forward, running her fingers through her hair in frustration. "I've been trying to keep my students calm, but it's so much harder doing everything from home," she said, her eyes reflecting the strain of her new remote-teaching reality. "Video teaching just isn't the same as being in the classroom."

"March break is coming up, though," Sarah said, reaching out to squeeze Leah's hand. "You'll have a chance to recharge and refocus."

Leah's eyes brightened at the thought. "Yes, I can really do something to help stop the apocalypse by picking up things on my trip to the Holy Land and The Vatican." There was a fire in her gaze, a determination that burned away some of the weight that moments ago had seemed unshakeable.

"Speaking of which," Becky said, her voice tinged with both exhaustion and pride, "I've been busy with reports on the global response to the disease. Countries are finally cooperating to combat this shared threat. It's just a shame it took something like this for them to realize we're all on team humanity."

"Agreed," Sarah said, her mind racing. "We need those clinical trials to happen soon. The virus is mutating, and the probability of it turning hemorrhagic has increased." As she spoke, the urgency in her tone reverberated throughout the loft, each word a stark reminder of the ticking clock they were all racing against.

Before any of them could dwell too long on that chilling prospect, Leah's phone rang, its shrill tone slicing through the air. She picked it up hesitantly, her eyes flicking toward Sarah, who gave an encouraging nod. Leah swallowed hard before answering. "Hello?"

A pause. Then her face lit up with a mixture of relief and excitement. "The ancient grains we need to send Famine back to Limbo have arrived," she announced, her voice quivering with anticipation. "We can finally make some real progress."

A week after Rachel tried to take care of Conquest alone, the limestone from Mt. Hermon had come in. The grains were the last item on back order they needed.

As Leah hung up, Sarah felt a renewed sense of hope surge through her veins. Maybe, just maybe, they could still save the world.

The Sunday afternoon sunlight streamed through the windows of the loft, casting a warm glow on the kitchen. Sarah looked up from her work as Leah entered, her arms full of ancient grains. The once cozy and familiar space now resembled a chemistry lab, with glass beakers, tubes, and Bunsen burners scattered throughout the countertops. Aromatic concoctions bubbled away in their containers, filling the air with an otherworldly scent.

Leah raised an eyebrow and quirked a small smile. "That's not how the kitchen looked when I left."

"Used some power to convert it temporarily into a lab

so we could make the serum," Sarah explained, trying to keep her voice steady. "It was faster than going to the CNML."

"What about the lab downstairs?" Leah asked. "You didn't want to take the thirty seconds to walk down there?"

Sarah shrugged. "Something like that."

Leah set the ancient grains down and eyed Sarah's wings, which were spread out behind her. "All the white is still there." Rachel, who had been silent in the corner, nodded in agreement.

"Yes. I guess using a little doesn't affect it much," she said, her tone carrying the weight of their collective relief.

Sarah couldn't help but feel a surge of gratitude for her sister's dedication. She asked about the holy water.

"Stopped on the way home and had a good priest bless it," Leah said, placing the small flask on the counter. "Here you go."

Sarah's insides quivered like an overstrung violin, but she managed a tight-lipped smile of thanks. Before she could voice her next question, Leah produced a small set of scales from her bag.

"And the scales, blessed by the same priest," she said, her eyes twinkling with amusement. "I could see in his eyes that he wanted to ask why I needed these things."

Sarah reached for the scales, her hand trembling ever so slightly. The weight of their mission pressed down on her like an unseen force. In the back of her mind, doubt gnawed at her resolve. She was a healer, a guardian of life, but could she truly be the one to save humanity? And what would it cost them all?

Sarah drew a deep breath, her hands still trembling slightly as she set to work on the serum. With practiced precision, she measured out the ancient grains and holy water, using the blessed scales Leah provided. As she combined the ingredients, she couldn't help but notice how her sisters watched her every move, their expressions tense yet trusting. This trust only served to amplify the pressure Sarah felt.

"All right," she said, steadying her hand as she carefully extracted the essence from the ancient grains.

"Are you okay?" Rachel asked, concern for her sister momentarily replacing her stern demeanor.

"Fine." Sarah's voice was low and determined, though not entirely convincing. "Just... focused."

Once the serum was complete, Sarah filled a syringe with the precious liquid and set it aside. She turned to face the other angels and asked, "Is everyone ready?"

The angels nodded in unison, each visibly steeling themselves for the task ahead. Sarah could see the nervousness in their eyes, but also the resolve. They'd waited too long to do this summoning, but they had no choice—they needed to regain their power after helping save Rachel from Conquest. And Rachel, especially, needed more power back in her wings.

"Let's gather everything we need," Rachel said, heading to the cupboard where they kept the items for summoning the horsemen. She removed the pewter bowl, the athame, the sigil for Famine, a lighter, and pillar candles. Then she added a bundle of sacred herbs that would serve as an offering during the ritual.

While Rachel collected the items, Sarah grabbed the scales and the syringe filled with the serum. Leah took the bottle of holy oil and sprinted to her bedroom to retrieve a fine paintbrush. Becky, ever the supportive sister, held the door for everyone as they exited the loft.

As they prepared to face Famine, Sarah couldn't shake the feeling that their lives were about to change irreversibly. But there was no turning back now—the fate of humanity rested squarely on their shoulders. And whether they emerged victorious or met their end trying, one thing was clear: they would give it everything they had.

The sun dipped low in the sky, casting long shadows over the rooftop as the angels began their preparations. Leah's paintbrush glided effortlessly across the concrete surface, leaving a gleaming trail of holy oil as she drew the large protective circle. The air seemed to crackle with energy, heightening Sarah's nerves and making her heart race.

"Is it big enough?" Sarah asked, her voice tight with tension as she surveyed the circle, large enough for them all, including Famine.

"Perfect," Leah said. "But wait, don't summon him yet."

Leah exited the circle and using her knowledge of ancient symbols, she painted a warding around the rooftop against the other horsemen so only Famine could appear. Rachel, meanwhile, set up the altar for summoning Famine with practiced precision.

"Here, Sarah," Rachel said, handing her the athame and ingredients. "It's time."

Sarah nodded, her fingers trembling slightly as she took the items from her older sister. She forced herself to focus on the task at hand, lighting the pillar candles that surrounded the pewter bowl. Their flickering flames danced in the growing twilight, casting eerie shadows around them.

One by one, Sarah added the ingredients to the bowl: the sacred herbs, the limestone, the sigil which she set alight before dropping it in the bowl, and finally, with a deep breath, she used the athame to prick her finger. A bead of blood welled up.

"Are you ready?" Becky asked, her eyes scanning the faces of her sisters, looking for any sign of doubt or fear.

"Ready," they all replied in unison.

"Then let's do this," Sarah said, her voice barely audible above the wind.

With a final flourish, she let five drops of blood drop into the bowl. The air grew heavy, charged with the power they were calling forth.

Suddenly, the sound of horse hooves echoed across the rooftop, their thunderous beat resonating in Sarah's chest. The air heated up, becoming almost stifling, and Famine wisped into existence like smoke, coalescing before them.

"*Circulus defensionis,*" Becky and Rachel chanted in unison, raising a protective barrier around the rooftop. Their voices mingled with the wind, weaving a spell of safety over them all.

Famine grinned wickedly, his eyes boring into Sarah's soul. "You can't win."

"Maybe not," Sarah said, her voice steady despite the fear that gripped her heart. "But we'll die trying."

As the words left her lips, she couldn't help but wonder if this would indeed be their final battle. And as Famine's laugh filled the air, the first stars appearing in the sky above them, she prayed they'd live to fight another day.

Leah's fingers flicked into action, striking the holy oil aflame. A brilliant circle of holy fire blazed around Famine and the angels, illuminating the dark rooftop. The fire cast eerie shadows on Famine's gaunt face, emphasizing his sickly pallor.

"Your fellow horsemen can't help you now," Sarah

said, her voice steady despite her heart pounding in her chest.

"Who needs them?" Famine sneered, his pale lips twisted into a cruel smile. "You pathetic angels will never be able to stop the apocalypse."

He lunged with a speed that belied his malnourished frame, charging toward Sarah. She dodged him, and he barreled into the holy fire, yelping in pain. Famine spun around, hatred flashing in his eyes.

"Get to work!" Sarah yelled at her sisters.

Rachel sprang into action, darting forward with fists clenched, trying to draw Famine's attention away from Sarah. As Rachel threw punch after punch, Sarah edged closer to Famine, every muscle tense and ready for attack. But his attention seemed to divide effortlessly between the two of them. With a wicked smile, he whipped around and sent Sarah flying through the barrier of holy fire.

Heat engulfed her like a ravenous beast, almost searing her skin as she passed through the flames. She barely had time to scream before slamming into the ground, gasping for breath.

"Sarah!" Becky cried, racing to her side, a grimace marring her face when she passed through the flames. Anxiety shone in her eyes as she helped Sarah to her feet. Sarah fought to steady her breathing, ignoring the pain that radiated through her body.

"Leah, Becky, get the spell ready. We're running out of time," she said.

"Got it," Becky said, her gaze flicking between Sarah and the ongoing battle between Rachel and Famine.

With a nod, Becky raced back to Leah in the circle of fire, leaving Sarah to gather her strength. As Rachel continued to fight, Sarah's thoughts raced. She needed to get closer. She had to stop him. Gritting her teeth, she pushed aside the pain and fear that threatened to overwhelm her. There was no time for doubt, not with the fate of humanity hanging in the balance.

Sarah's body ached from the impact, but she steeled herself and ran back into the circle. As she reached Becky and Leah at the altar, Sarah noticed the pewter bowl filled with a mixture of ingredients.

"Add the rest of the grains from Mt. Hermon and the holy water," Sarah instructed, her voice ragged.

With swift, practiced movements, Leah emptied its contents, making room for the ingredients they would need for the spell. As the remnants of the previous concoction sizzled on the floor, Leah and Becky began adding the new ingredients: the rest of the grains from Mt. Hermon, holy water, and other sacred items that would bind Famine and weaken him.

"Rachel, keep him busy!" she called out, her heart pounding in her chest. Rachel nodded, her fists clenched as she continued to throw punches at Famine. The thin, malnourished figure of Famine twisted and turned, evading her punches with an eerie grace.

Sarah summoned her power and launched balls of light at Famine, each one pulsating with divine energy. The projectiles flew toward him, some narrowly missing their target while others found their mark. Each impact sent waves of searing pain through Famine, his rage intensifying with every hit.

"Pathetic angels," Famine said, his voice like nails on a chalkboard. He retaliated by hurling fireballs at Sarah, who dodged and weaved through the deadly barrage. However, she couldn't avoid them all. The fireballs that struck her left her breathless, her energy draining out of her like water down a drain. A gnawing hunger clawed at her insides, leaving her weak and trembling.

"Sarah!" Leah shouted, her voice laced with concern. She and Becky abandoned the spell momentarily to rush to Sarah's aid. Rachel redoubled her efforts, landing punch after punch on Famine to keep him occupied.

"Rachel, don't stop!" Sarah gasped, gritting her teeth against the pain that wracked her body. "We're almost there!"

He gathered his strength and unleashed a torrent of fireballs at Leah and Becky, all his anger focused into making the projectiles more powerful. The immense power catching them off guard, both angels hurled through the air. They passed through the holy flames with a sizzle and bounced on the hard rooftop.

"Leah! Becky!" Sarah shouted, fear curling in her gut. But she couldn't afford to let Famine see her falter. With a deep breath, she squared her shoulders and focused all her remaining energy on defeating the horseman.

"Stay down, angels," Famine taunted. "You'll never stop the apocalypse."

"Never is an awfully long time," Sarah said. The weight of the world pressed down on her shoulders, and she refused to fail.

With her heart pounding in her ears, Sarah drew from the depths of her being to create more potent balls of light. Famine continued his relentless assault, launching fireballs and arrows at her with a wicked grin. The heat singed the air around her, making it difficult to breathe.

"Is this all you've got?" Famine taunted, unfazed by the onslaught.

As she hurled the orbs of brilliance toward him, searing pain erupted in her arm as an arrow found its mark. Blood welled from the wound, dripping down her forearm and staining the ground below. Her face contorted with agony, but she refused to let it slow her down.

"Sarah!" Rachel called out, her voice laced with fear. But Sarah couldn't afford to falter now; she needed to get closer to Famine. With every step, the pain intensified, throbbing in time with her heartbeat.

"Rachel, keep him busy!" Sarah shouted, forcing herself to ignore the agony coursing through her veins. Rachel nodded grimly, launching herself at Famine with renewed vigor. Her fists were a blur as she pummeled the horseman, forcing him back on his heels.

"NOW!" Sarah screamed, her voice cracking under the strain. As Rachel kept Famine occupied, Sarah lunged forward, using her remaining strength to hurl the blessed scales at Famine's neck. A touch of magic guiding them, they wrapped around his throat as if they possessed a life of their own. Famine gagged, clawing at the scales in a futile attempt to remove them. Sarah rallied her strength and plunged the serum-filled syringe into Famine's leg.

A vengeful fireball aimed point blank at Sarah's chest swiftly followed a yelp of pain. The searing heat slammed into her, forcing the air from her lungs and igniting every nerve ending with a blaze of agony. Through gritted teeth, Sarah fought back the urge to cry out, knowing that she couldn't afford to falter now.

"Rachel, Leah, Becky!" she managed to choke out, her voice raw and strained. "Incantation, now!"

"*Ex tenebris ad lucem, redde nos in locum tuum,*" they chanted, their words echoing across the rooftop, filling the air with an electric charge. The power of their combined wills pressed down on Famine, tightening like a vice around him. His face contorted in fury, and he attempted to hurl another fireball at them, but the flames sputtered and died in mid-air, the force of their incantation snuffing them out.

"*Ex tenebris ad lucem, redde nos in locum tuum!*" the angels repeated, their voices growing louder and more confident with each repetition. Sarah's arm shook as she lifted it, gathering the remnants of her strength to hurl one final barrage of light at Famine. The orbs of pure energy streaked through the air, colliding with Famine's frail form and sending him hurtling backward.

"NO!" he screamed, his voice a shrill, desperate howl. But it was too late - his body began to disintegrate before their eyes, fading into nothingness like ashes caught in a gust of wind.

"Ex tenebris ad lucem, redde nos in locum tuum!" the angels cried one last time. And then, suddenly, Famine was gone.

"Is... is he gone?" Becky asked, her voice barely a whisper.

"Back to limbo," Rachel said, her gaze fixed on the spot where Famine had stood moments before.

As the adrenaline began to ebb from Sarah's body, she became acutely aware of her injuries. Pain throbbed in her chest; blood ran slick and warm down her arm where an arrow had pierced her flesh. Exhaustion weighed down her limbs like lead, dragging her to her knees. Her body trembled, no longer able to support her, and she crumpled to the ground.

"Sarah!" Leah's cry pierced through the haze.

"Is she... alive?" Becky's voice trembled as she hovered over Sarah.

Sarah coughed weakly, her body convulsing with the effort. It felt like a thousand needles pierced her lungs with each breath, but she clung to life, refusing to surrender that easily.

"Hey there," Rachel said softly, squatting down beside her sister. "You're one stubborn angel, you know that?"

Sarah managed a small smirk, despite the pain. "I've

been told." She forced herself to focus on the sounds around her: the distant sirens, the wind rattling windows, and the steady beating of her own heart. Each painful throb reminded her that she still had a purpose here on Earth, and she couldn't afford to give up.

Her sisters watched, eyes wide with concern, as Sarah's power began to surge back into her—slowly at first, but then an unstoppable torrent. The blackened feathers of her wings transformed before their eyes, glowing white once more. The pain and hunger that had threatened to consume her vanished, a renewed strength that coursed through her veins replacing them.

"Whoa," Leah said, unable to contain her surprise. "That's... incredible."

"More than incredible," Rachel said, her pride momentarily forgotten in the face of her sister's miraculous recovery. "It's a miracle."

Feeling steadier now, Sarah gratefully accepted Rachel's offered arm and pushed herself up from the ground, her legs trembling only slightly. Her sisters formed a protective circle around her, ready to support her if she faltered.

"Thank you," she said, her gaze meeting each of theirs in turn as gratitude welled up within her.

"Always," Rachel said, her grip on Sarah's arm unyielding. "We're a team, remember?"

"Definitely," Leah said, her smile bright and reassuring. "We'll face whatever comes our way, just like we always have."

"Hey, don't forget about me," Becky said, winking at Sarah as she gently squeezed her sister's other hand. "I'm not going anywhere either."

As they stood together on the rooftop, battered and bruised but unbroken, Sarah couldn't help but feel a surge of hope that they might actually stand a chance against the impending apocalypse.

"That was a close one," she admitted, her words met with relieved laughter from her sisters. And despite the overwhelming odds they faced, Sarah knew that together, they could overcome anything.

The loft door slammed shut as Sarah, Rachel, Becky, and Leah stumbled inside, their breaths heavy and ragged after the intense battle with Famine. Relief washed over them like a cool rain, but it didn't last long.

"Father Ianetti will just summon Famine again," Sarah said, her heart pounding against her chest. "Then all the horsemen will be back."

"Summoning Death's reapers had to have been draining for him," Rachel said, leaning against the wall for support. Her once confident demeanor was now replaced with exhaustion and worry.

"Hopefully Father Ianetti won't be able to bring Famine back immediately," Leah said, her voice shaky yet hopeful.

With the excitement over, Sarah dragged herself toward the breakfast island in the kitchen, her legs feeling like lead. She collapsed onto a stool, her head resting on her arms. The cold marble countertop provided some comfort to her overheated skin.

Becky hurried to her side, concern etched on her face. She handed Sarah a glass of water, which she gratefully accepted, gulping down mouthfuls desperately.

"Are you sure you don't need anything else?" Becky asked, fussing over her.

"Really, I'm fine." Sarah forced a smile, secretly

enjoying the attention. "All of my power came back, remember?"

"But it looked like you died," Leah said, her eyes wide with lingering fear.

"Trust me, I didn't die," Sarah reassured the youngest angel, placing a hand on her shoulder. "We've got this."

As they caught their breaths and felt the adrenaline slowly leaving their bodies, Sarah's thoughts were consumed by what lay ahead. No matter how drained Father Ianetti might be, he wouldn't give up without a fight. They would have to be stronger than ever if they were going to save humanity.

The air in the loft crackled with tension as if each breath they took held the weight of their mission. Sarah studied her sisters' weary faces, a mix of determination and fear etched on each one. Now, more than ever, they needed to recharge.

"Listen," she said, her voice firm but gentle. "We all need to rest and power up. Especially you, Rachel. We'll be dealing with all the horsemen next time, and they won't be as easily separated."

Rachel's eyes flashed with defiance, but beneath it, Sarah could see the vulnerability she tried so hard to hide. Pride may have been Rachel's downfall, but it was also her driving force.

"Wherever Death is," Sarah said, "that's where we'll need to be."

Leah's brow furrowed in thought, her fingers unconsciously tapping on the countertop. "But where will Death be?"

"Somewhere with mass casualties," Sarah said solemnly, feeling the heavy burden of their task settle in her chest. "Death feeds off of human suffering—it gives him power."

"Then we should start researching," Becky said, her reporter instincts kicking in. "We can't afford any missteps."

Sarah nodded, grateful for Becky's unwavering support. As the others began pulling up news articles and scouring social media for any signs of impending disaster, Sarah's gaze lingered on Rachel.

She knew her sister was struggling, grappling with the weight of her own perceived failure. It was important to show her that they were stronger together—that they could rely on each other.

"Rachel," Sarah said softly, placing a hand on her shoulder. "Remember, you don't have to do it all by yourself."

Rachel's eyes met hers, and for a moment, the mask slipped away. Sarah saw the fear and uncertainty lurking beneath her sister's tough exterior. She squeezed Rachel's shoulder reassuringly, hoping to convey the unspoken words of comfort.

With a nod, Rachel turned back to the task at hand, her jaw set in determination. As they delved into their research, Sarah couldn't help but feel a sense of unity forming among them. It was as if each victory brought them closer together, knitting their bond tighter and stronger than ever before.

They were racing against time. The final battle loomed closer with every heartbeat, and there would be no turning back once it began.

"Whatever happens," she said, "we'll face it together."

Sarah watched her sisters huddle over a sprawling map on the table, their features marred by concern and determination. Rachel was the most visibly tense among them, her hands gripping the edges of the map as if trying to draw strength from it.

"Rachel," Sarah said, "what's wrong?"

Rachel looked up, her green eyes giving away the turmoil within her. "I'm just... I'm worried about failing. About not earning my wings back." Her voice wavered, uncharacteristic of the usually stoic eldest angel.

"Hey," Sarah said, stepping closer to place a comforting hand on Rachel's arm. "We'll succeed and you'll get your wings back. We couldn't do this without you."

A flicker of gratitude flashed across Rachel's face, surprise lighting her eyes, and a shiver rippled through her. Sarah leaned back to peer at Rachel's wings in time to see a new white spot bloom in a patch of black feathers at the top of the limb.

Rachel smiled. "Looks like you were right." She pulled the limb forward to admire the evidence of her humbleness.

As the silence stretched between them, Sarah's thoughts raced. They needed a respite from the crushing weight of their mission, even if only for a moment. A way to remember that despite the darkness surrounding them, there was still light left to fight for.

"Let's take a break," Sarah said, her voice full of conviction. "We should celebrate our small victories, too."

Becky, ever the optimist, quickly caught on to Sarah's intentions. "Great idea!" she said, heading to the freezer and emerging with a tub of ice cream. Leah, always eager to help, grabbed bowls from the cupboard while Rachel hesitated for a moment before retrieving chocolate sauce from the fridge.

As they each prepared their own sundaes on a small spot on the island not taken up by lab equipment, the tension in the room gradually dissipated. Laughter bubbled up like a soothing balm, filling the space where worry and doubt had once festered.

"Hey, this ice cream is just what the doctor ordered," Sarah said, a playful grin tugging at the corners of her mouth. The sound of her sisters' laughter wrapped around her like a warm embrace, igniting a spark of hope within her chest.

Half an hour later, dirty bowls littering the breakfast island, they cleaned up the loft, each movement methodical and purposeful. As they prepared for the battles to come, there was a newfound sense of unity and confidence that pulsed through them. They were stronger together, and no matter what horrors awaited them, they would face them head-on—as one.

Dear Reader,

Thank you for reading my book!

If you read Black Feathers, you know the original plan was to have one book with four angels all dealing with the four horsemen. Figuring out the points of view, and getting the whole story in the way I wanted to tell it, would have resulted in a huge tome. Deciding to give each angel her own book, dealing with her own horseman, and trying to figure out why she was exiled was a breakthrough for me. It allowed me to delve into the characters in more depth.

I really hope you loved the book as much as I did. White Feathers took longer to write because I was writing about a pandemic during a pandemic. At one point in the process I just couldn't deal with a fictional pandemic so the book went on a back burner. I am so happy with how Sarah's story turned out and I'm happy I took that time away. I am currently working on the last book in the series and can't wait for you to see how it all turns out.

There are four books in the series, but I suspect there will be more series in the angels' world. Stay tuned for that. You can sign up for my mailing list at https://cindycarroll. com/angelslist to be notified when new stories come out, plus get a copy of Fallen, the prequel short story.

Happy Reading,

Cindy

Acknowledgments

Writing a book is a solitary endeavour, but with a book like this one, research is required. I wanted to send a huge thanks to Dr. Adina Bujold, PhD for answering my many questions about diseases and bringing back a virus with a twist. The answers I received from Dr. Bujold were invaluable with developing Sarah's character and progressing the plot. Any errors regarding infectious disease and protocols are mine.

Thanks should also go to my writing group, Guelph Write Now, who keep me going when I just want to procrastinate. Those twice a month goals meetings help me stay on track.

About the Author

Cindy is a member of Sisters in Crime and a graduate of Hal Croasmun's screenwriting ProSeries. She writes screenplays, thrillers, horror, urban fantasy, science fiction and paranormals, occasionally exploring an erotic twist. A background in banking and IT doesn't allow much in the way of excitement so she turns to writing stories that are a little dark and usually have a dead body. She lives in Ontario, Canada with her husband and two cats. When she's not writing you can usually find her painting land-scapes in oil, playing video games (Sims 3 and Sims 4 are favourites), or watching her favourite television shows marathon style.

Check out Cindy's website:
https://www.cindycarroll.com
Check out Cindy's other books:
https://books2read.com/cindycarroll

facebook.com/AuthorCindyCarroll

instagram.com/CindyPCarroll

goodreads.com/writesbooks

bookbub.com/authors/cindy-carroll

bsky.app/profile/cindypcarroll.bsky.social